THE MINECRAFT-INSPIRED MISADVENTURES OF

FRIGIEL AND FLUFFY

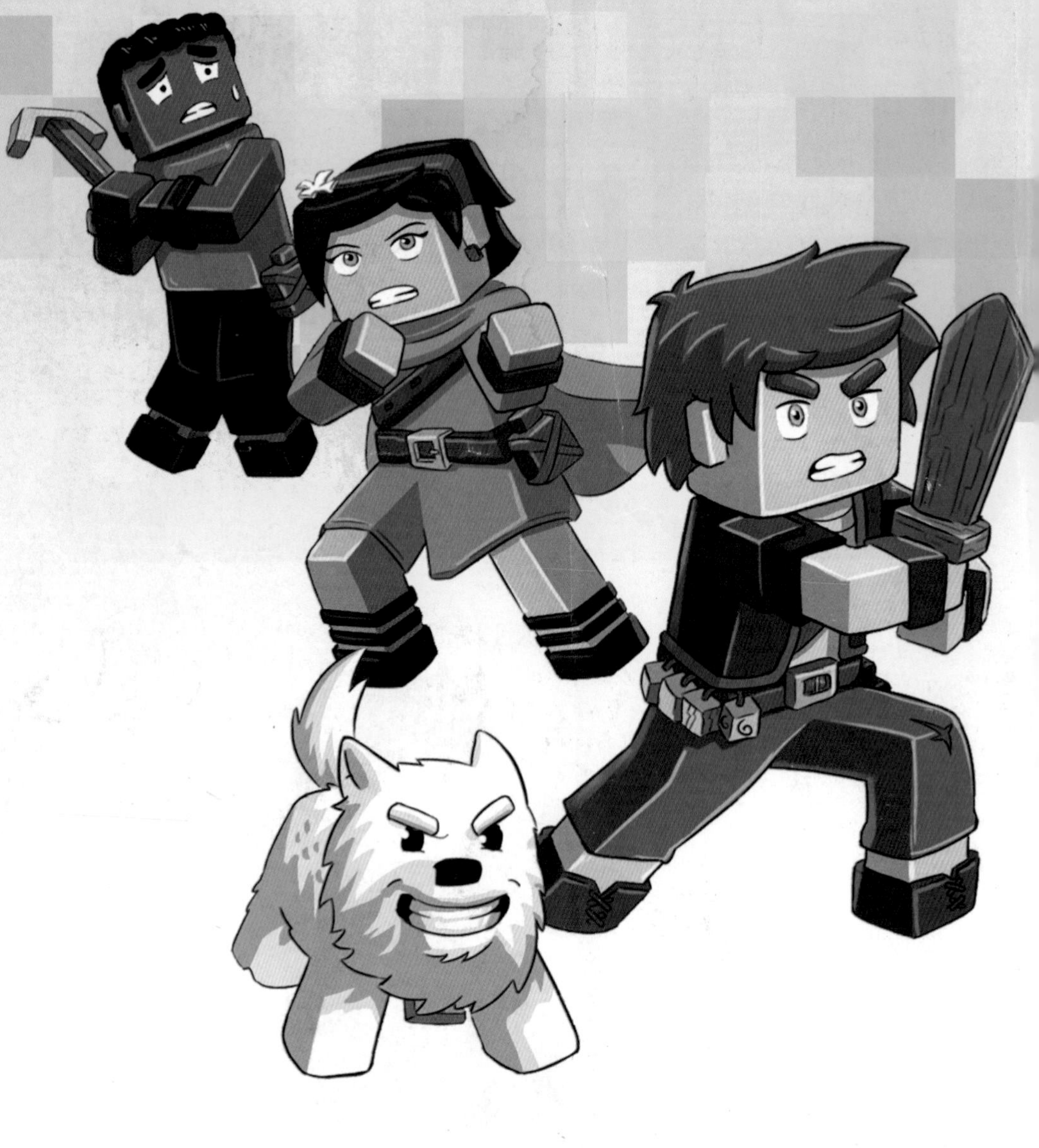

THE MINECRAFT-INSPIRED MISADVENTURES OF

FRIGIEL AND FLUFFY

VOL 1

WRITERS:
JEAN-CHRISTOPHE DERRIEN, FRIGIEL

ARTISTS:
STUDIO MINTE

FOR ABLAZE

MANAGING EDITOR
RICH YOUNG

DESIGNER
RODOLFO MURAGUCHI

Publisher's Cataloging-in-Publication Data

Names: Derrien, Jean-Christophe, author. | Frigiel, author. | Minte, illustrator.
Title: The Minecraft-Inspired Misadventures of Frigiel and Fluffy, vol. 1 /
[written by] Jean-Christophe Derrien and Frigiel; [illustrated by] Minte.
Description: Portland, OR: Ablaze Publishing, 2020.
Identifiers: ISBN 978-1-950912-22-3
Subjects: LCSH Minecraft (Game)—Comic books, strips, etc. | Video game characters—Comic books, strips, etc. | Video games—Comic books, strips, etc. | Graphic novels. | BISAC JUVENILE FICTION / Comics & Graphic Novels / Media Tie-In
Classification: LCC PZ7.7 .D502 Un 2020 | DDC 741.5—dc23

For advertising and licensing email: info@ablazepublishing.com

THE MYSTERY OF THE LOST WATERMELONS

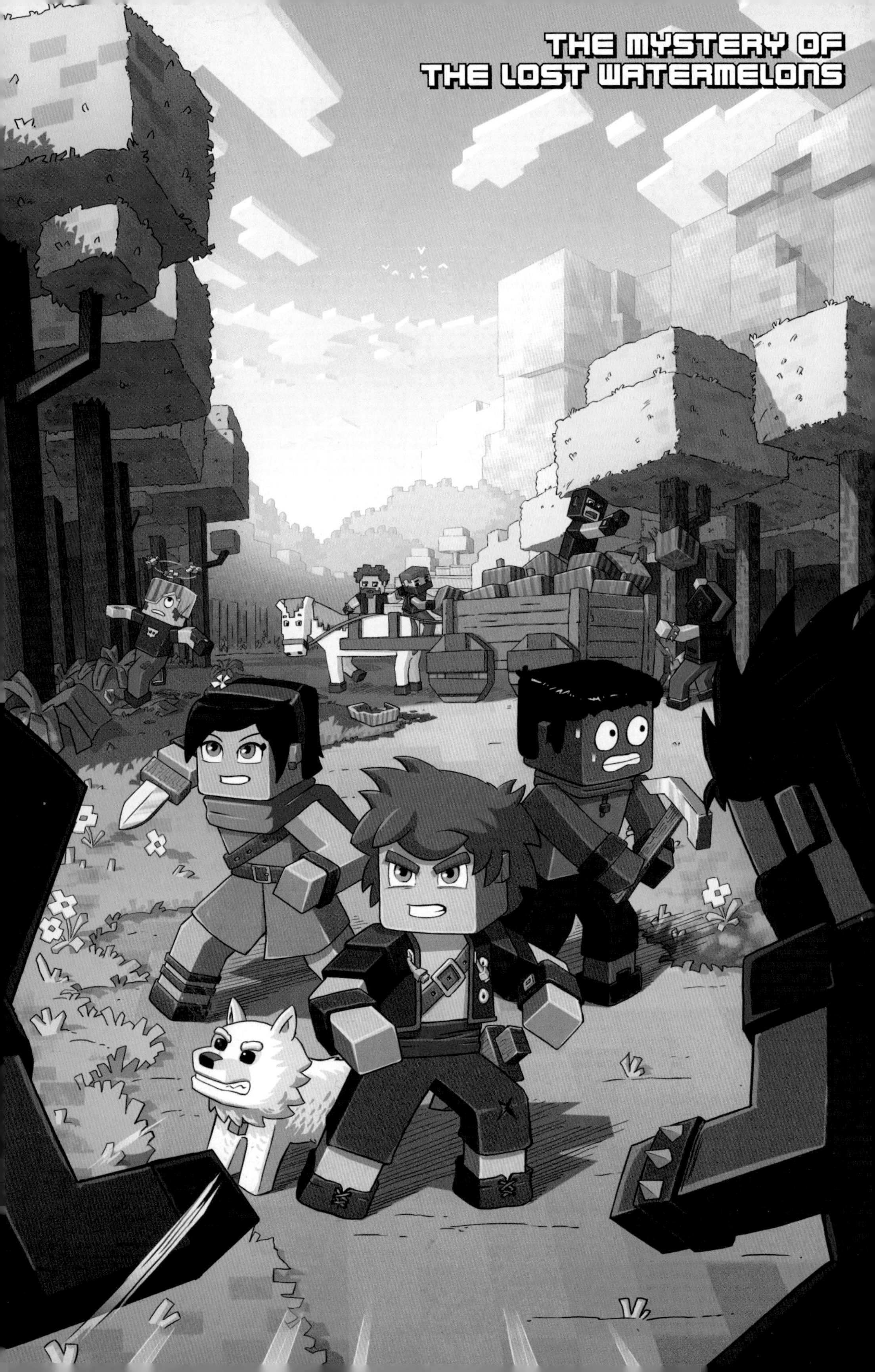

Dramatis Personae

■ Frigiel

A brave sorcerer's apprentice ever-ready to give his all for his friends. He dreams of one day becoming a true adventurer. His chance to discover the world begins today...

■ Fluffy

Frigiel's faithful canine companion, as cuddly with his master as he is bitey with the bad guys.

■ Alice

Proud and passionate, this thief-in-training keeps her secrets close to her heart...

■ Abel

A clever builder, and a somewhat mocking friend, he doesn't always see the irony of the situation.

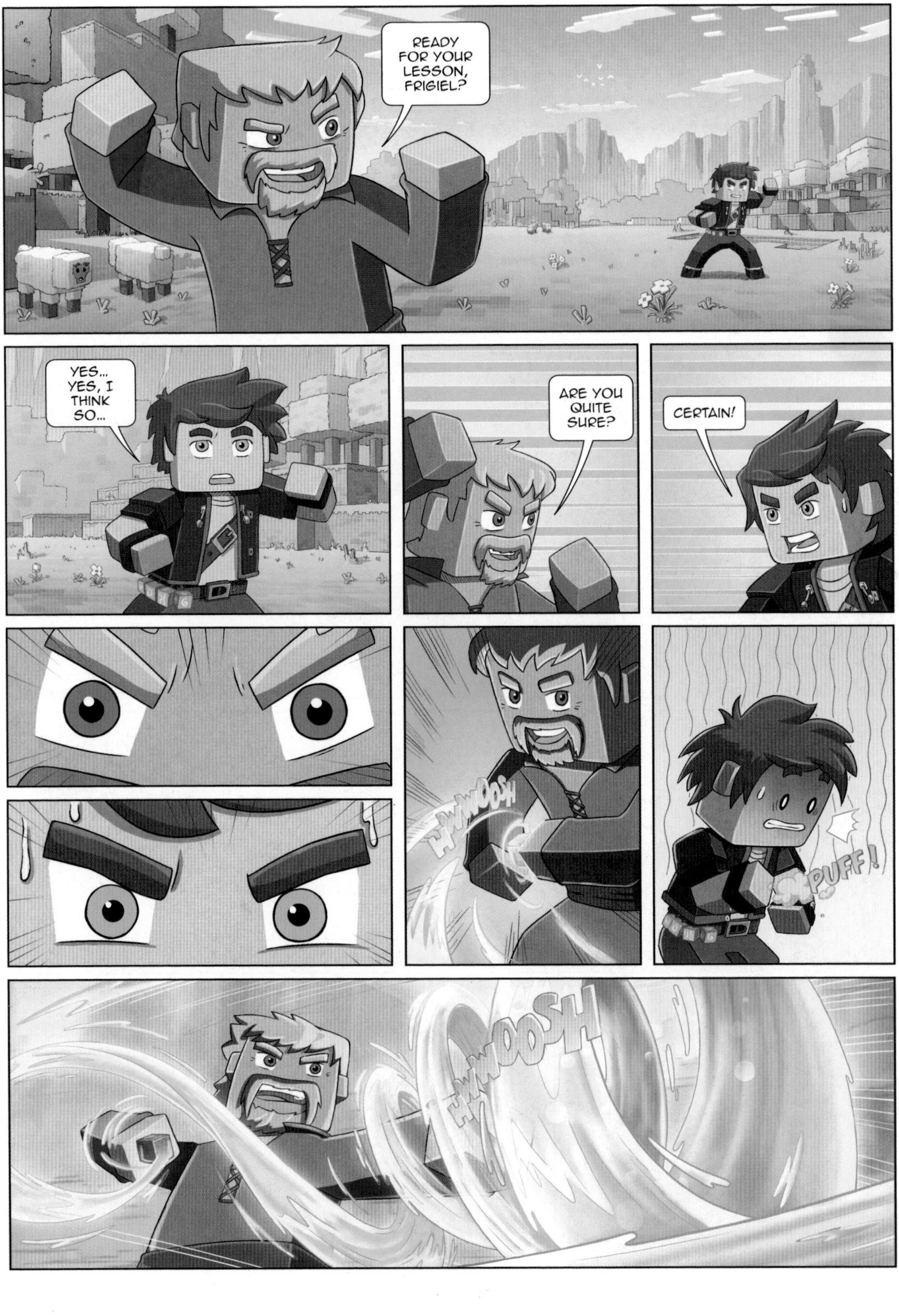
READY FOR YOUR LESSON, FRIGIEL?
YES... YES, I THINK SO...
ARE YOU QUITE SURE?
CERTAIN!
WHWOOSH
PUFF!
WHWOOSH

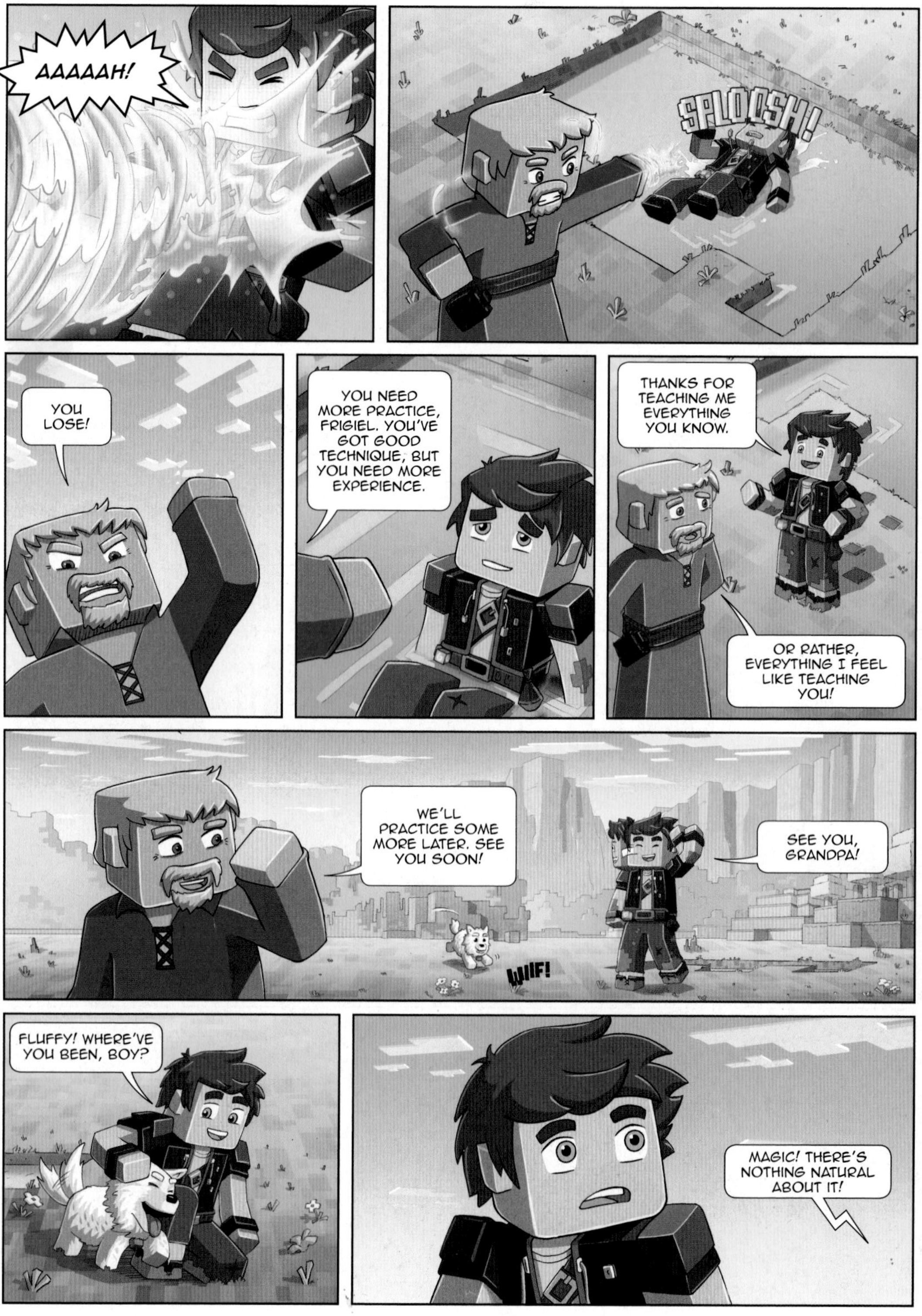
AAAAAH!
SPLOOSH!
YOU LOSE!
YOU NEED MORE PRACTICE, FRIGIEL. YOU'VE GOT GOOD TECHNIQUE, BUT YOU NEED MORE EXPERIENCE.
THANKS FOR TEACHING ME EVERYTHING YOU KNOW.
OR RATHER, EVERYTHING I FEEL LIKE TEACHING YOU!
WE'LL PRACTICE SOME MORE LATER. SEE YOU SOON!
SEE YOU, GRANDPA!
WIF!
FLUFFY! WHERE'VE YOU BEEN, BOY?
MAGIC! THERE'S NOTHING NATURAL ABOUT IT!

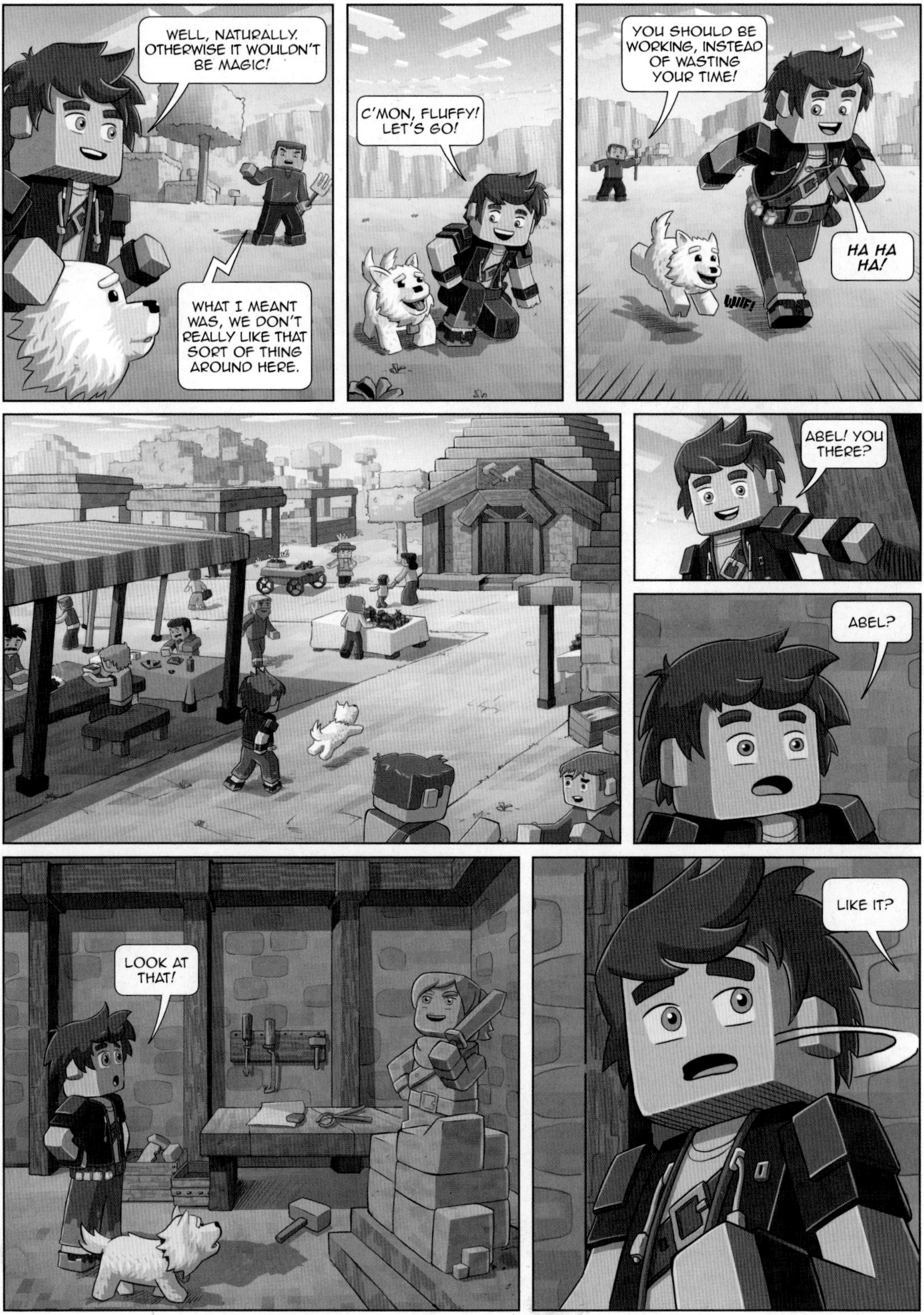
WELL, NATURALLY. OTHERWISE IT WOULDN'T BE MAGIC!
WHAT I MEANT WAS, WE DON'T REALLY LIKE THAT SORT OF THING AROUND HERE.
C'MON, FLUFFY! LET'S GO!
YOU SHOULD BE WORKING, INSTEAD OF WASTING YOUR TIME!
HA HA HA!
WUF!
ABEL! YOU THERE?
ABEL?
LOOK AT THAT!
LIKE IT?

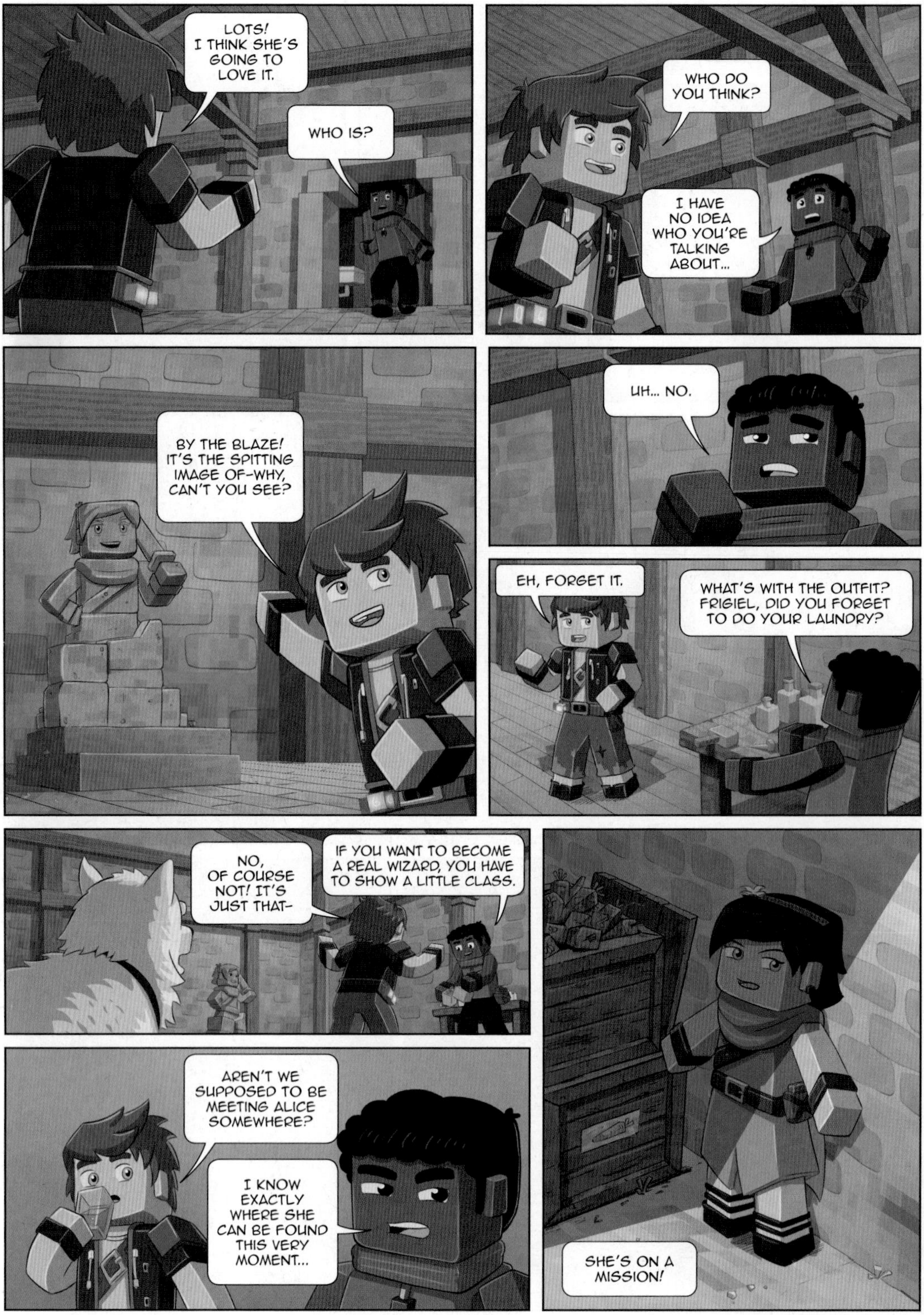
LOTS! I THINK SHE'S GOING TO LOVE IT.
WHO IS?
WHO DO YOU THINK?
I HAVE NO IDEA WHO YOU'RE TALKING ABOUT...
BY THE BLAZE! IT'S THE SPITTING IMAGE OF-WHY, CAN'T YOU SEE?
UH... NO.
EH, FORGET IT.
WHAT'S WITH THE OUTFIT? FRIGIEL, DID YOU FORGET TO DO YOUR LAUNDRY?
NO, OF COURSE NOT! IT'S JUST THAT-
IF YOU WANT TO BECOME A REAL WIZARD, YOU HAVE TO SHOW A LITTLE CLASS.
AREN'T WE SUPPOSED TO BE MEETING ALICE SOMEWHERE?
I KNOW EXACTLY WHERE SHE CAN BE FOUND THIS VERY MOMENT...
SHE'S ON A MISSION!

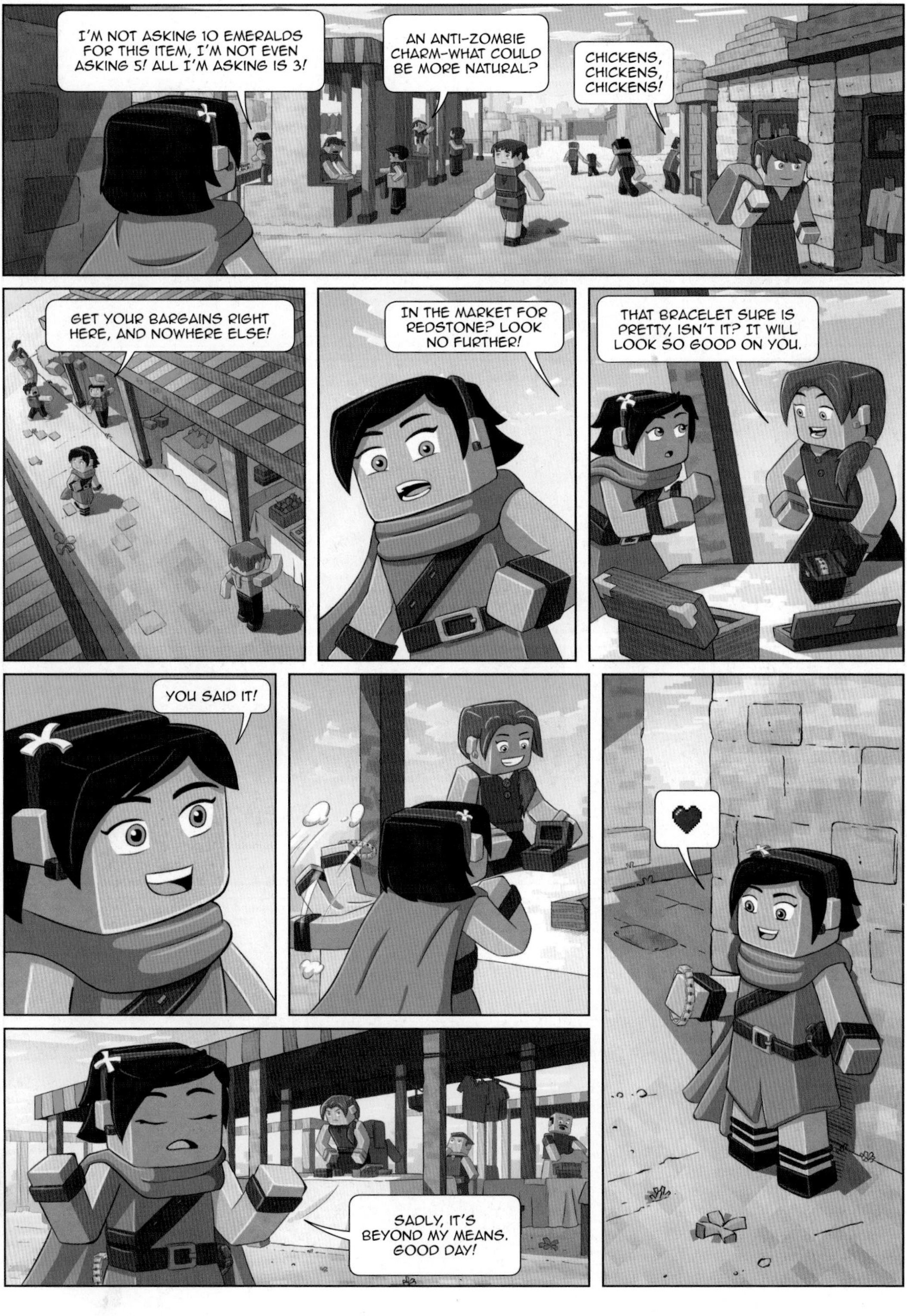
I'M NOT ASKING 10 EMERALDS FOR THIS ITEM, I'M NOT EVEN ASKING 5! ALL I'M ASKING IS 3!
AN ANTI-ZOMBIE CHARM–WHAT COULD BE MORE NATURAL?
CHICKENS, CHICKENS, CHICKENS!
GET YOUR BARGAINS RIGHT HERE, AND NOWHERE ELSE!
IN THE MARKET FOR REDSTONE? LOOK NO FURTHER!
THAT BRACELET SURE IS PRETTY, ISN'T IT? IT WILL LOOK SO GOOD ON YOU.
YOU SAID IT!
SADLY, IT'S BEYOND MY MEANS. GOOD DAY!

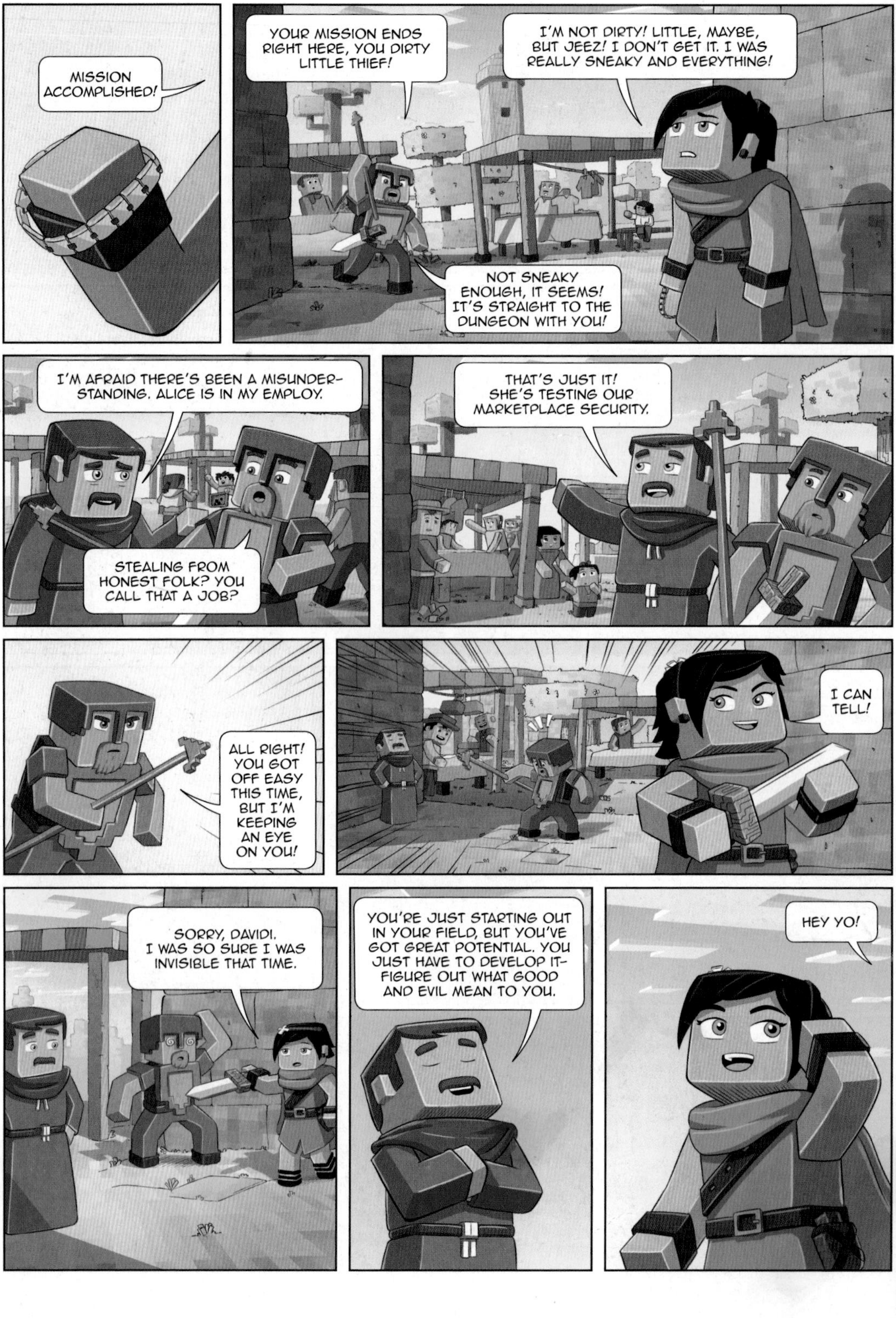
MISSION ACCOMPLISHED!
YOUR MISSION ENDS RIGHT HERE, YOU DIRTY LITTLE THIEF!
I'M NOT DIRTY! LITTLE, MAYBE, BUT JEEZ! I DON'T GET IT. I WAS REALLY SNEAKY AND EVERYTHING!
NOT SNEAKY ENOUGH, IT SEEMS! IT'S STRAIGHT TO THE DUNGEON WITH YOU!
I'M AFRAID THERE'S BEEN A MISUNDER-STANDING. ALICE IS IN MY EMPLOY.
STEALING FROM HONEST FOLK? YOU CALL THAT A JOB?
THAT'S JUST IT! SHE'S TESTING OUR MARKETPLACE SECURITY.
ALL RIGHT! YOU GOT OFF EASY THIS TIME, BUT I'M KEEPING AN EYE ON YOU!
I CAN TELL!
SORRY, DAVID! I WAS SO SURE I WAS INVISIBLE THAT TIME.
YOU'RE JUST STARTING OUT IN YOUR FIELD, BUT YOU'VE GOT GREAT POTENTIAL. YOU JUST HAVE TO DEVELOP IT-FIGURE OUT WHAT GOOD AND EVIL MEAN TO YOU.
HEY YO!

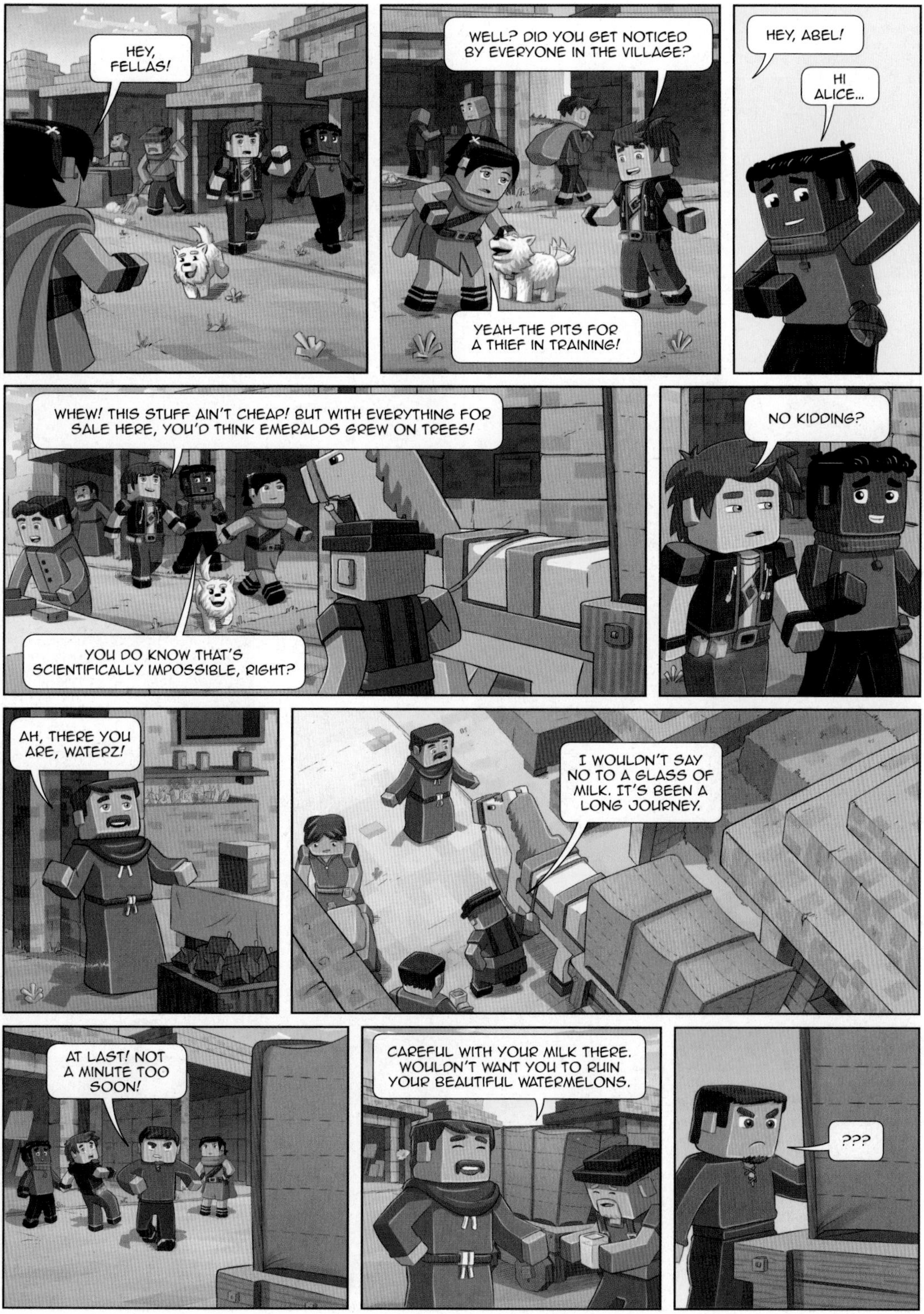
HEY, FELLAS!
WELL? DID YOU GET NOTICED BY EVERYONE IN THE VILLAGE?
YEAH–THE PITS FOR A THIEF IN TRAINING!
HEY, ABEL!
HI ALICE...
WHEW! THIS STUFF AIN'T CHEAP! BUT WITH EVERYTHING FOR SALE HERE, YOU'D THINK EMERALDS GREW ON TREES!
YOU DO KNOW THAT'S SCIENTIFICALLY IMPOSSIBLE, RIGHT?
NO KIDDING?
AH, THERE YOU ARE, WATERZ!
I WOULDN'T SAY NO TO A GLASS OF MILK. IT'S BEEN A LONG JOURNEY.
AT LAST! NOT A MINUTE TOO SOON!
CAREFUL WITH YOUR MILK THERE. WOULDN'T WANT YOU TO RUIN YOUR BEAUTIFUL WATERMELONS.
???

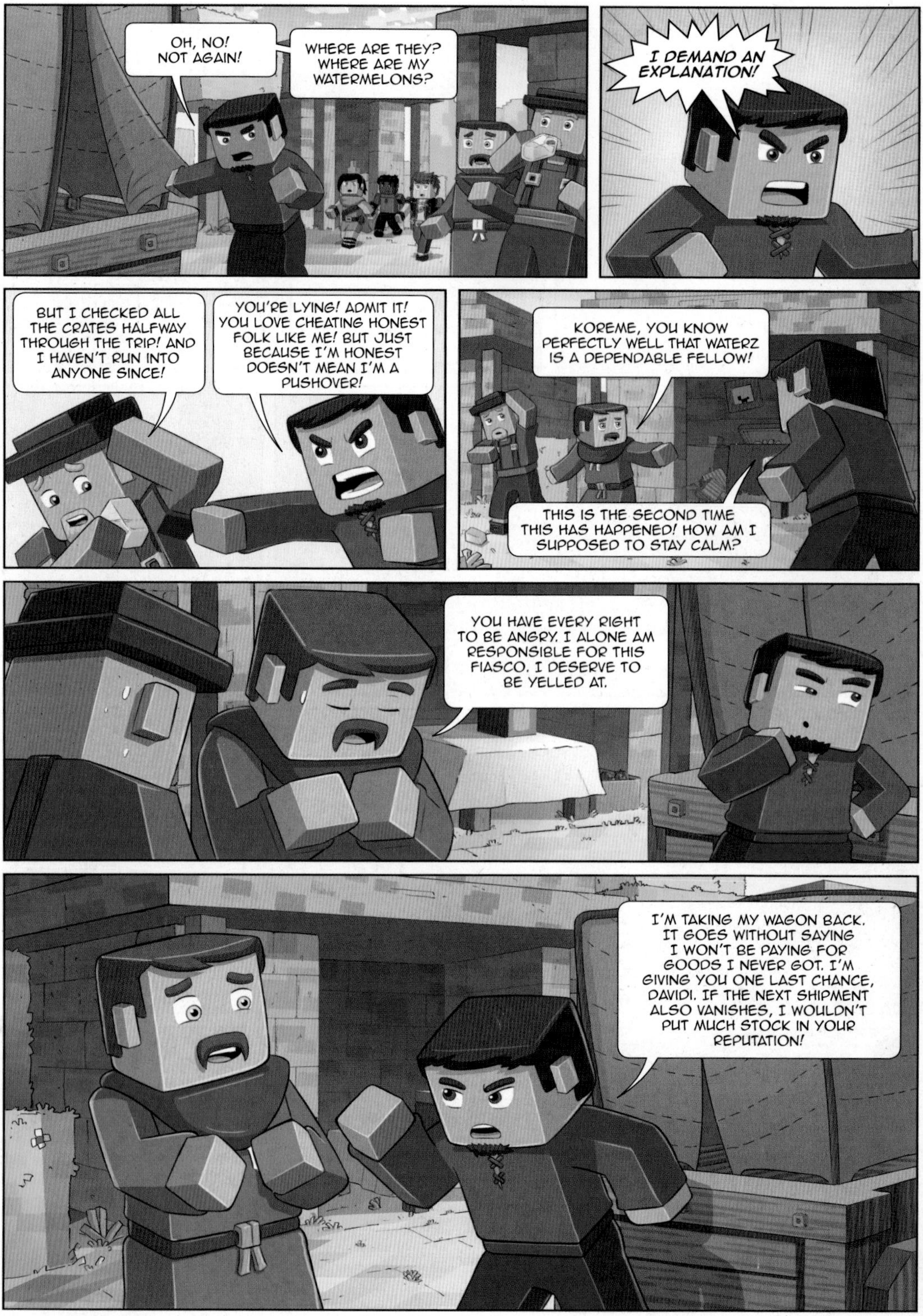
OH, NO! NOT AGAIN!
WHERE ARE THEY? WHERE ARE MY WATERMELONS?
I DEMAND AN EXPLANATION!
BUT I CHECKED ALL THE CRATES HALFWAY THROUGH THE TRIP! AND I HAVEN'T RUN INTO ANYONE SINCE!
YOU'RE LYING! ADMIT IT! YOU LOVE CHEATING HONEST FOLK LIKE ME! BUT JUST BECAUSE I'M HONEST DOESN'T MEAN I'M A PUSHOVER!
KOREME, YOU KNOW PERFECTLY WELL THAT WATERZ IS A DEPENDABLE FELLOW!
THIS IS THE SECOND TIME THIS HAS HAPPENED! HOW AM I SUPPOSED TO STAY CALM?
YOU HAVE EVERY RIGHT TO BE ANGRY. I ALONE AM RESPONSIBLE FOR THIS FIASCO. I DESERVE TO BE YELLED AT.
I'M TAKING MY WAGON BACK. IT GOES WITHOUT SAYING I WON'T BE PAYING FOR GOODS I NEVER GOT. I'M GIVING YOU ONE LAST CHANCE, DAVIDI. IF THE NEXT SHIPMENT ALSO VANISHES, I WOULDN'T PUT MUCH STOCK IN YOUR REPUTATION!

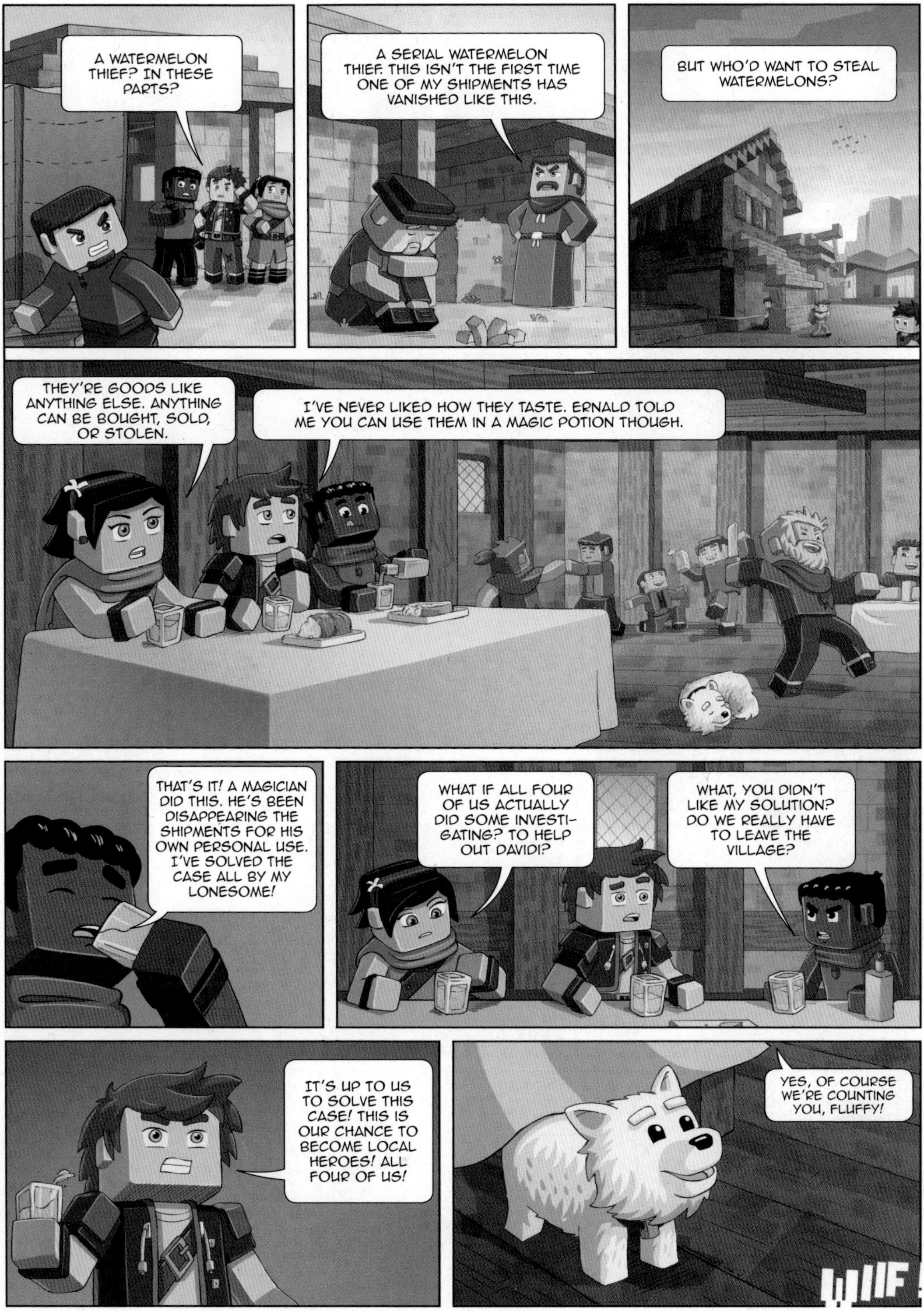
A WATERMELON THIEF? IN THESE PARTS?
A SERIAL WATERMELON THIEF. THIS ISN'T THE FIRST TIME ONE OF MY SHIPMENTS HAS VANISHED LIKE THIS.
BUT WHO'D WANT TO STEAL WATERMELONS?
THEY'RE GOODS LIKE ANYTHING ELSE. ANYTHING CAN BE BOUGHT, SOLD, OR STOLEN.
I'VE NEVER LIKED HOW THEY TASTE. ERNALD TOLD ME YOU CAN USE THEM IN A MAGIC POTION THOUGH.
THAT'S IT! A MAGICIAN DID THIS. HE'S BEEN DISAPPEARING THE SHIPMENTS FOR HIS OWN PERSONAL USE. I'VE SOLVED THE CASE ALL BY MY LONESOME!
WHAT IF ALL FOUR OF US ACTUALLY DID SOME INVESTI-GATING? TO HELP OUT DAVIDI?
WHAT, YOU DIDN'T LIKE MY SOLUTION? DO WE REALLY HAVE TO LEAVE THE VILLAGE?
IT'S UP TO US TO SOLVE THIS CASE! THIS IS OUR CHANCE TO BECOME LOCAL HEROES! ALL FOUR OF US!
YES, OF COURSE WE'RE COUNTING YOU, FLUFFY!
WIIF !

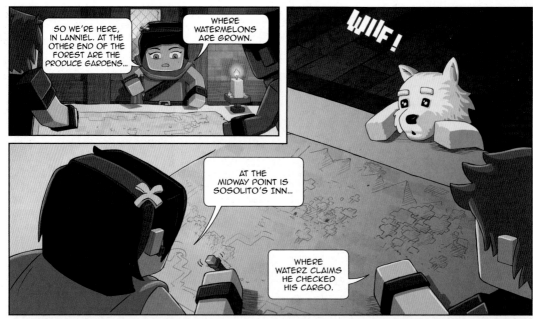

SO WE'RE HERE, IN LANNIEL. AT THE OTHER END OF THE FOREST ARE THE PRODUCE GARDENS...

WHERE WATERMELONS ARE GROWN.

WIIF!

AT THE MIDWAY POINT IS SOSOLITO'S INN...

WHERE WATERZ CLAIMS HE CHECKED HIS CARGO.

EXACTLY. I DOUBT THERE'S ANY POINT GOING FARTHER THAN SOSOLITO ON OUR MISSION. DAVIDI BELIEVES WATERZ IS TELLING THE TRUTH.

SO DO WE TELL DAVIDI? WE SHOULD, RIGHT?

ABSOLUTELY NOT! THIS IS OUR SECRET MISSION.

HOW ABOUT WE CALL IT "OPERATION WATERMELON"?

LET'S MEET UP TOMORROW MORNING AT DAWN. REMEMBER TO WEAR YOUR BEST BOOTS. WE'VE GOT A LONG HIKE AHEAD.

I DON'T KNOW IF ABEL CAN GET UP THIS EARLY.

HAVE FAITH IN HIM. HE'LL COME.

LOOK, THERE HE IS!

16

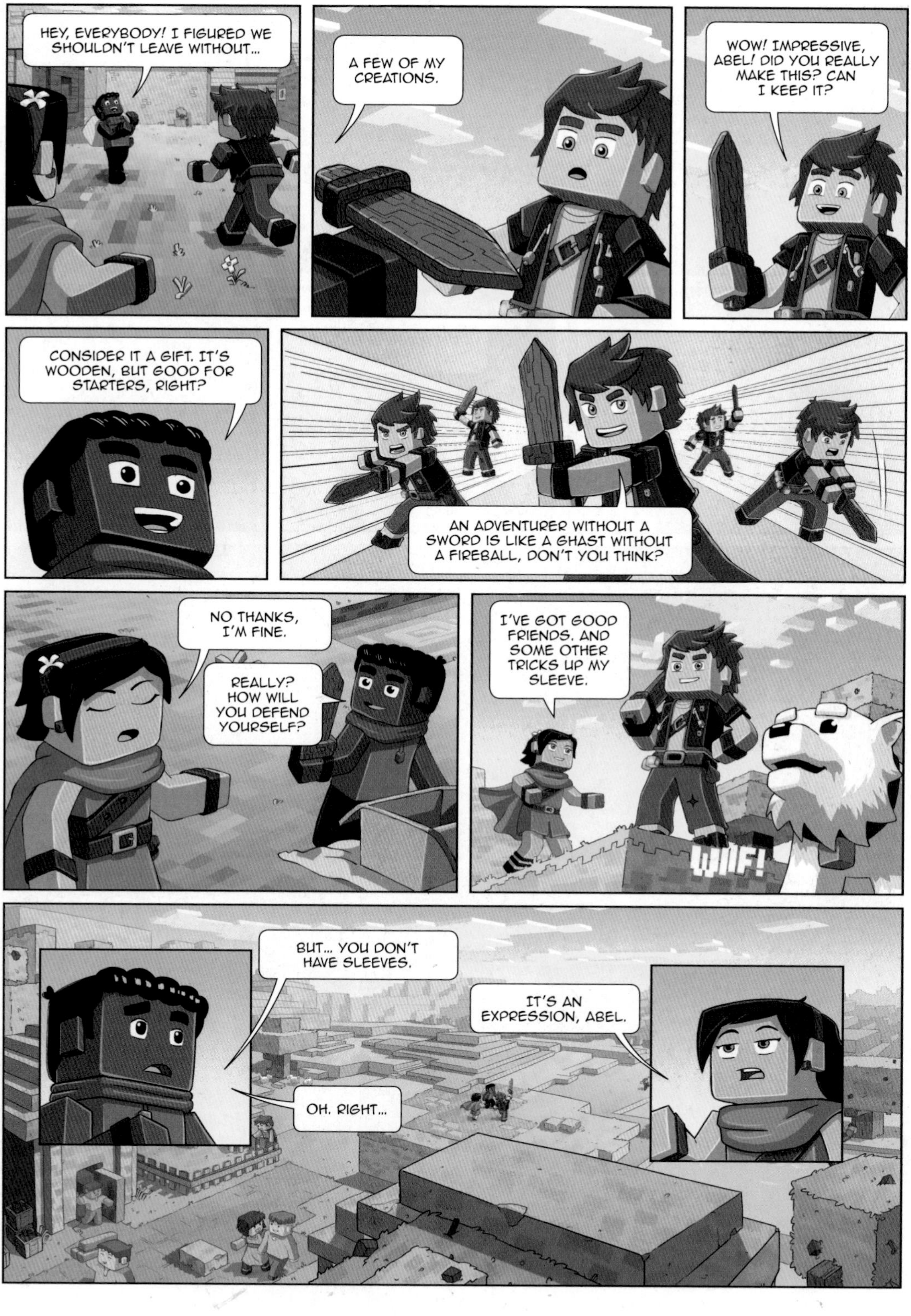
HEY, EVERYBODY! I FIGURED WE SHOULDN'T LEAVE WITHOUT...
A FEW OF MY CREATIONS.
WOW! IMPRESSIVE, ABEL! DID YOU REALLY MAKE THIS? CAN I KEEP IT?
CONSIDER IT A GIFT. IT'S WOODEN, BUT GOOD FOR STARTERS, RIGHT?
AN ADVENTURER WITHOUT A SWORD IS LIKE A GHAST WITHOUT A FIREBALL, DON'T YOU THINK?
NO THANKS, I'M FINE.
REALLY? HOW WILL YOU DEFEND YOURSELF?
I'VE GOT GOOD FRIENDS. AND SOME OTHER TRICKS UP MY SLEEVE.
WIIF!
BUT... YOU DON'T HAVE SLEEVES.
IT'S AN EXPRESSION, ABEL.
OH. RIGHT...

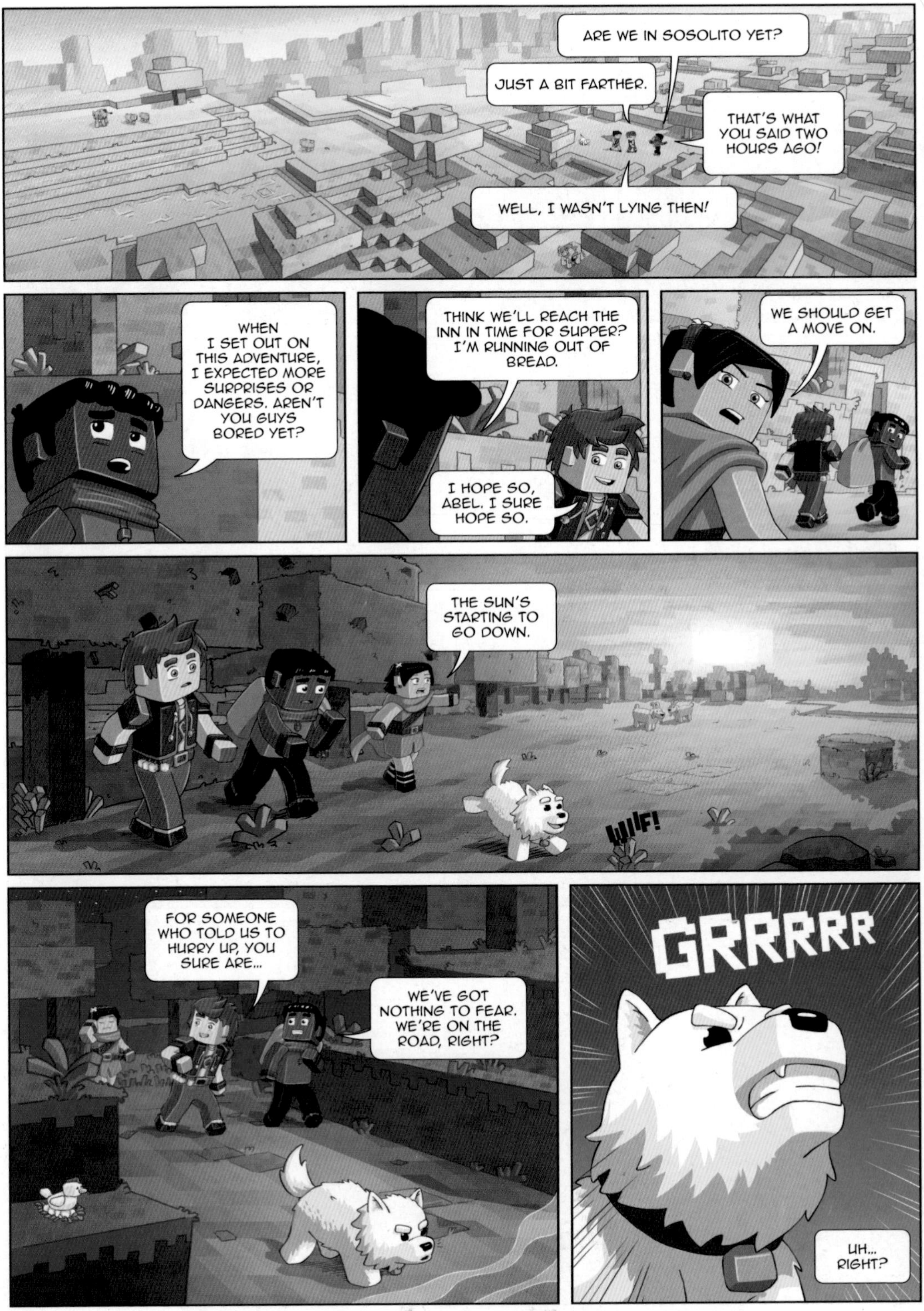
ARE WE IN SOSOLITO YET?
JUST A BIT FARTHER.
THAT'S WHAT YOU SAID TWO HOURS AGO!
WELL, I WASN'T LYING THEN!
WHEN I SET OUT ON THIS ADVENTURE, I EXPECTED MORE SURPRISES OR DANGERS. AREN'T YOU GUYS BORED YET?
THINK WE'LL REACH THE INN IN TIME FOR SUPPER? I'M RUNNING OUT OF BREAD.
I HOPE SO, ABEL. I SURE HOPE SO.
WE SHOULD GET A MOVE ON.
THE SUN'S STARTING TO GO DOWN.
WUF!
FOR SOMEONE WHO TOLD US TO HURRY UP, YOU SURE ARE...
WE'VE GOT NOTHING TO FEAR. WE'RE ON THE ROAD, RIGHT?
GRRRRR
UH... RIGHT?

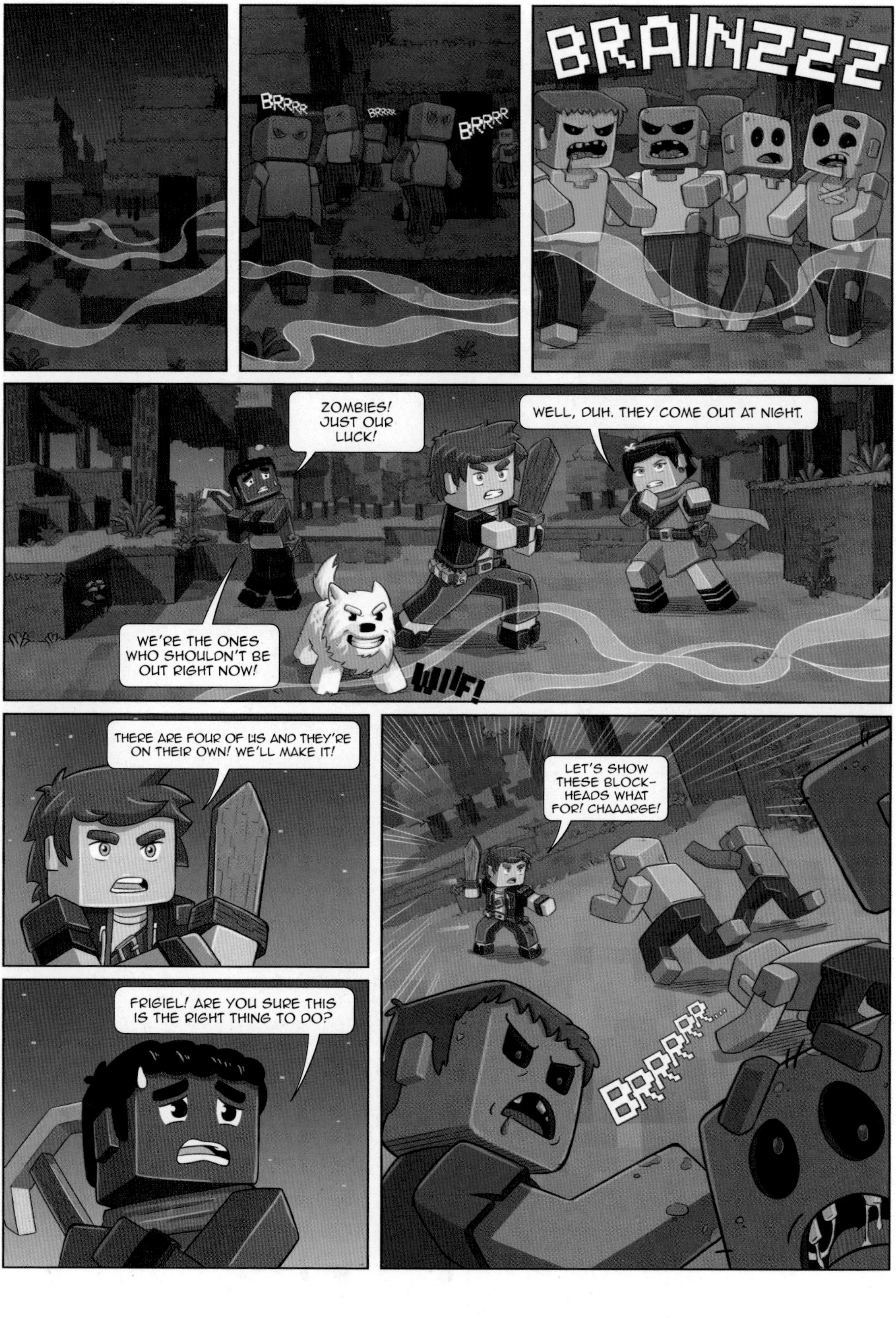
BRRRR...
BRRRR
BRRRR
BRAINZZZ
ZOMBIES! JUST OUR LUCK!
WELL, DUH. THEY COME OUT AT NIGHT.
WE'RE THE ONES WHO SHOULDN'T BE OUT RIGHT NOW!
WIIF!
THERE ARE FOUR OF US AND THEY'RE ON THEIR OWN! WE'LL MAKE IT!
FRIGIEL! ARE YOU SURE THIS IS THE RIGHT THING TO DO?
LET'S SHOW THESE BLOCK-HEADS WHAT FOR! CHAAARGE!
BRRRR...

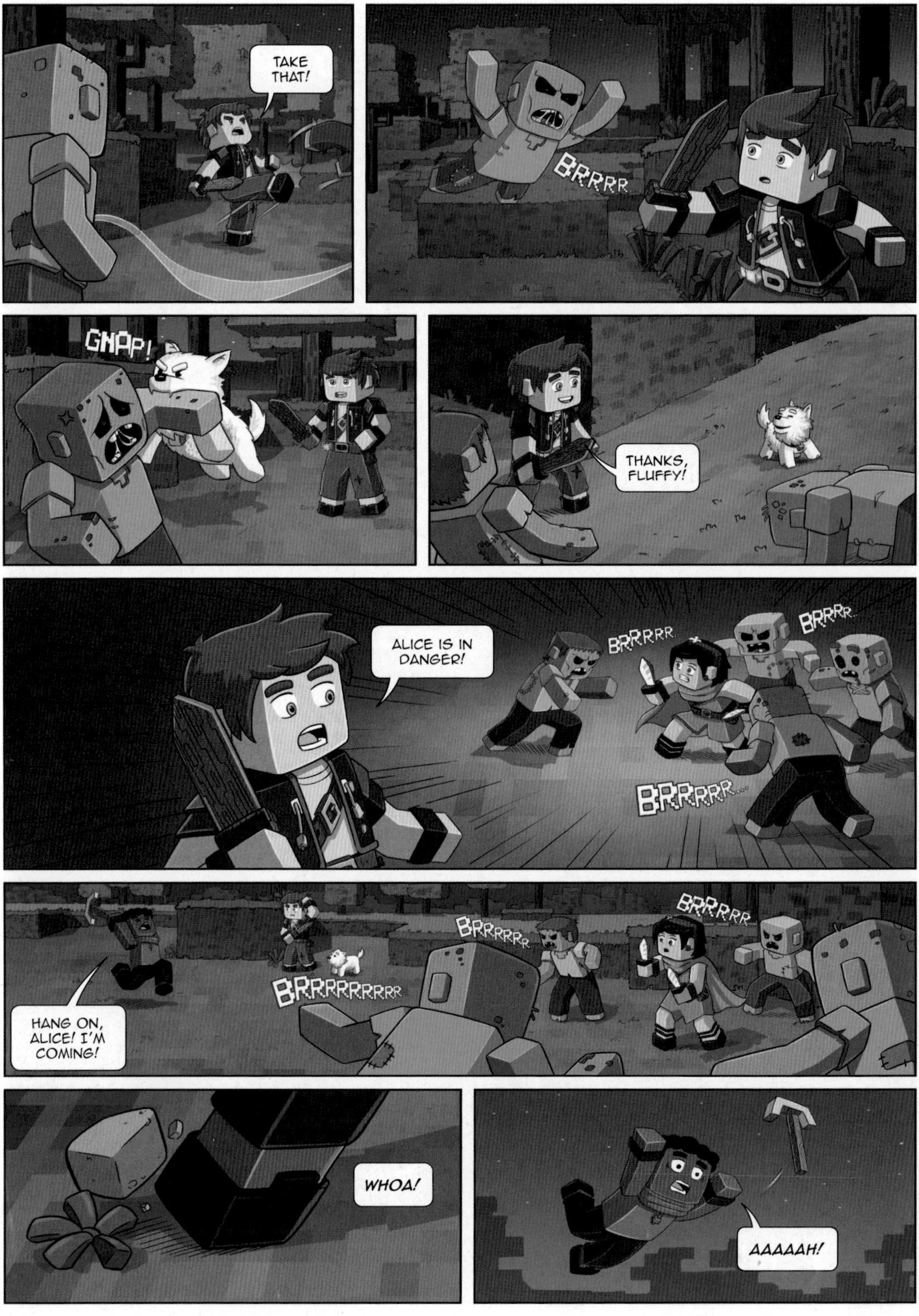
TAKE THAT!
BRRRR...
GNAP!
THANKS, FLUFFY!
ALICE IS IN DANGER!
BRRRRR...
BRRRR...
BRRRRR...
HANG ON, ALICE! I'M COMING!
BRRRRRRRRR
BRRRRRRR
BRRRRR
WHOA!
AAAAAH!

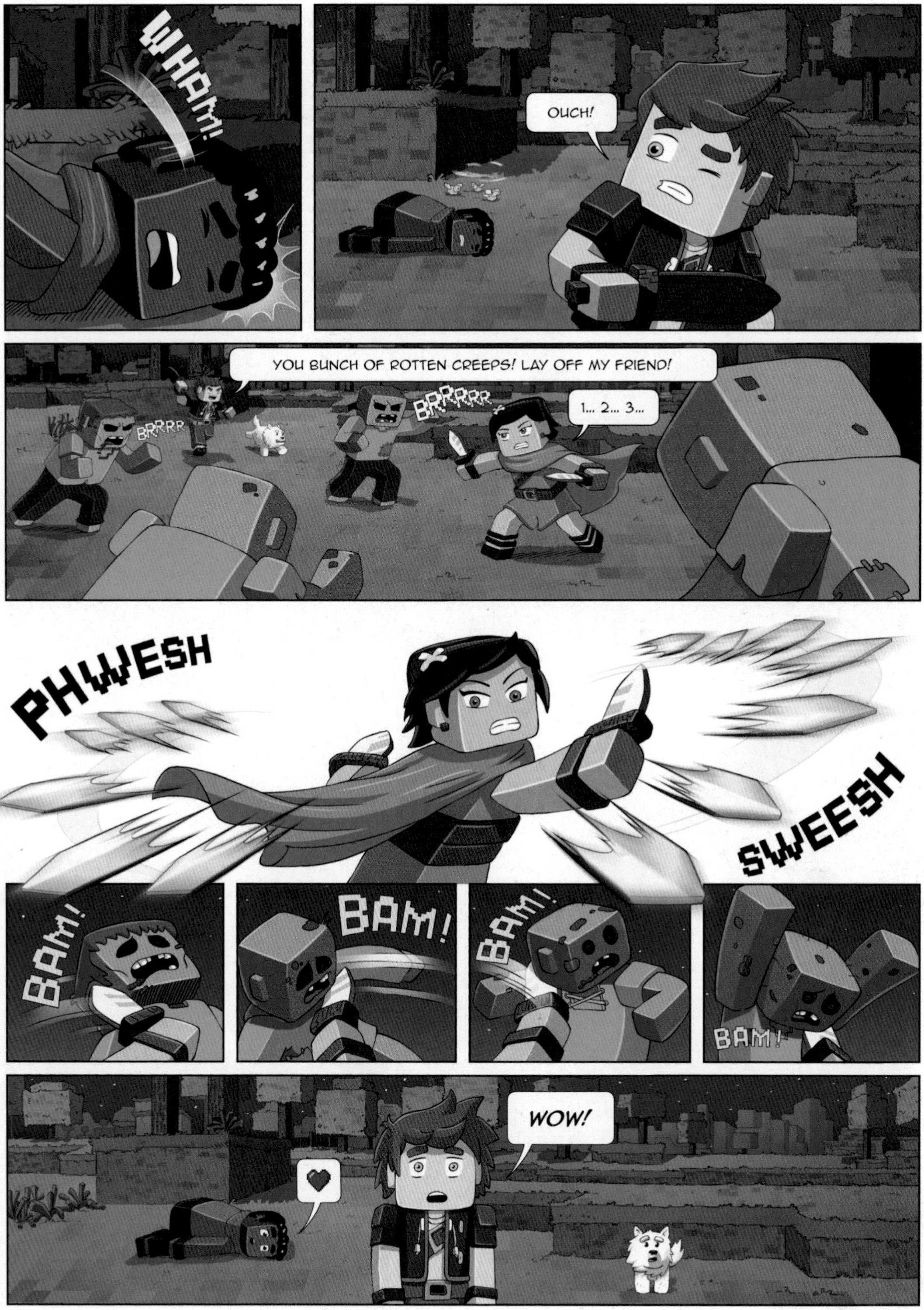
WHAM!
OUCH!
YOU BUNCH OF ROTTEN CREEPS! LAY OFF MY FRIEND!
BRRRR
BRRRRRR
1... 2... 3...
PHWESH
SWEESH
BAM!
BAM!
BAM!
BAM!
WOW!

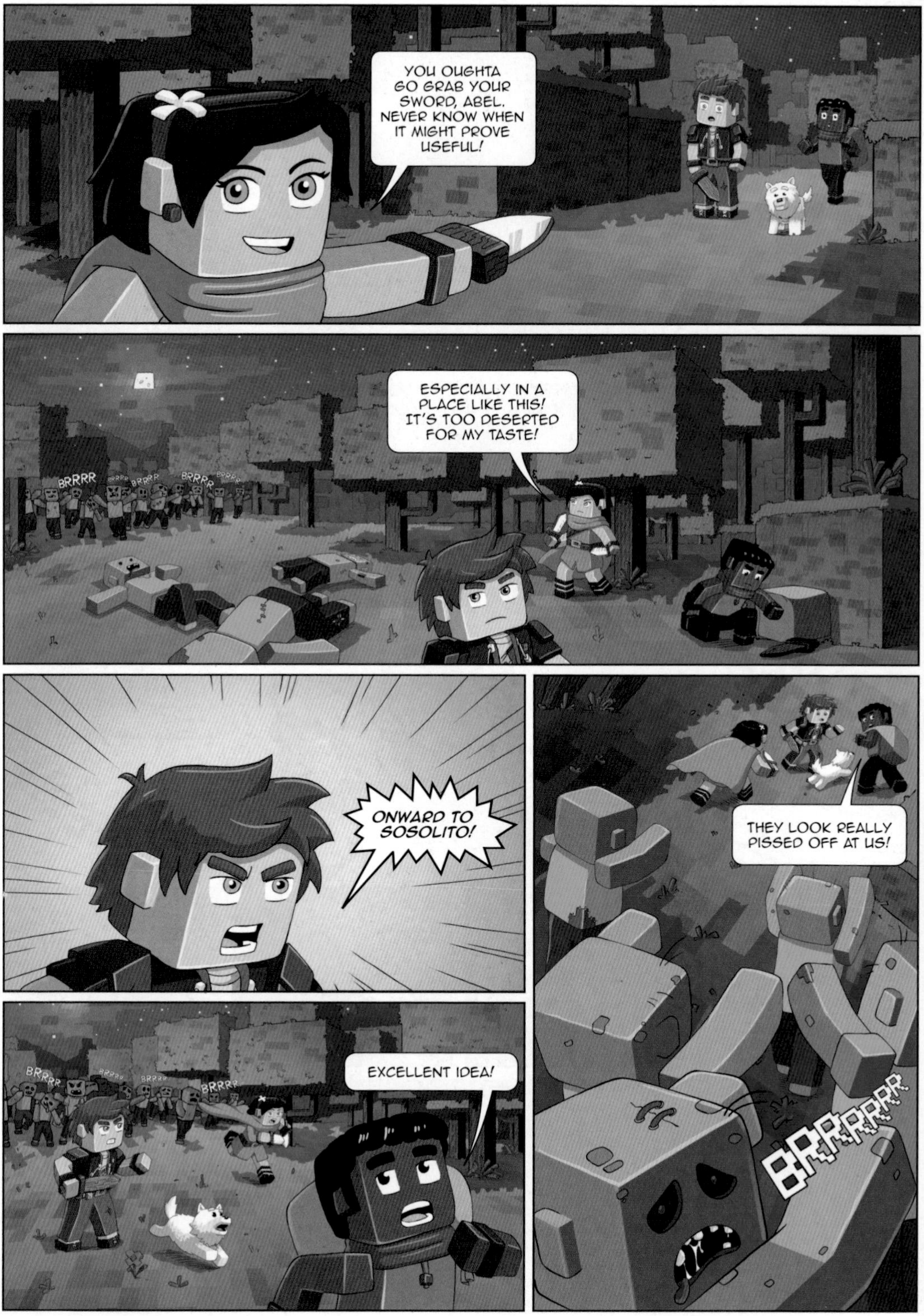
YOU OUGHTA GO GRAB YOUR SWORD, ABEL. NEVER KNOW WHEN IT MIGHT PROVE USEFUL!
ESPECIALLY IN A PLACE LIKE THIS! IT'S TOO DESERTED FOR MY TASTE!
BRRRR
ONWARD TO SOSOLITO!
EXCELLENT IDEA!
THEY LOOK REALLY PISSED OFF AT US!
BRRRRRR

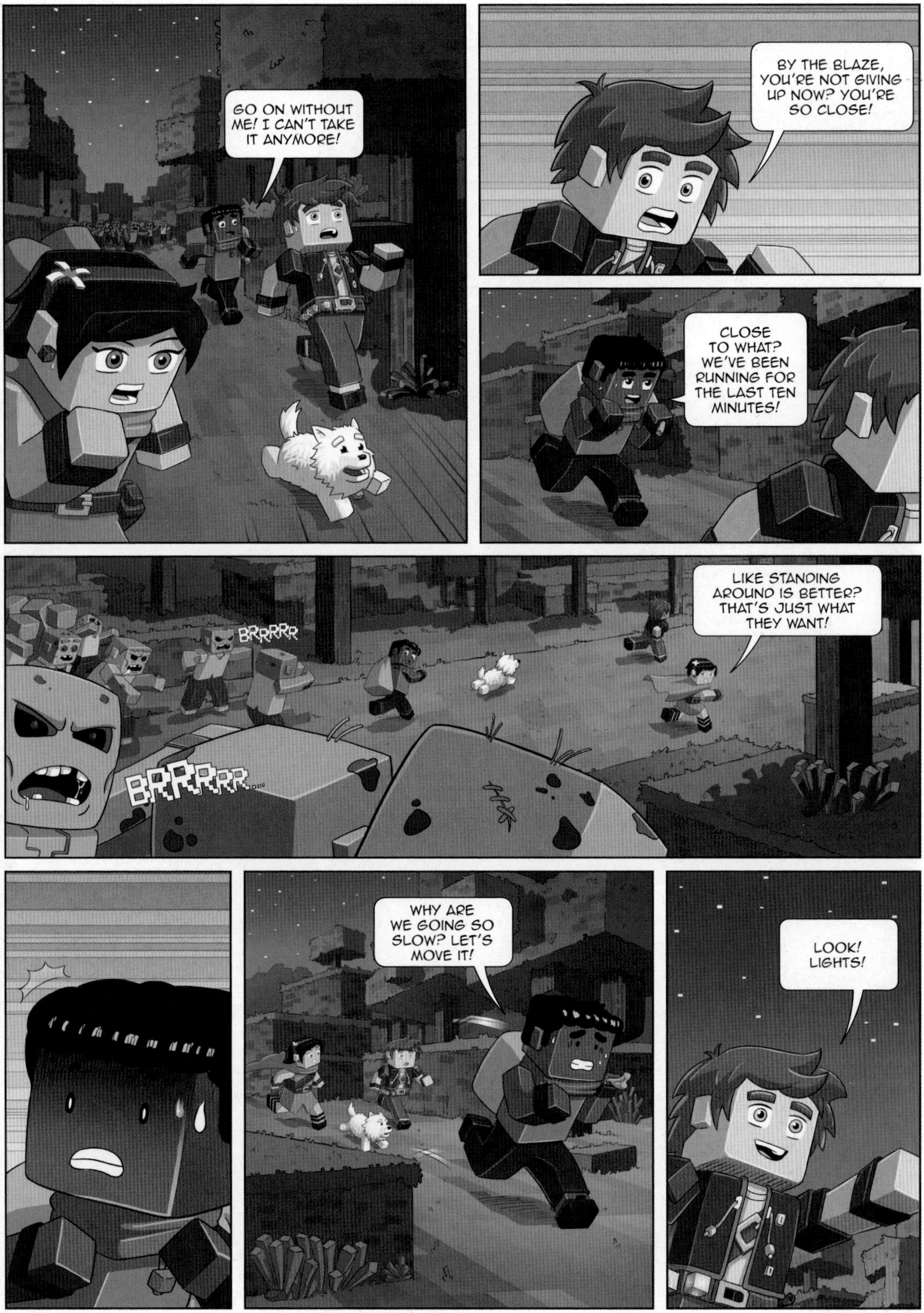
GO ON WITHOUT ME! I CAN'T TAKE IT ANYMORE!
BY THE BLAZE, YOU'RE NOT GIVING UP NOW? YOU'RE SO CLOSE!
CLOSE TO WHAT? WE'VE BEEN RUNNING FOR THE LAST TEN MINUTES!
BRRRRR
BRRRRR...
LIKE STANDING AROUND IS BETTER? THAT'S JUST WHAT THEY WANT!
WHY ARE WE GOING SO SLOW? LET'S MOVE IT!
LOOK! LIGHTS!

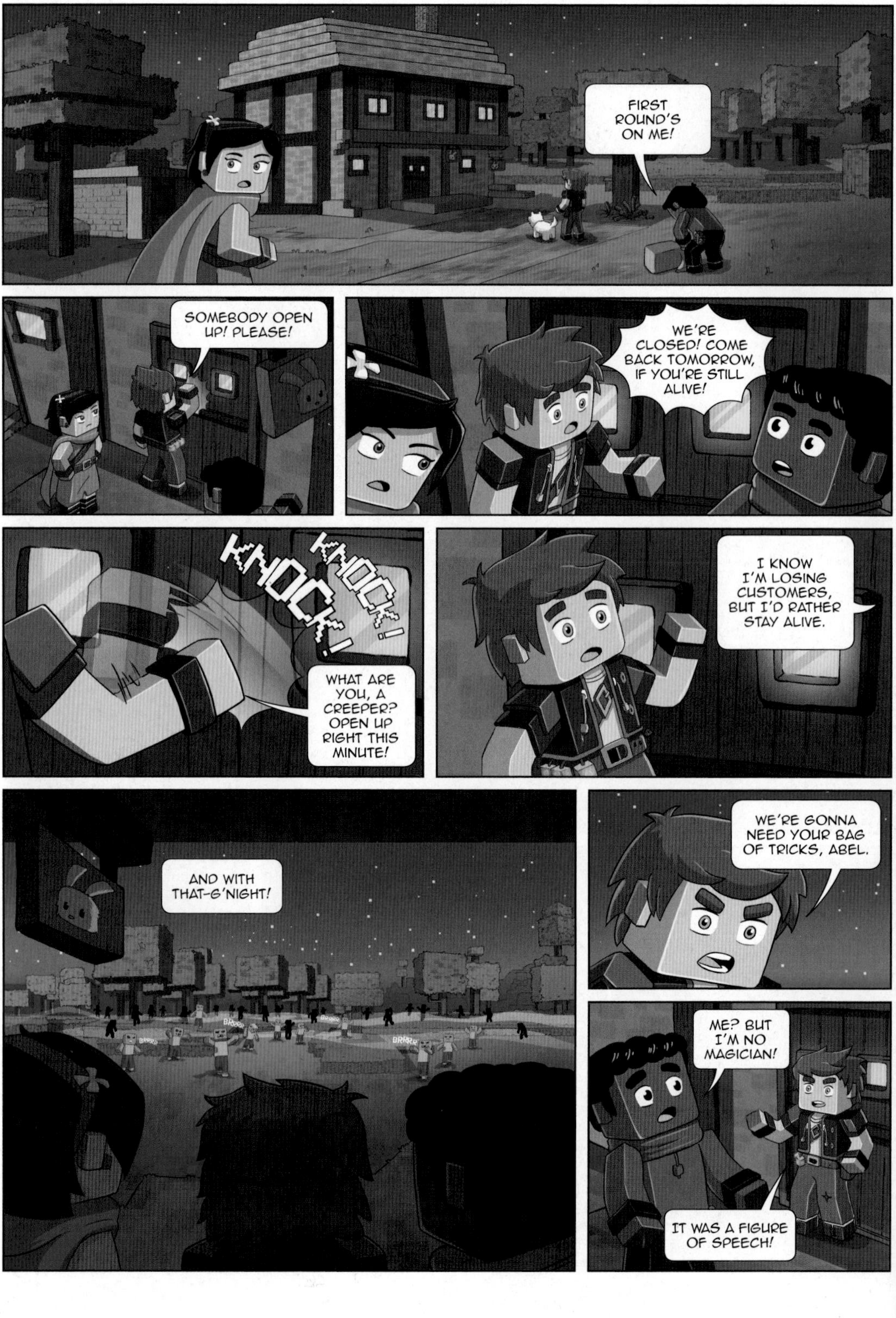
FIRST ROUND'S ON ME!
SOMEBODY OPEN UP! PLEASE!
WE'RE CLOSED! COME BACK TOMORROW, IF YOU'RE STILL ALIVE!
KNOCK! KNOCK!
WHAT ARE YOU, A CREEPER? OPEN UP RIGHT THIS MINUTE!
I KNOW I'M LOSING CUSTOMERS, BUT I'D RATHER STAY ALIVE.
AND WITH THAT-G'NIGHT!
WE'RE GONNA NEED YOUR BAG OF TRICKS, ABEL.
ME? BUT I'M NO MAGICIAN!
IT WAS A FIGURE OF SPEECH!

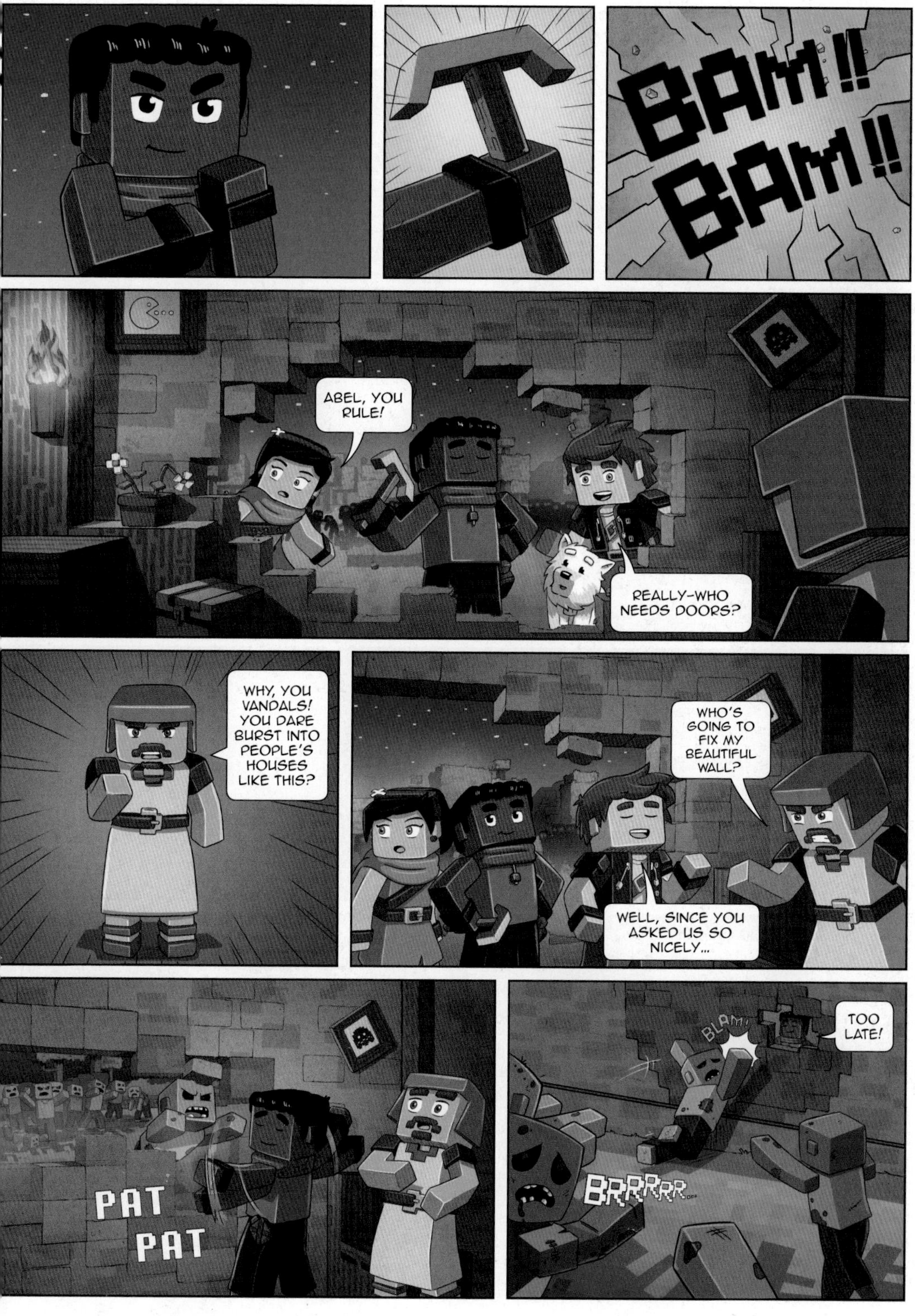
BAM!!
BAM!!
ABEL, YOU RULE!
REALLY–WHO NEEDS DOORS?
WHY, YOU VANDALS! YOU DARE BURST INTO PEOPLE'S HOUSES LIKE THIS?
WHO'S GOING TO FIX MY BEAUTIFUL WALL?
WELL, SINCE YOU ASKED US SO NICELY...
PAT
PAT
BLAM!
TOO LATE!
BRRRRR...

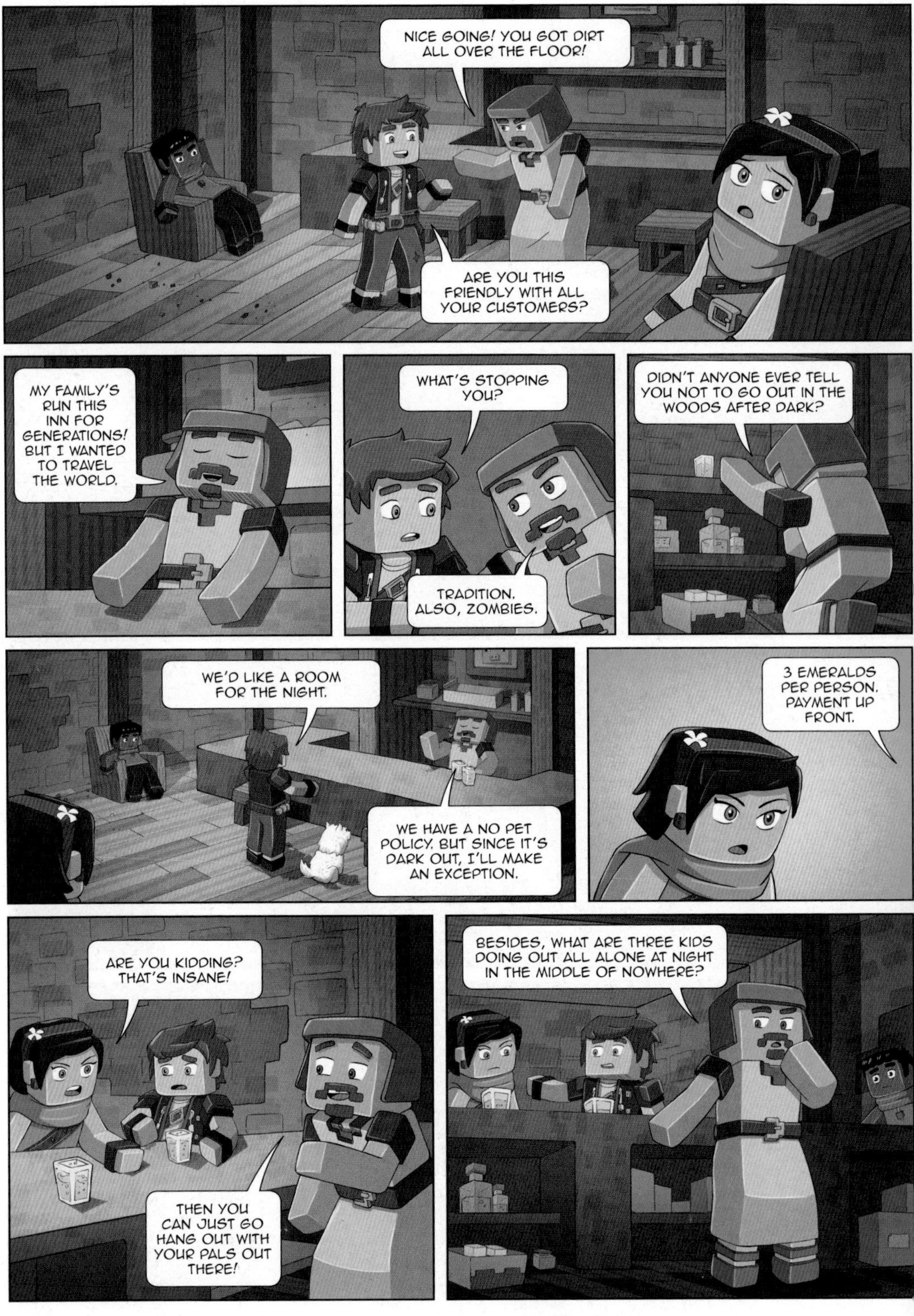
NICE GOING! YOU GOT DIRT ALL OVER THE FLOOR!
ARE YOU THIS FRIENDLY WITH ALL YOUR CUSTOMERS?
MY FAMILY'S RUN THIS INN FOR GENERATIONS! BUT I WANTED TO TRAVEL THE WORLD.
WHAT'S STOPPING YOU?
TRADITION. ALSO, ZOMBIES.
DIDN'T ANYONE EVER TELL YOU NOT TO GO OUT IN THE WOODS AFTER DARK?
WE'D LIKE A ROOM FOR THE NIGHT.
WE HAVE A NO PET POLICY. BUT SINCE IT'S DARK OUT, I'LL MAKE AN EXCEPTION.
3 EMERALDS PER PERSON. PAYMENT UP FRONT.
ARE YOU KIDDING? THAT'S INSANE!
THEN YOU CAN JUST GO HANG OUT WITH YOUR PALS OUT THERE!
BESIDES, WHAT ARE THREE KIDS DOING OUT ALL ALONE AT NIGHT IN THE MIDDLE OF NOWHERE?

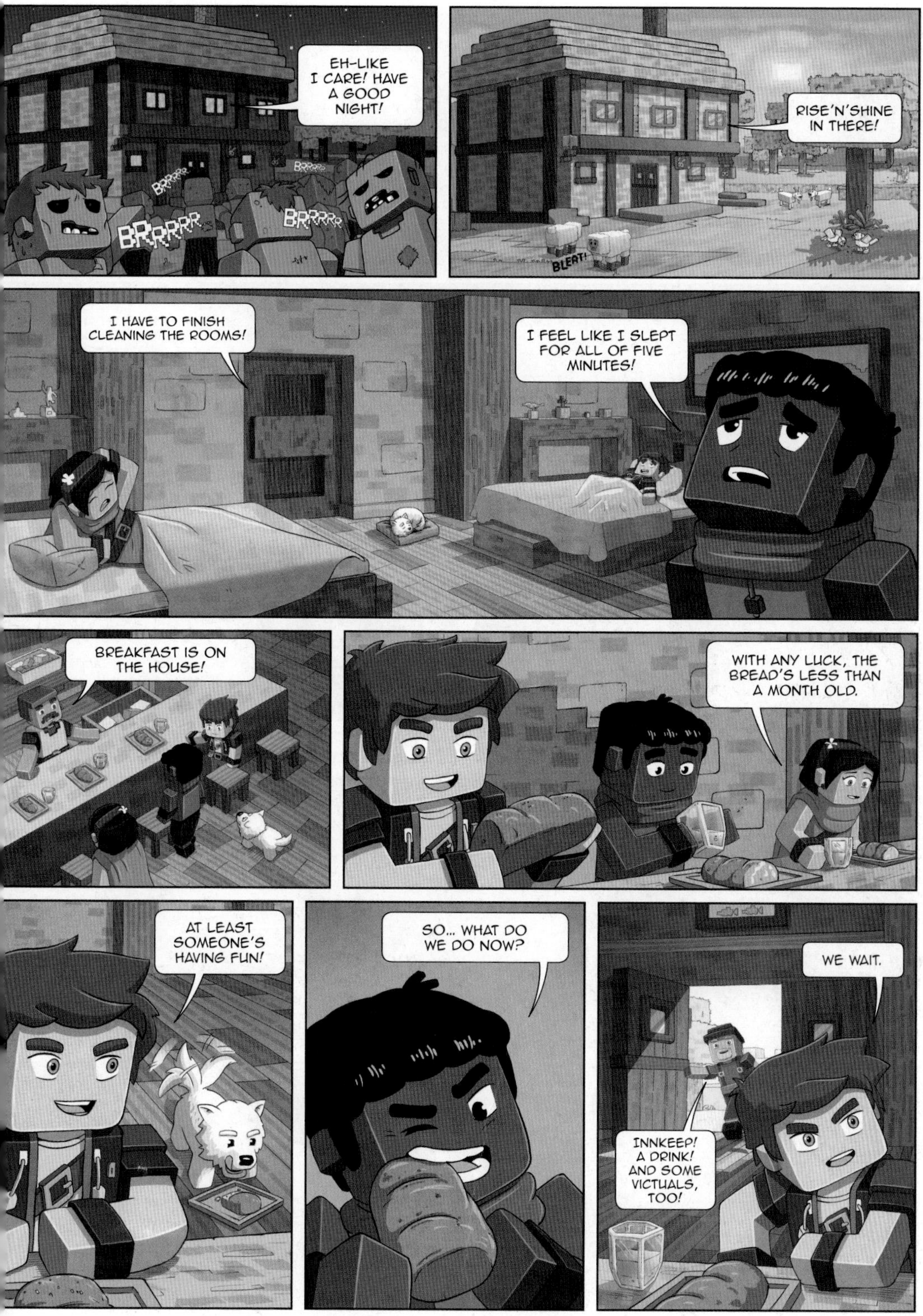
EH-LIKE I CARE! HAVE A GOOD NIGHT!
BRRRRR
BRRRRR
BRRRRR
BRRRRR
RISE'N'SHINE IN THERE!
BLEAT!
I HAVE TO FINISH CLEANING THE ROOMS!
I FEEL LIKE I SLEPT FOR ALL OF FIVE MINUTES!
BREAKFAST IS ON THE HOUSE!
WITH ANY LUCK, THE BREAD'S LESS THAN A MONTH OLD.
AT LEAST SOMEONE'S HAVING FUN!
SO... WHAT DO WE DO NOW?
WE WAIT.
INNKEEP! A DRINK! AND SOME VICTUALS, TOO!

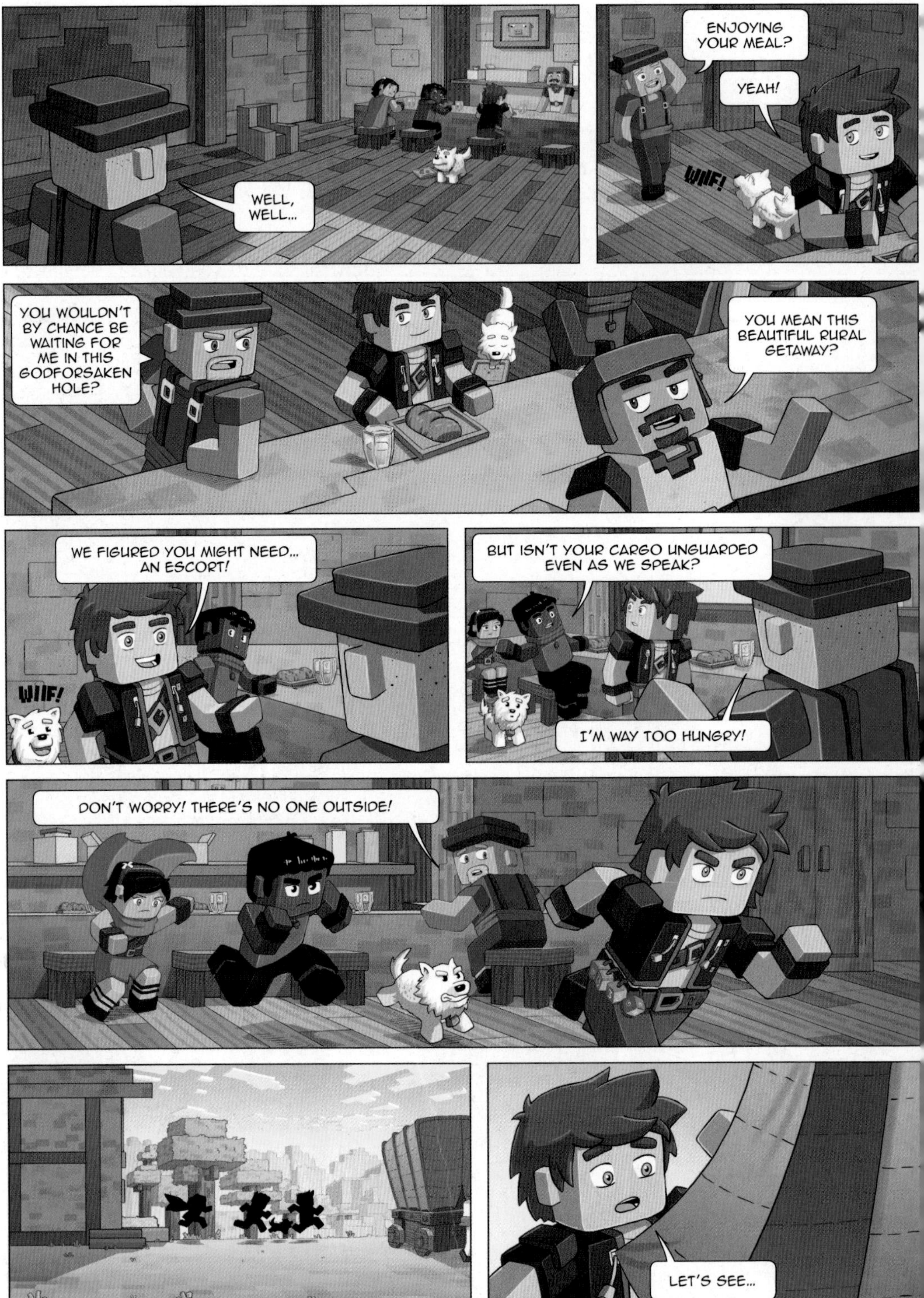
WELL, WELL...
ENJOYING YOUR MEAL?
YEAH!
WIIF!
YOU WOULDN'T BY CHANCE BE WAITING FOR ME IN THIS GODFORSAKEN HOLE?
YOU MEAN THIS BEAUTIFUL RURAL GETAWAY?
WE FIGURED YOU MIGHT NEED... AN ESCORT!
WIIF!
BUT ISN'T YOUR CARGO UNGUARDED EVEN AS WE SPEAK?
I'M WAY TOO HUNGRY!
DON'T WORRY! THERE'S NO ONE OUTSIDE!
LET'S SEE...

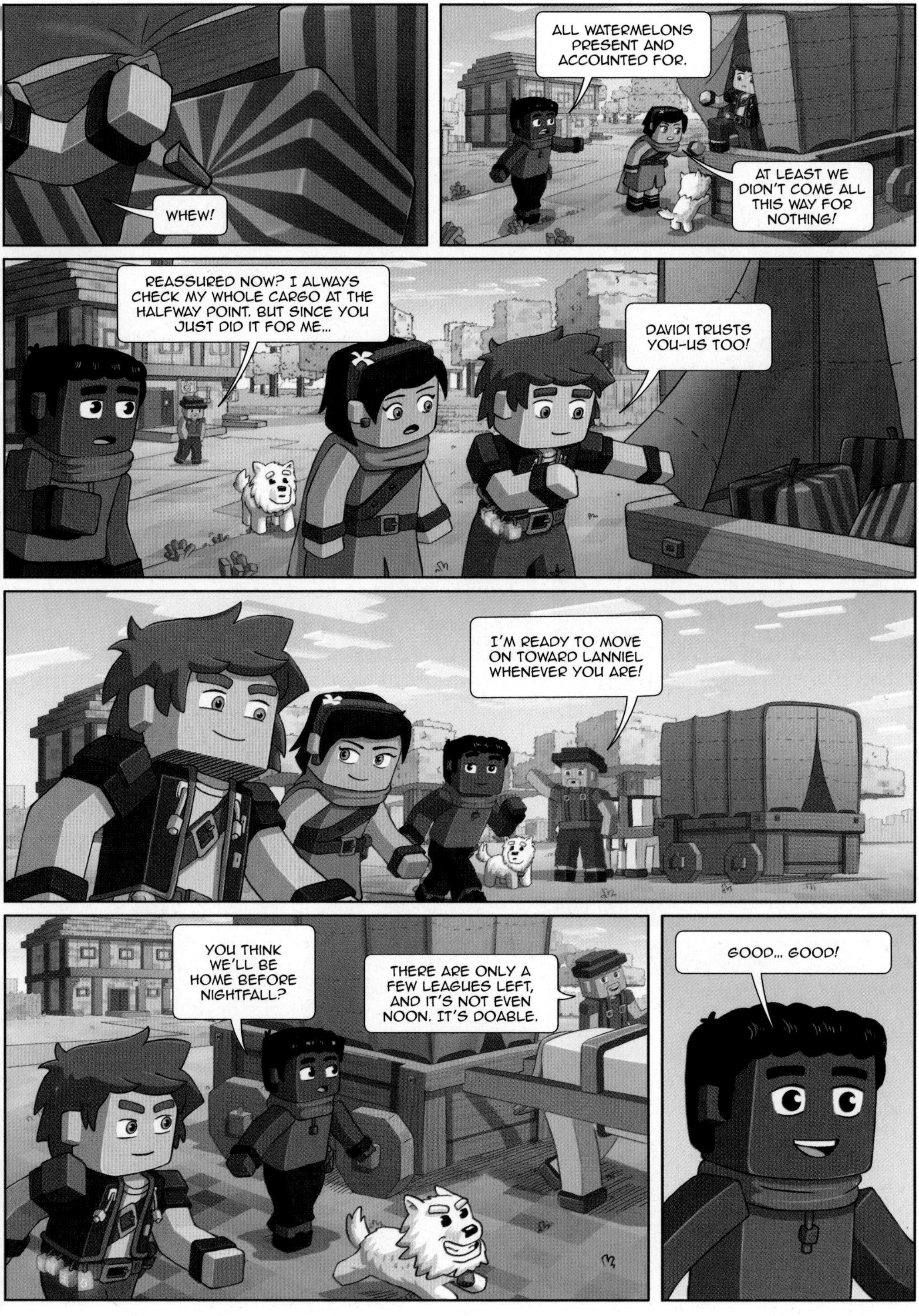
WHEW!
ALL WATERMELONS PRESENT AND ACCOUNTED FOR.
AT LEAST WE DIDN'T COME ALL THIS WAY FOR NOTHING!
REASSURED NOW? I ALWAYS CHECK MY WHOLE CARGO AT THE HALFWAY POINT. BUT SINCE YOU JUST DID IT FOR ME...
DAVIDI TRUSTS YOU-US TOO!
I'M READY TO MOVE ON TOWARD LANNIEL WHENEVER YOU ARE!
YOU THINK WE'LL BE HOME BEFORE NIGHTFALL?
THERE ARE ONLY A FEW LEAGUES LEFT, AND IT'S NOT EVEN NOON. IT'S DOABLE.
GOOD... GOOD!

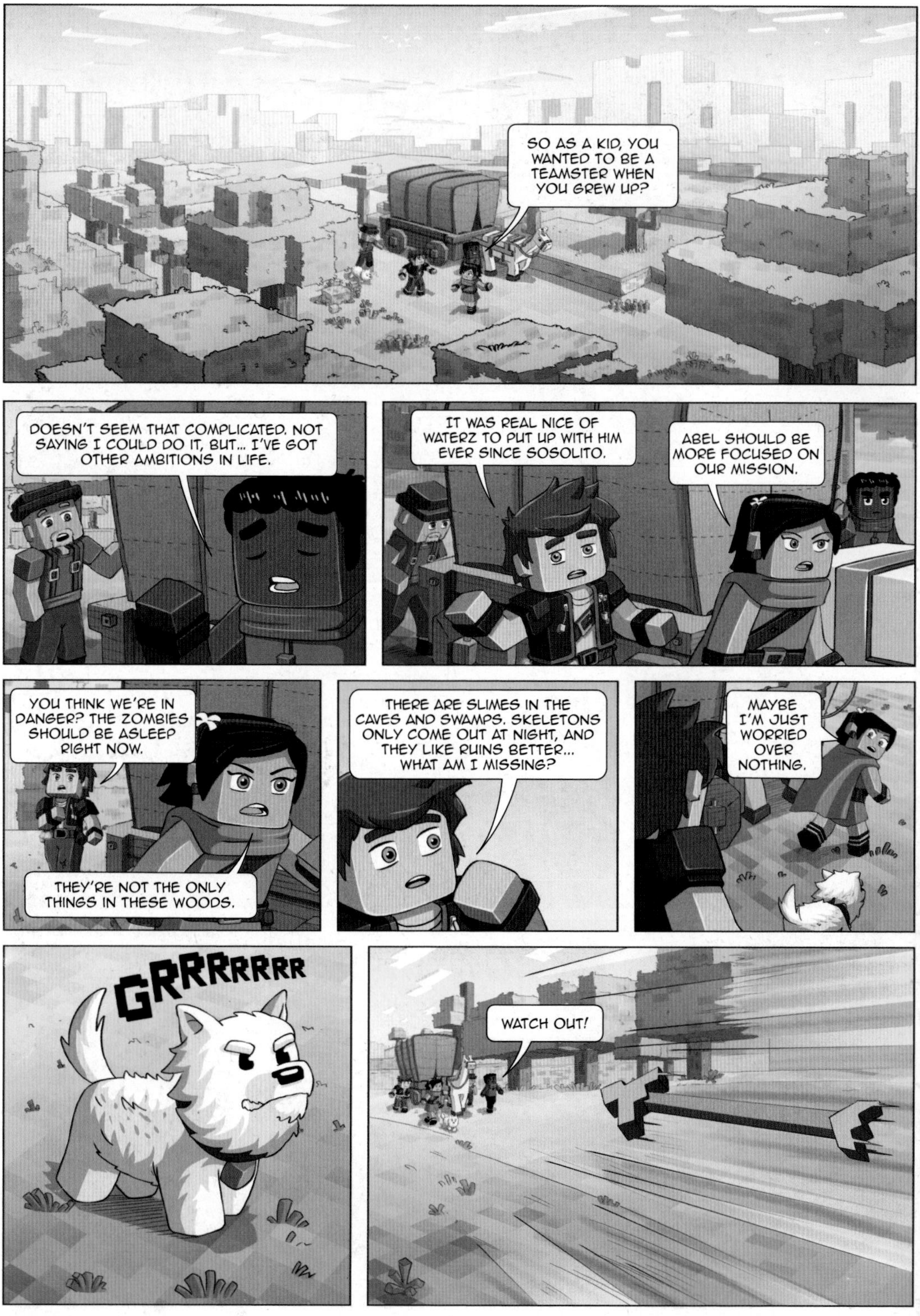
SO AS A KID, YOU WANTED TO BE A TEAMSTER WHEN YOU GREW UP?
DOESN'T SEEM THAT COMPLICATED. NOT SAYING I COULD DO IT, BUT... I'VE GOT OTHER AMBITIONS IN LIFE.
IT WAS REAL NICE OF WATERZ TO PUT UP WITH HIM EVER SINCE SOSOLITO.
ABEL SHOULD BE MORE FOCUSED ON OUR MISSION.
YOU THINK WE'RE IN DANGER? THE ZOMBIES SHOULD BE ASLEEP RIGHT NOW.
THEY'RE NOT THE ONLY THINGS IN THESE WOODS.
THERE ARE SLIMES IN THE CAVES AND SWAMPS. SKELETONS ONLY COME OUT AT NIGHT, AND THEY LIKE RUINS BETTER... WHAT AM I MISSING?
MAYBE I'M JUST WORRIED OVER NOTHING.
GRRRRRRR
WATCH OUT!

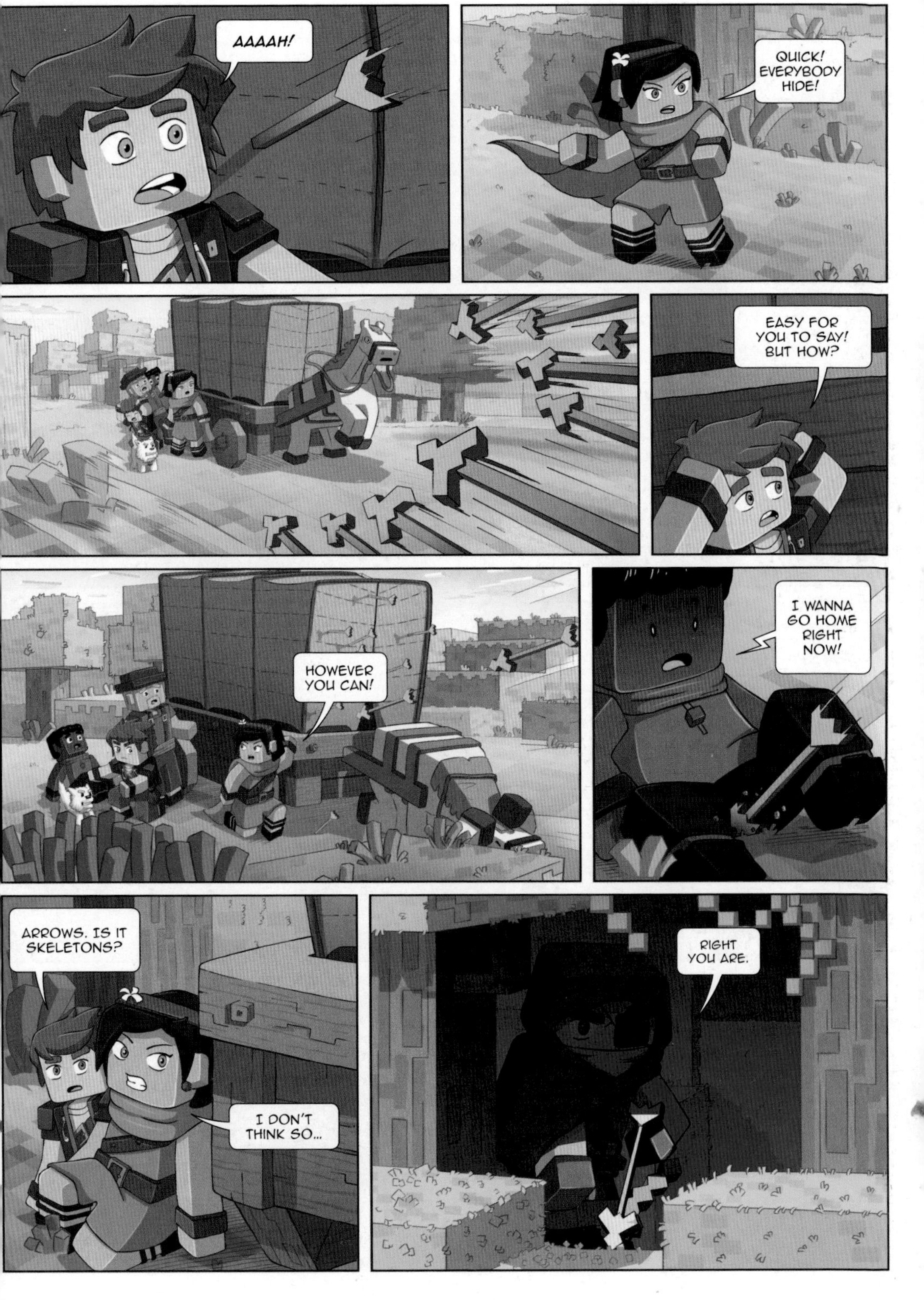
AAAAH!
QUICK! EVERYBODY HIDE!
EASY FOR YOU TO SAY! BUT HOW?
HOWEVER YOU CAN!
I WANNA GO HOME RIGHT NOW!
ARROWS. IS IT SKELETONS?
I DON'T THINK SO...
RIGHT YOU ARE.

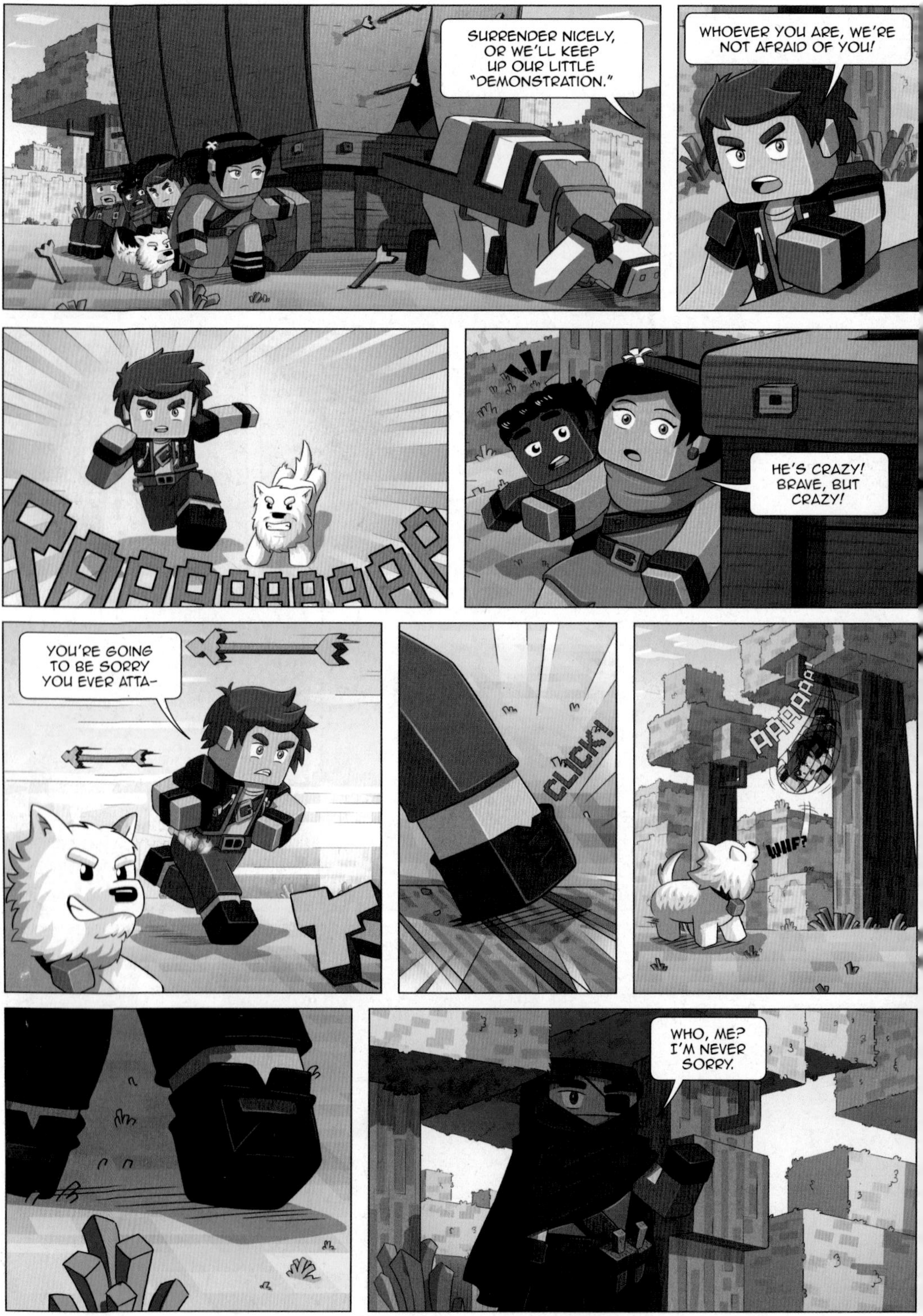
SURRENDER NICELY, OR WE'LL KEEP UP OUR LITTLE "DEMONSTRATION."
WHOEVER YOU ARE, WE'RE NOT AFRAID OF YOU!
RAAAAAAAAAP
HE'S CRAZY! BRAVE, BUT CRAZY!
YOU'RE GOING TO BE SORRY YOU EVER ATTA-
CLICK!
AAAAAA!
WHIF?
WHO, ME? I'M NEVER SORRY.

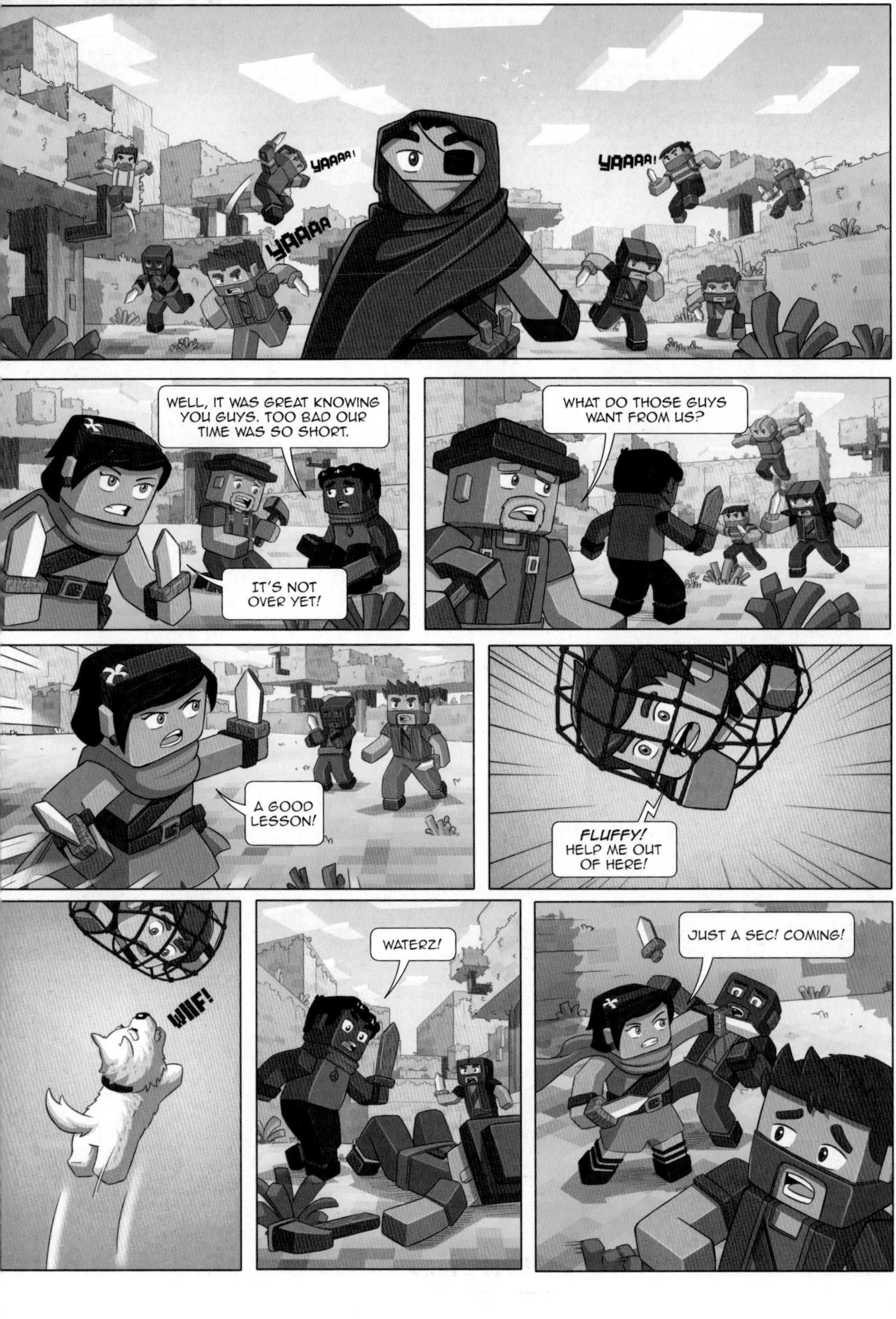
YAAAA!
YAAAA
YAAAA!
WELL, IT WAS GREAT KNOWING YOU GUYS. TOO BAD OUR TIME WAS SO SHORT.
IT'S NOT OVER YET!
WHAT DO THOSE GUYS WANT FROM US?
A GOOD LESSON!
FLUFFY! HELP ME OUT OF HERE!
WIIF!
WATERZ!
JUST A SEC! COMING!

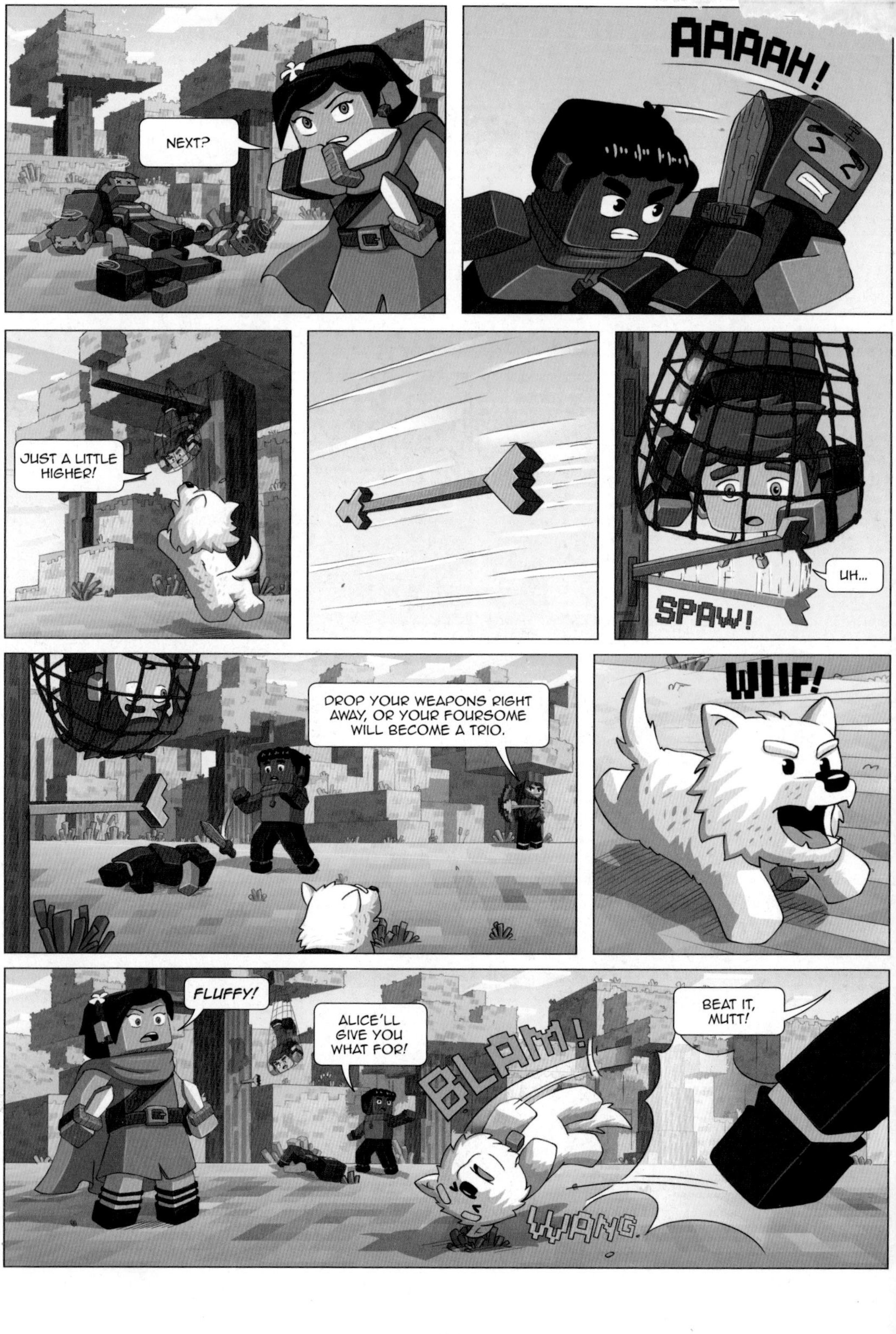
NEXT?
AAAAH!
JUST A LITTLE HIGHER!
UH...
SPAW!
DROP YOUR WEAPONS RIGHT AWAY, OR YOUR FOURSOME WILL BECOME A TRIO.
WIIF!
FLUFFY!
ALICE'LL GIVE YOU WHAT FOR!
BEAT IT, MUTT!
BLAM!
WANG.

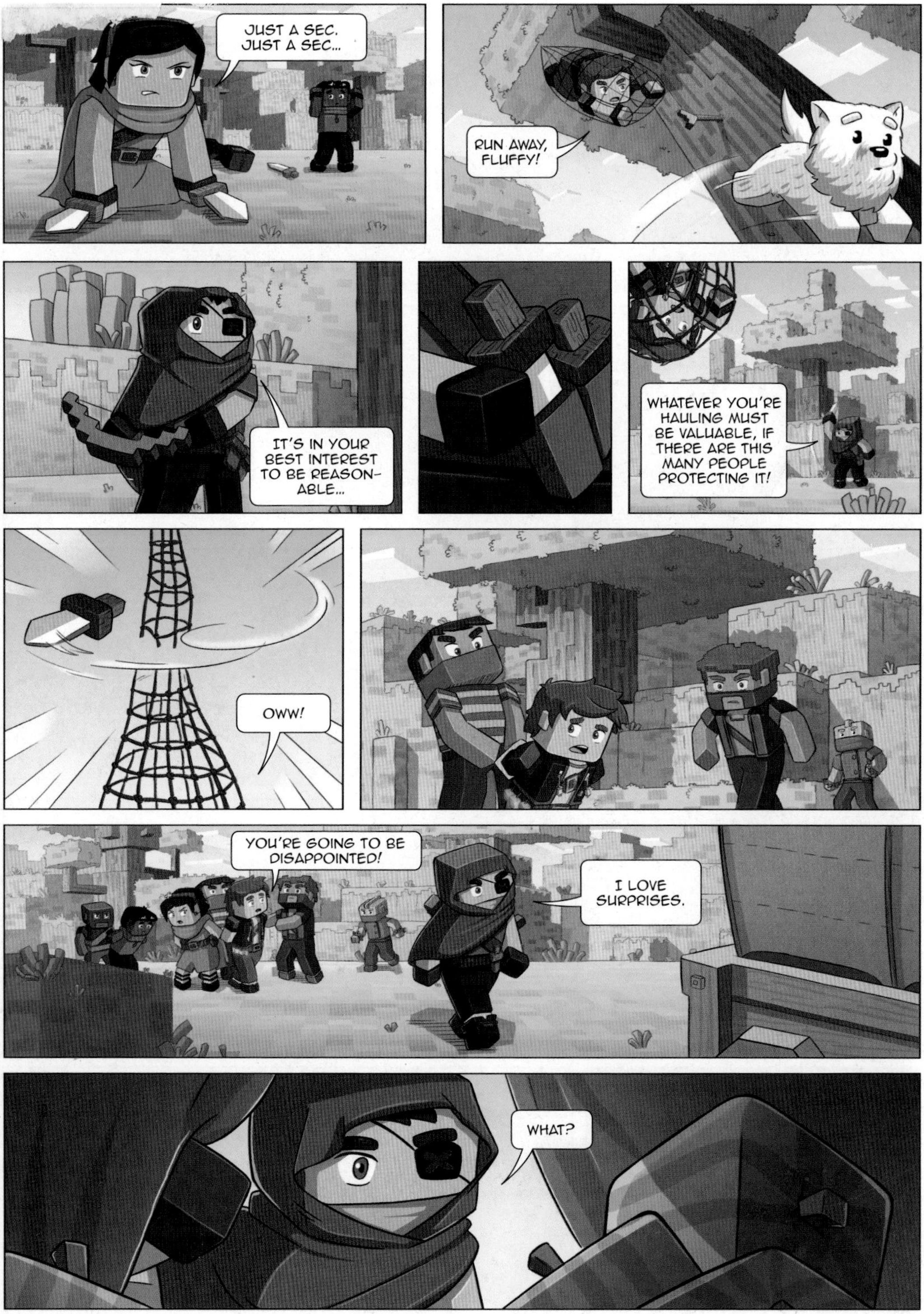
JUST A SEC. JUST A SEC...
RUN AWAY, FLUFFY!
IT'S IN YOUR BEST INTEREST TO BE REASON-ABLE...
WHATEVER YOU'RE HAULING MUST BE VALUABLE, IF THERE ARE THIS MANY PEOPLE PROTECTING IT!
OWW!
YOU'RE GOING TO BE DISAPPOINTED!
I LOVE SURPRISES.
WHAT?

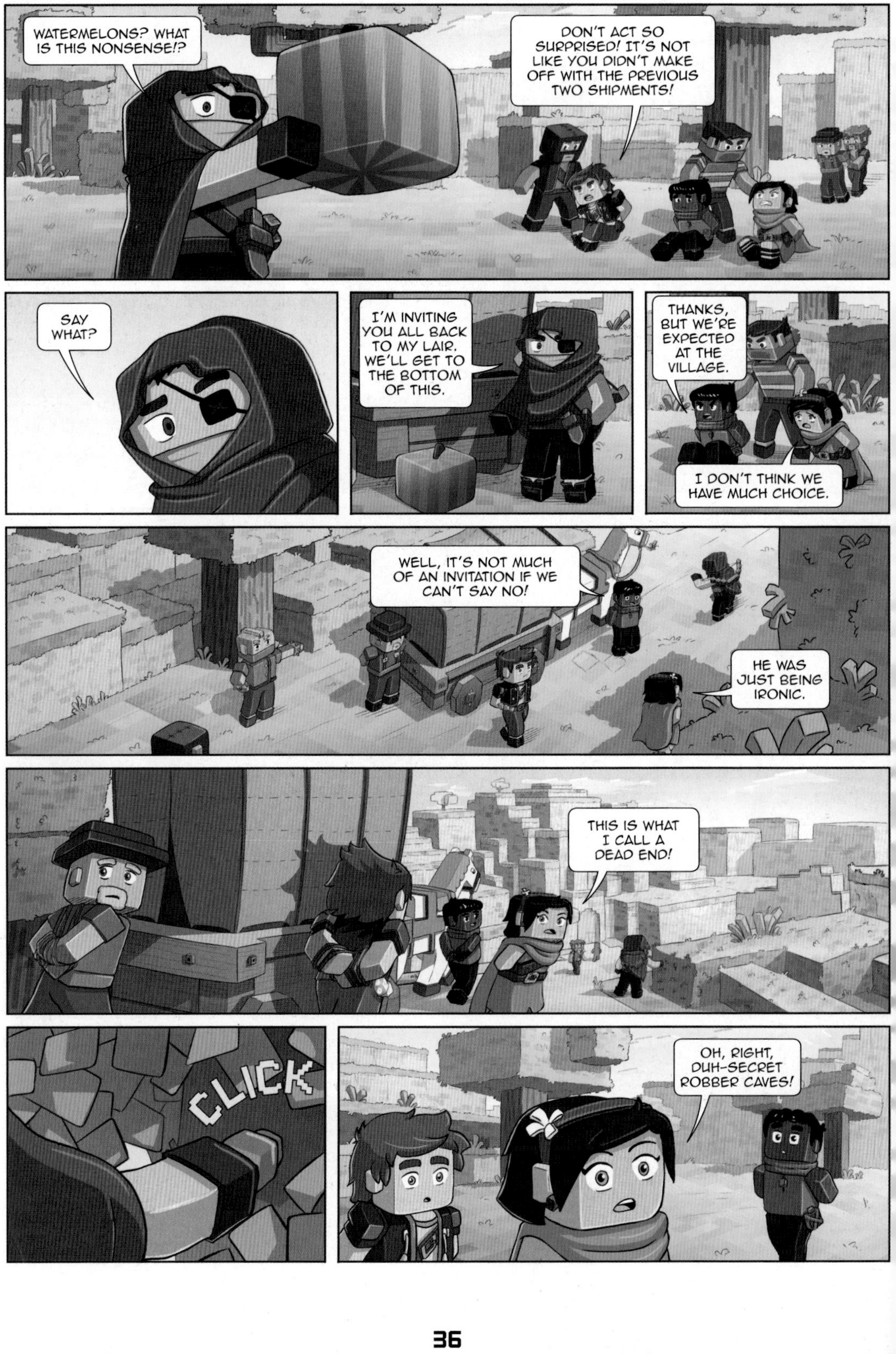
WATERMELONS? WHAT IS THIS NONSENSE!?
DON'T ACT SO SURPRISED! IT'S NOT LIKE YOU DIDN'T MAKE OFF WITH THE PREVIOUS TWO SHIPMENTS!
SAY WHAT?
I'M INVITING YOU ALL BACK TO MY LAIR. WE'LL GET TO THE BOTTOM OF THIS.
THANKS, BUT WE'RE EXPECTED AT THE VILLAGE.
I DON'T THINK WE HAVE MUCH CHOICE.
WELL, IT'S NOT MUCH OF AN INVITATION IF WE CAN'T SAY NO!
HE WAS JUST BEING IRONIC.
THIS IS WHAT I CALL A DEAD END!
CLICK
OH, RIGHT, DUH-SECRET ROBBER CAVES!

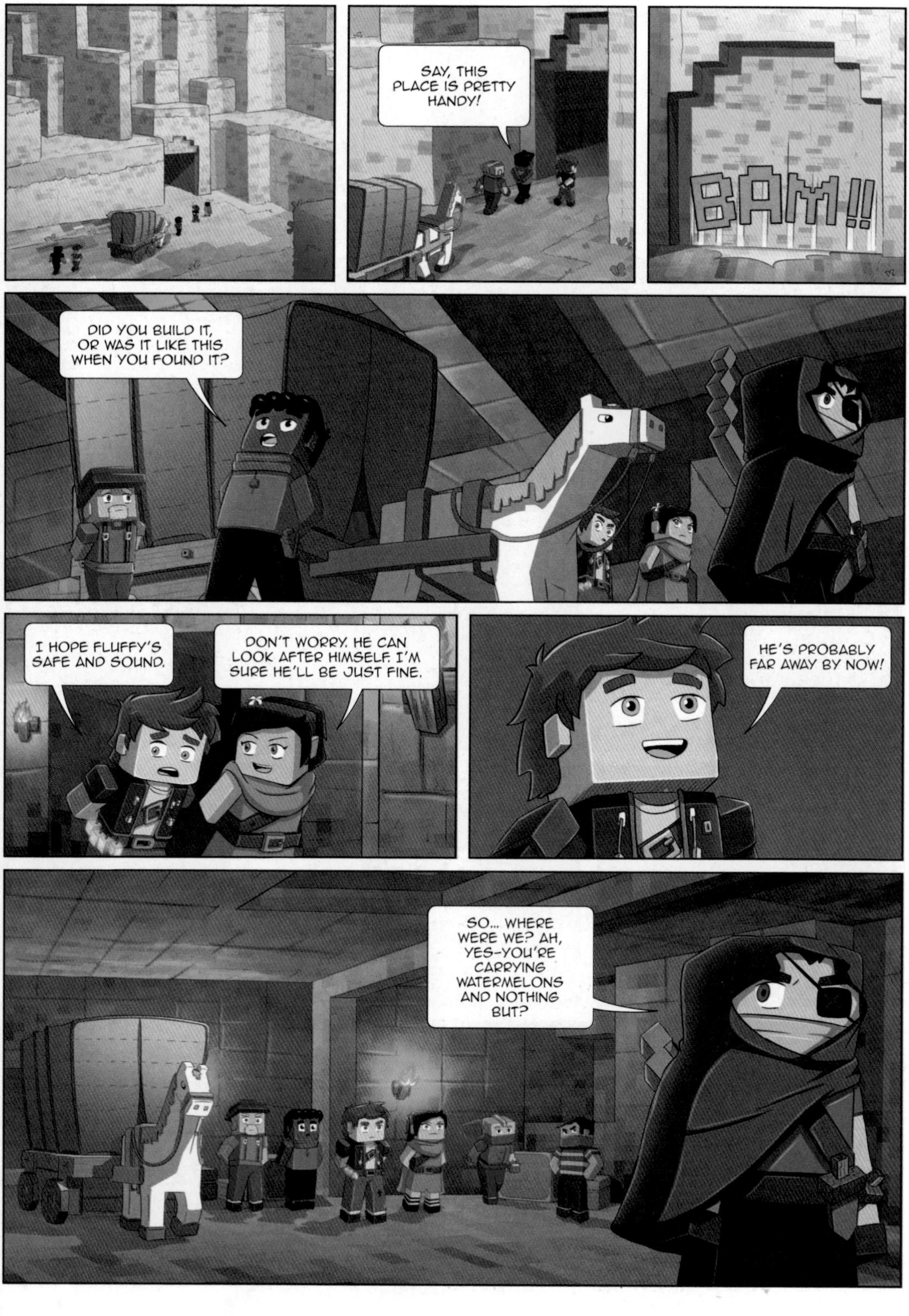
SAY, THIS PLACE IS PRETTY HANDY!
BAM!!
DID YOU BUILD IT, OR WAS IT LIKE THIS WHEN YOU FOUND IT?
I HOPE FLUFFY'S SAFE AND SOUND.
DON'T WORRY. HE CAN LOOK AFTER HIMSELF. I'M SURE HE'LL BE JUST FINE.
HE'S PROBABLY FAR AWAY BY NOW!
SO... WHERE WERE WE? AH, YES–YOU'RE CARRYING WATERMELONS AND NOTHING BUT?

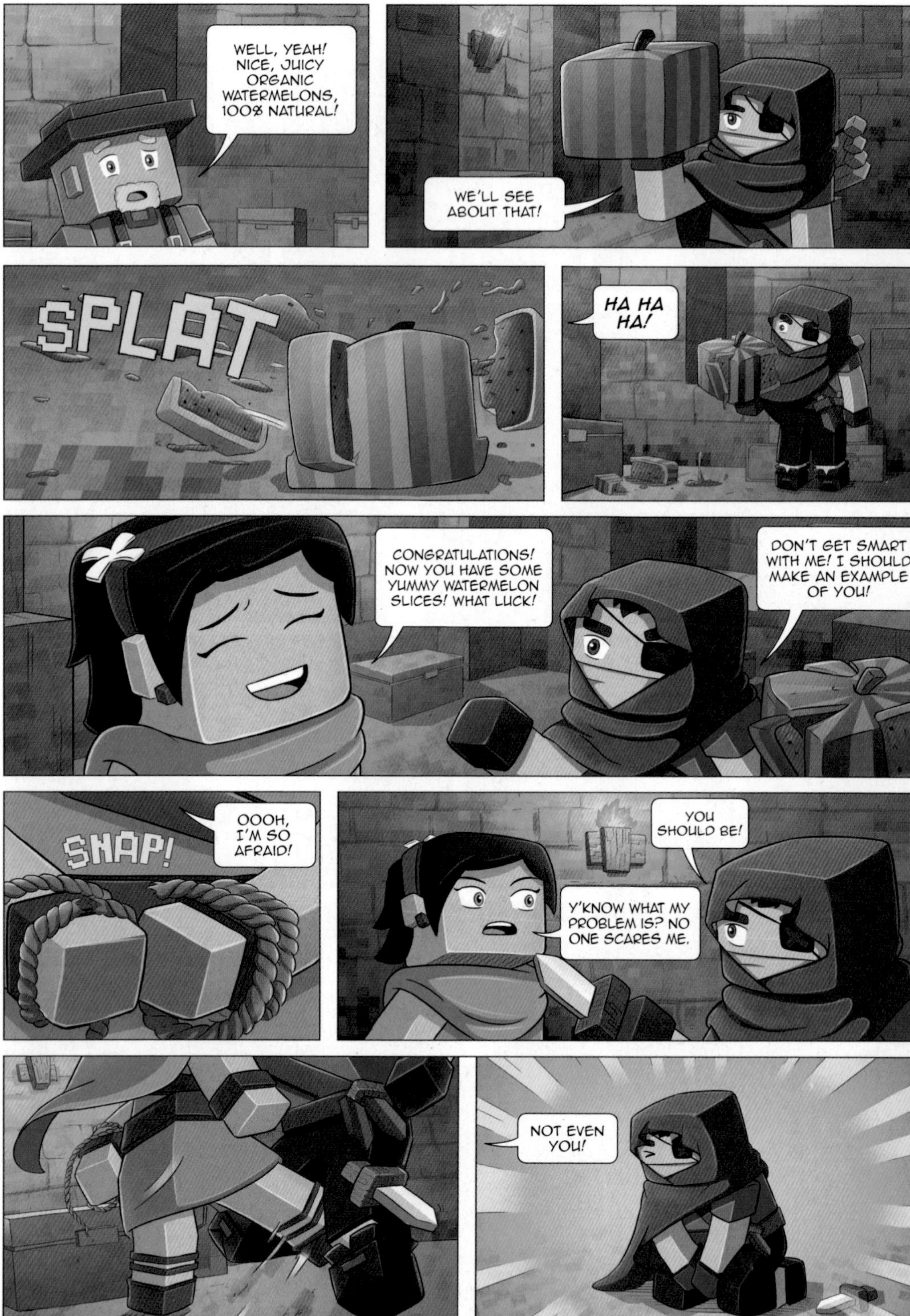
WELL, YEAH! NICE, JUICY ORGANIC WATERMELONS, 100% NATURAL!
WE'LL SEE ABOUT THAT!
SPLAT
HA HA HA!
CONGRATULATIONS! NOW YOU HAVE SOME YUMMY WATERMELON SLICES! WHAT LUCK!
DON'T GET SMART WITH ME! I SHOULD MAKE AN EXAMPLE OF YOU!
SNAP!
OOOH, I'M SO AFRAID!
YOU SHOULD BE!
Y'KNOW WHAT MY PROBLEM IS? NO ONE SCARES ME.
NOT EVEN YOU!

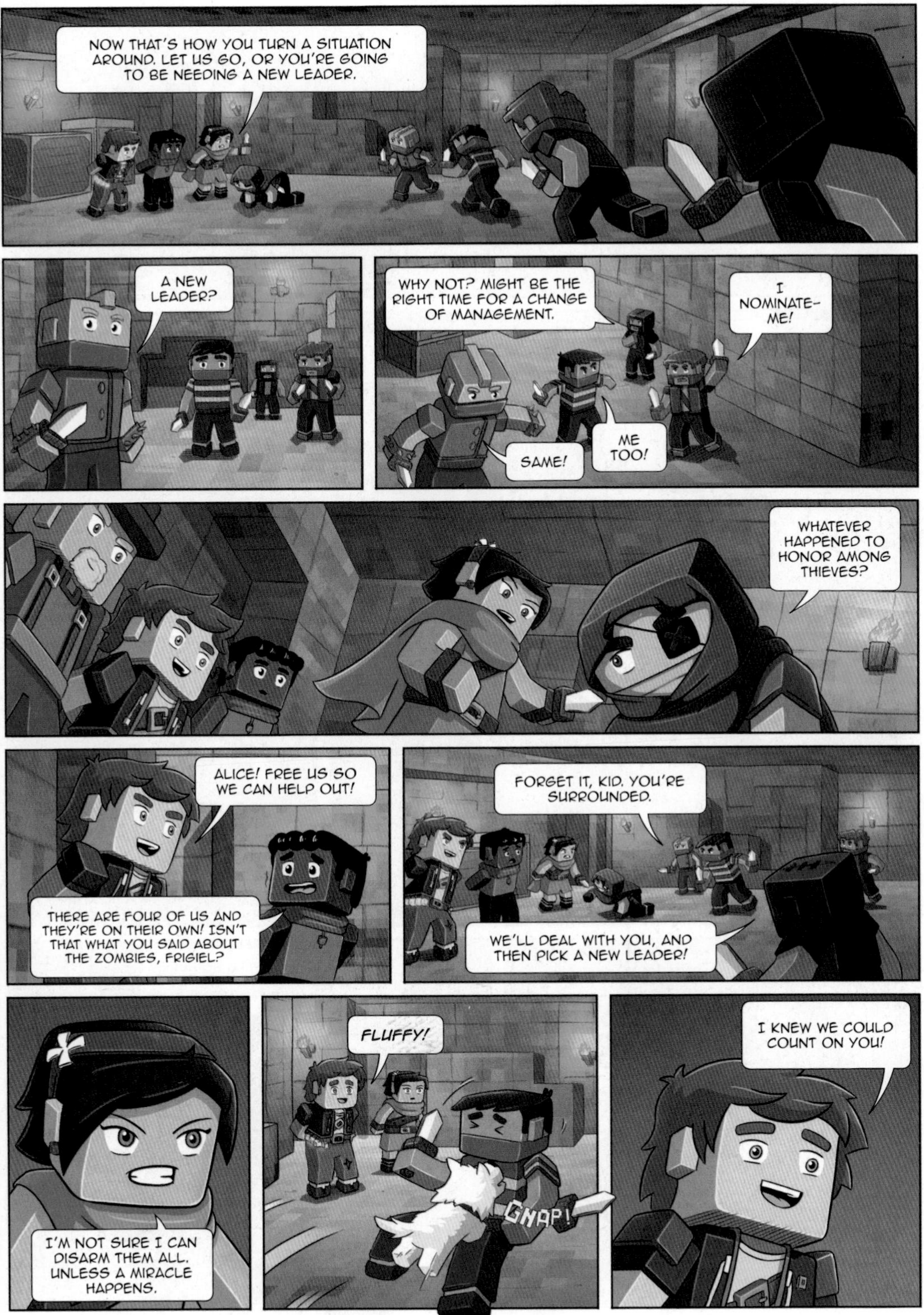
NOW THAT'S HOW YOU TURN A SITUATION AROUND. LET US GO, OR YOU'RE GOING TO BE NEEDING A NEW LEADER.
A NEW LEADER?
WHY NOT? MIGHT BE THE RIGHT TIME FOR A CHANGE OF MANAGEMENT.
I NOMINATE- ME!
SAME!
ME TOO!
WHATEVER HAPPENED TO HONOR AMONG THIEVES?
ALICE! FREE US SO WE CAN HELP OUT!
THERE ARE FOUR OF US AND THEY'RE ON THEIR OWN! ISN'T THAT WHAT YOU SAID ABOUT THE ZOMBIES, FRIGIEL?
FORGET IT, KID. YOU'RE SURROUNDED.
WE'LL DEAL WITH YOU, AND THEN PICK A NEW LEADER!
I'M NOT SURE I CAN DISARM THEM ALL. UNLESS A MIRACLE HAPPENS.
FLUFFY!
GNAP!
I KNEW WE COULD COUNT ON YOU!

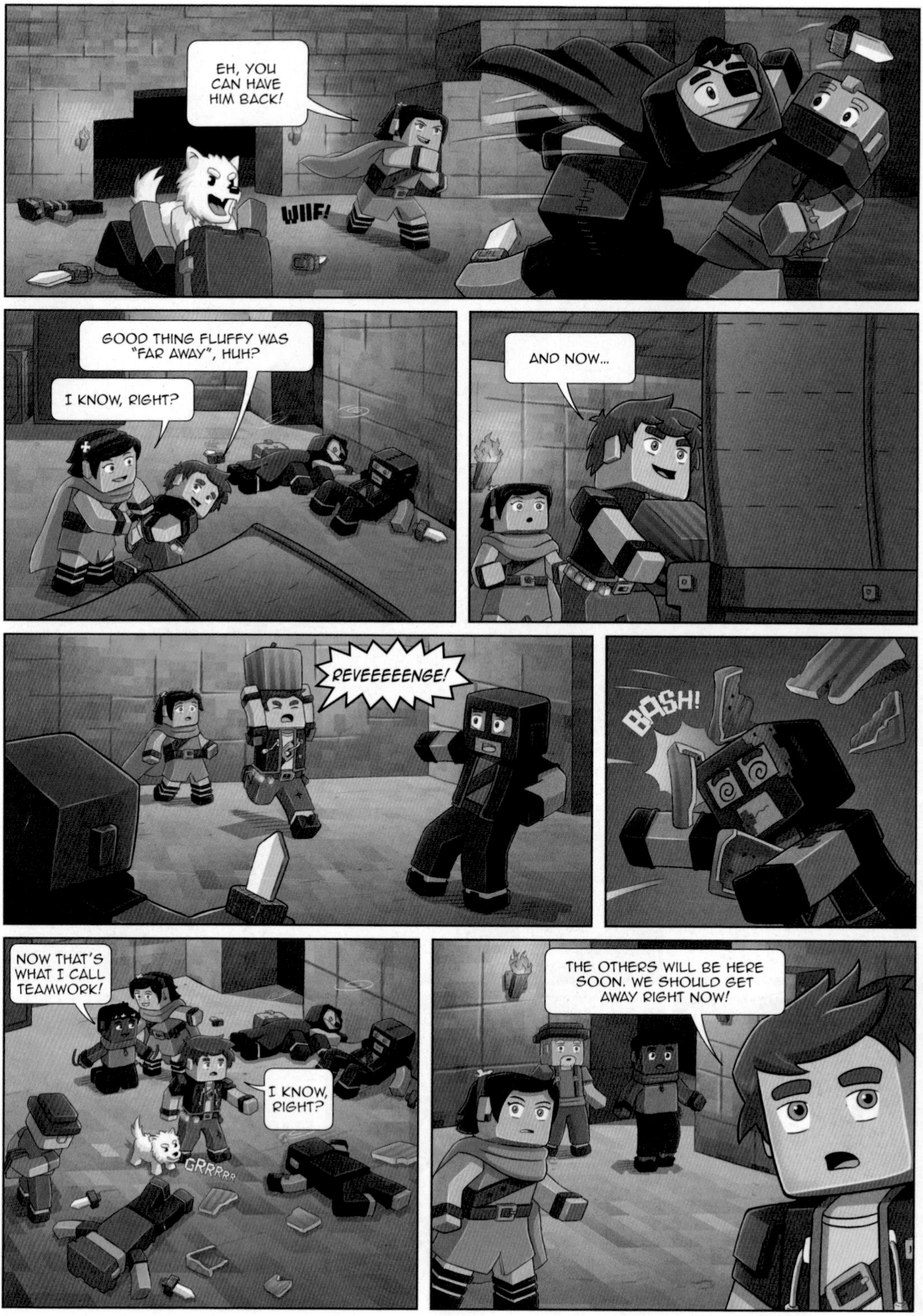
EH, YOU CAN HAVE HIM BACK!
WIIF!
GOOD THING FLUFFY WAS "FAR AWAY", HUH?
I KNOW, RIGHT?
AND NOW...
REVEEEEEENGE!
BASH!
NOW THAT'S WHAT I CALL TEAMWORK!
I KNOW, RIGHT?
GRRRRR
THE OTHERS WILL BE HERE SOON. WE SHOULD GET AWAY RIGHT NOW!

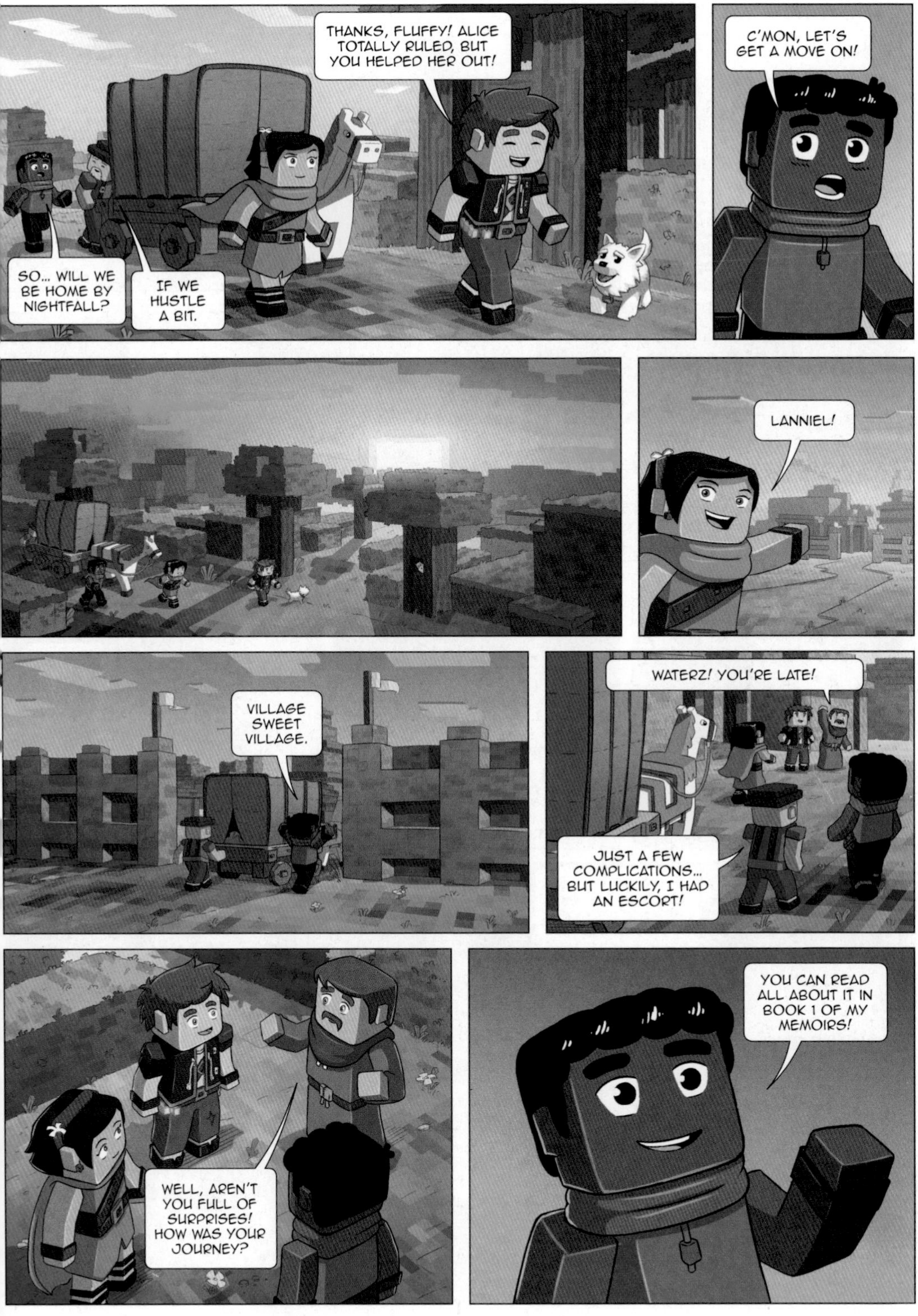
THANKS, FLUFFY! ALICE TOTALLY RULED, BUT YOU HELPED HER OUT!
SO... WILL WE BE HOME BY NIGHTFALL?
IF WE HUSTLE A BIT.
C'MON, LET'S GET A MOVE ON!
LANNIEL!
VILLAGE SWEET VILLAGE.
WATERZ! YOU'RE LATE!
JUST A FEW COMPLICATIONS... BUT LUCKILY, I HAD AN ESCORT!
WELL, AREN'T YOU FULL OF SURPRISES! HOW WAS YOUR JOURNEY?
YOU CAN READ ALL ABOUT IT IN BOOK 1 OF MY MEMOIRS!

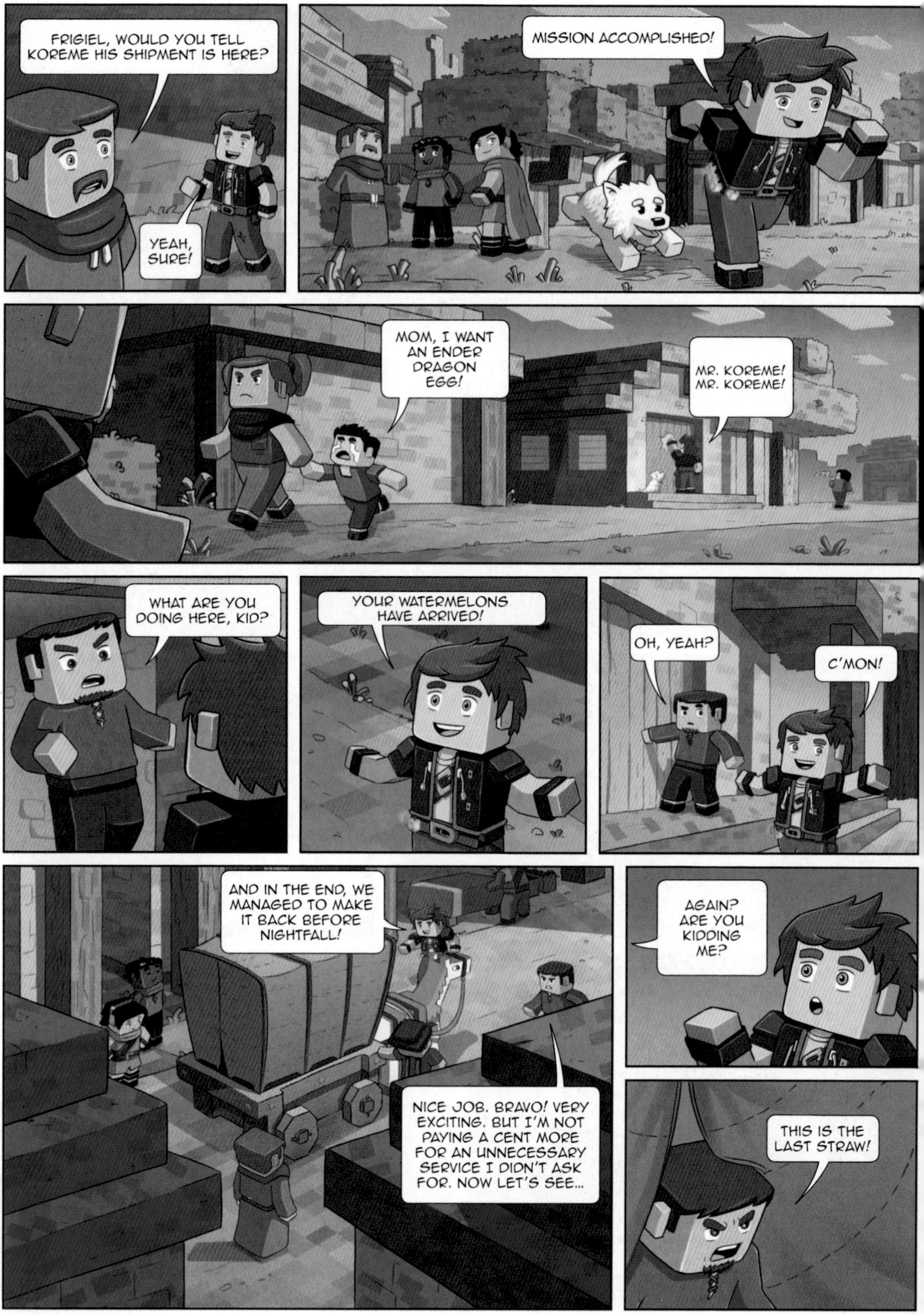

FRIGIEL, WOULD YOU TELL KOREME HIS SHIPMENT IS HERE?
YEAH, SURE!
MISSION ACCOMPLISHED!
MOM, I WANT AN ENDER DRAGON EGG!
MR. KOREME! MR. KOREME!
WHAT ARE YOU DOING HERE, KID?
YOUR WATERMELONS HAVE ARRIVED!
OH, YEAH?
C'MON!
AND IN THE END, WE MANAGED TO MAKE IT BACK BEFORE NIGHTFALL!
NICE JOB. BRAVO! VERY EXCITING. BUT I'M NOT PAYING A CENT MORE FOR AN UNNECESSARY SERVICE I DIDN'T ASK FOR. NOW LET'S SEE...
AGAIN? ARE YOU KIDDING ME?
THIS IS THE LAST STRAW!

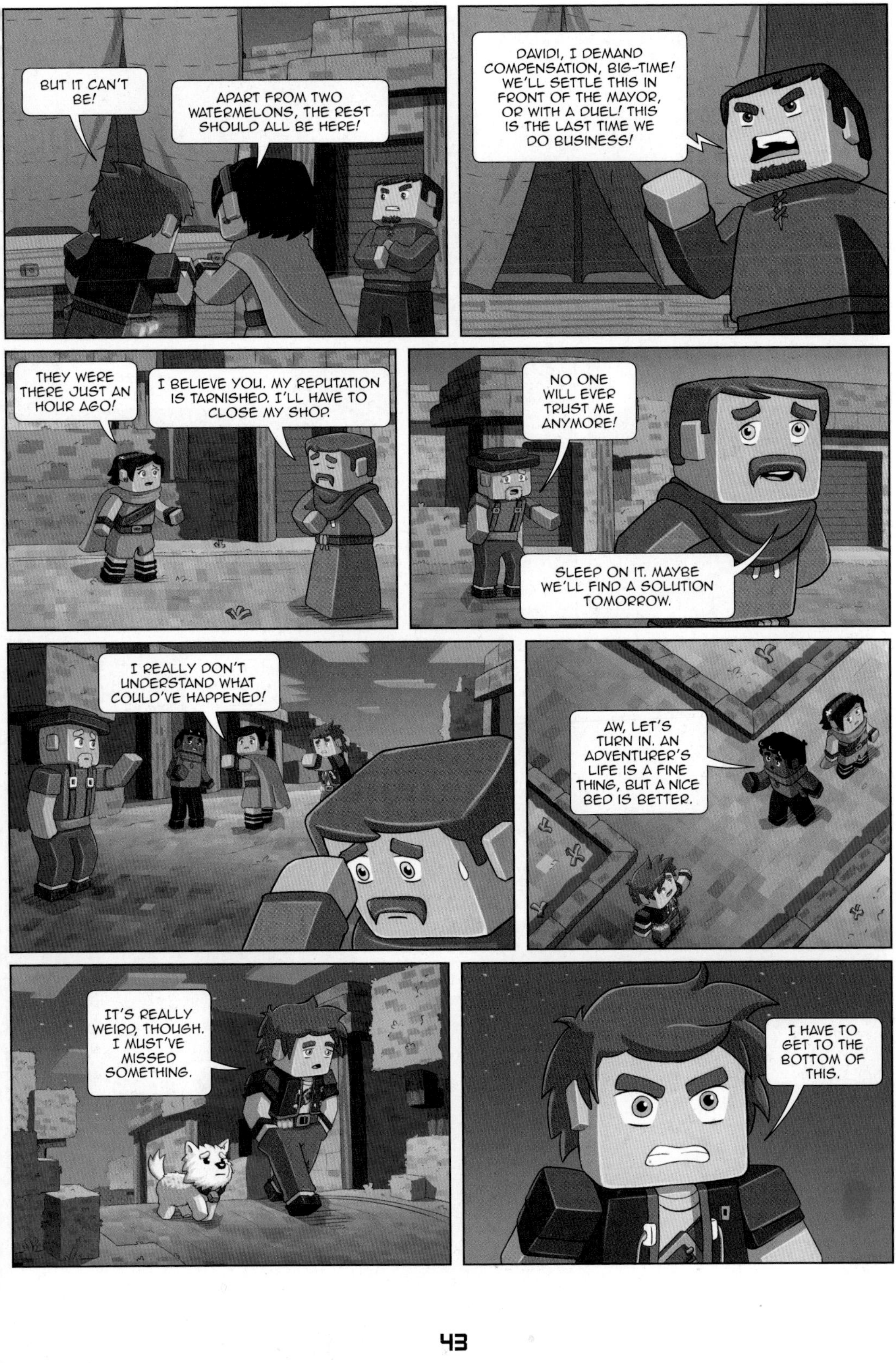
BUT IT CAN'T BE!
APART FROM TWO WATERMELONS, THE REST SHOULD ALL BE HERE!
DAVIDI, I DEMAND COMPENSATION, BIG-TIME! WE'LL SETTLE THIS IN FRONT OF THE MAYOR, OR WITH A DUEL! THIS IS THE LAST TIME WE DO BUSINESS!
THEY WERE THERE JUST AN HOUR AGO!
I BELIEVE YOU. MY REPUTATION IS TARNISHED. I'LL HAVE TO CLOSE MY SHOP.
NO ONE WILL EVER TRUST ME ANYMORE!
SLEEP ON IT. MAYBE WE'LL FIND A SOLUTION TOMORROW.
I REALLY DON'T UNDERSTAND WHAT COULD'VE HAPPENED!
AW, LET'S TURN IN. AN ADVENTURER'S LIFE IS A FINE THING, BUT A NICE BED IS BETTER.
IT'S REALLY WEIRD, THOUGH. I MUST'VE MISSED SOMETHING.
I HAVE TO GET TO THE BOTTOM OF THIS.

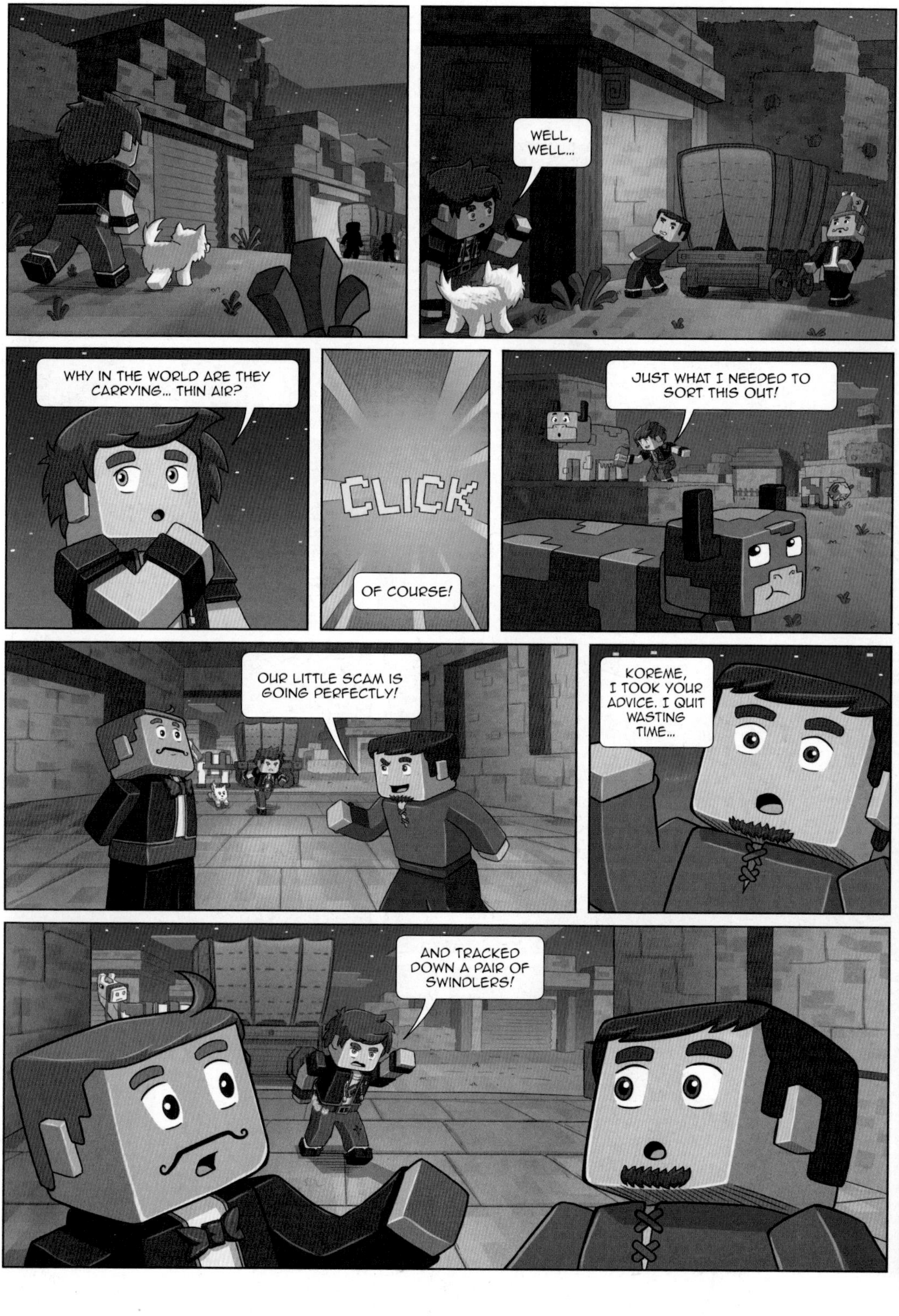
WELL, WELL...
WHY IN THE WORLD ARE THEY CARRYING... THIN AIR?
CLICK
OF COURSE!
JUST WHAT I NEEDED TO SORT THIS OUT!
OUR LITTLE SCAM IS GOING PERFECTLY!
KOREME, I TOOK YOUR ADVICE. I QUIT WASTING TIME...
AND TRACKED DOWN A PAIR OF SWINDLERS!

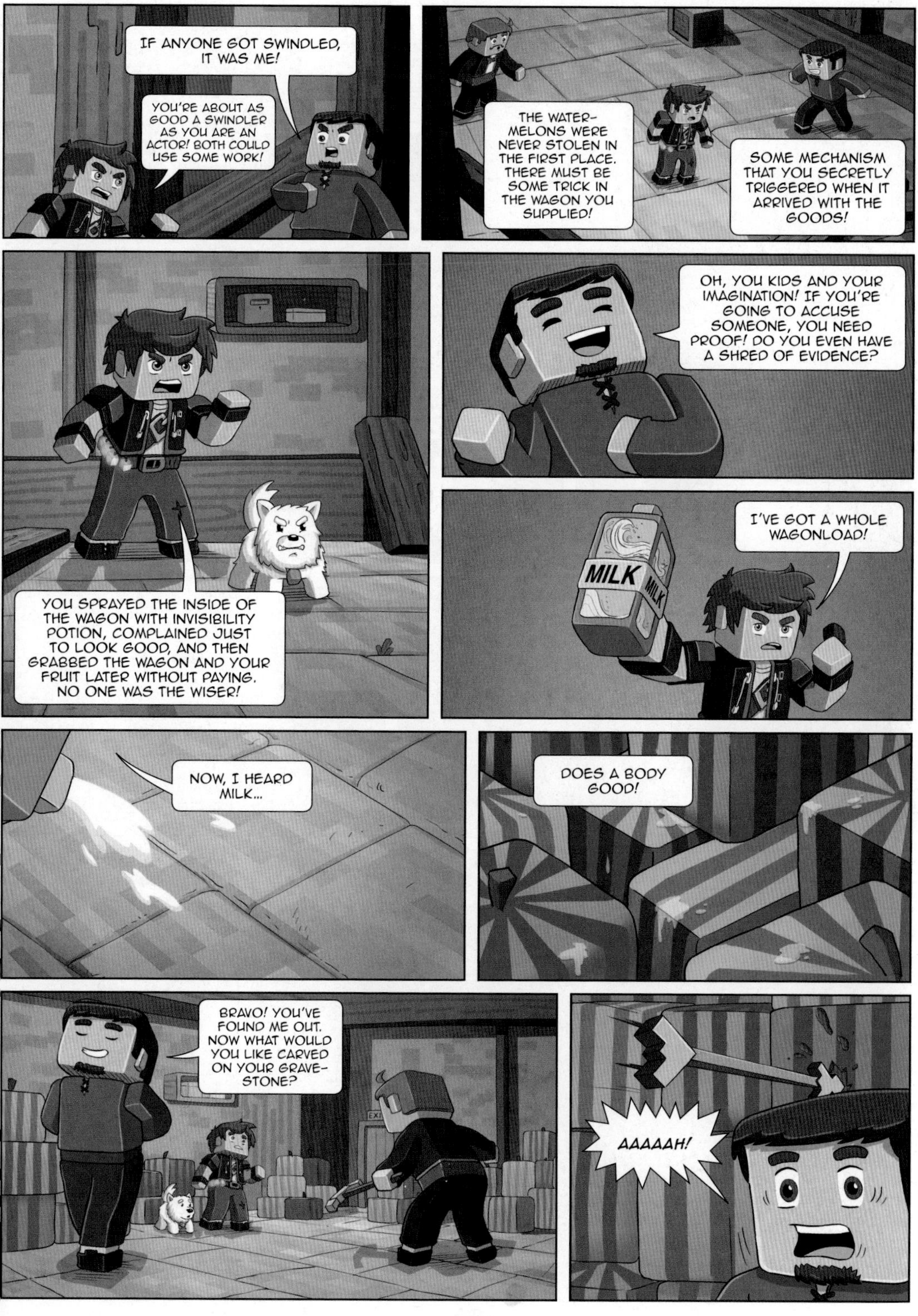
IF ANYONE GOT SWINDLED, IT WAS ME!
YOU'RE ABOUT AS GOOD A SWINDLER AS YOU ARE AN ACTOR! BOTH COULD USE SOME WORK!
THE WATER-MELONS WERE NEVER STOLEN IN THE FIRST PLACE. THERE MUST BE SOME TRICK IN THE WAGON YOU SUPPLIED!
SOME MECHANISM THAT YOU SECRETLY TRIGGERED WHEN IT ARRIVED WITH THE GOODS!
YOU SPRAYED THE INSIDE OF THE WAGON WITH INVISIBILITY POTION, COMPLAINED JUST TO LOOK GOOD, AND THEN GRABBED THE WAGON AND YOUR FRUIT LATER WITHOUT PAYING. NO ONE WAS THE WISER!
OH, YOU KIDS AND YOUR IMAGINATION! IF YOU'RE GOING TO ACCUSE SOMEONE, YOU NEED PROOF! DO YOU EVEN HAVE A SHRED OF EVIDENCE?
I'VE GOT A WHOLE WAGONLOAD!
MILK
MILK
NOW, I HEARD MILK...
DOES A BODY GOOD!
BRAVO! YOU'VE FOUND ME OUT. NOW WHAT WOULD YOU LIKE CARVED ON YOUR GRAVE-STONE?
AAAAAH!

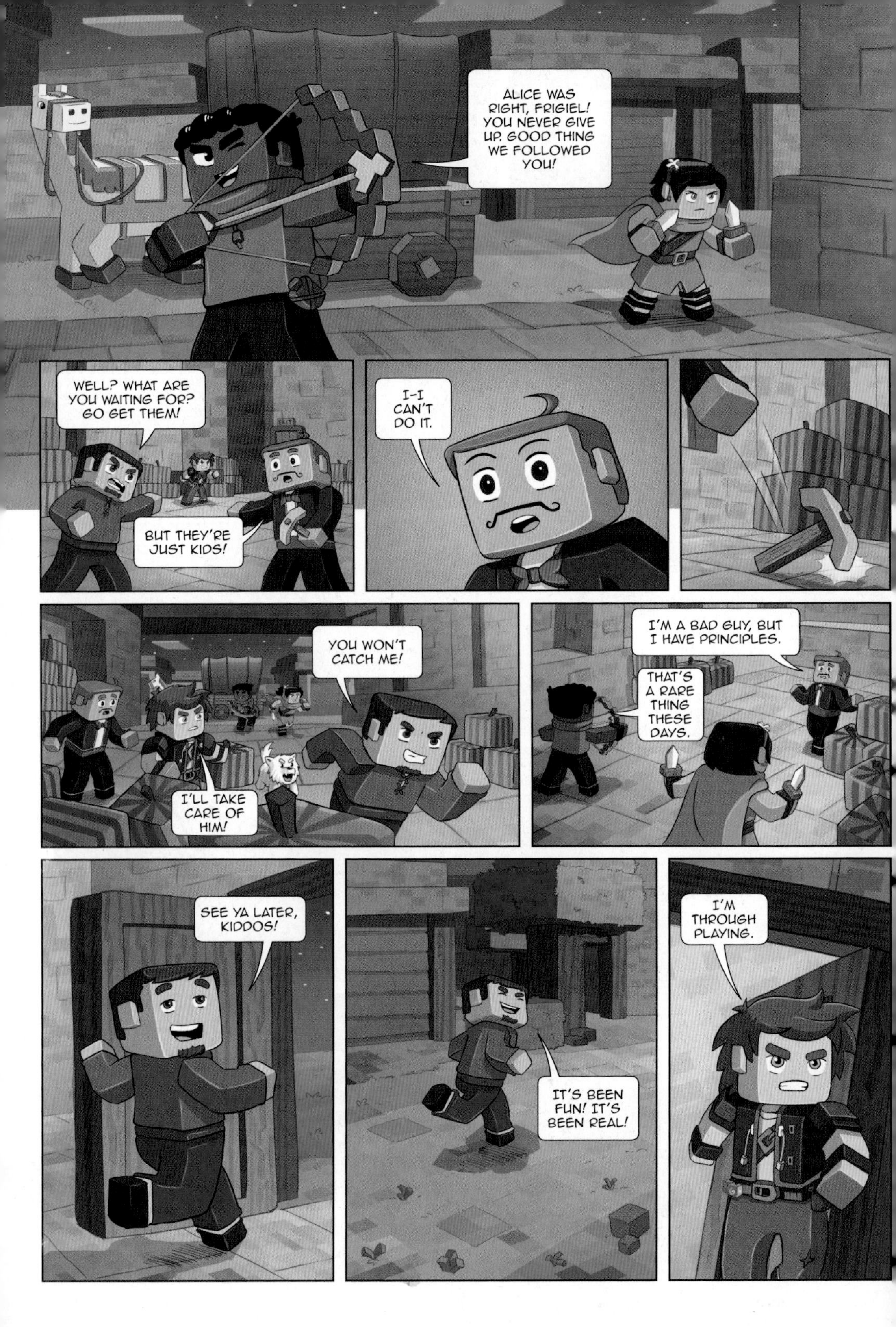

ALICE WAS RIGHT, FRIGIEL! YOU NEVER GIVE UP. GOOD THING WE FOLLOWED YOU!
WELL? WHAT ARE YOU WAITING FOR? GO GET THEM!
BUT THEY'RE JUST KIDS!
I-I CAN'T DO IT.
YOU WON'T CATCH ME!
I'LL TAKE CARE OF HIM!
I'M A BAD GUY, BUT I HAVE PRINCIPLES.
THAT'S A RARE THING THESE DAYS.
SEE YA LATER, KIDDOS!
IT'S BEEN FUN! IT'S BEEN REAL!
I'M THROUGH PLAYING.

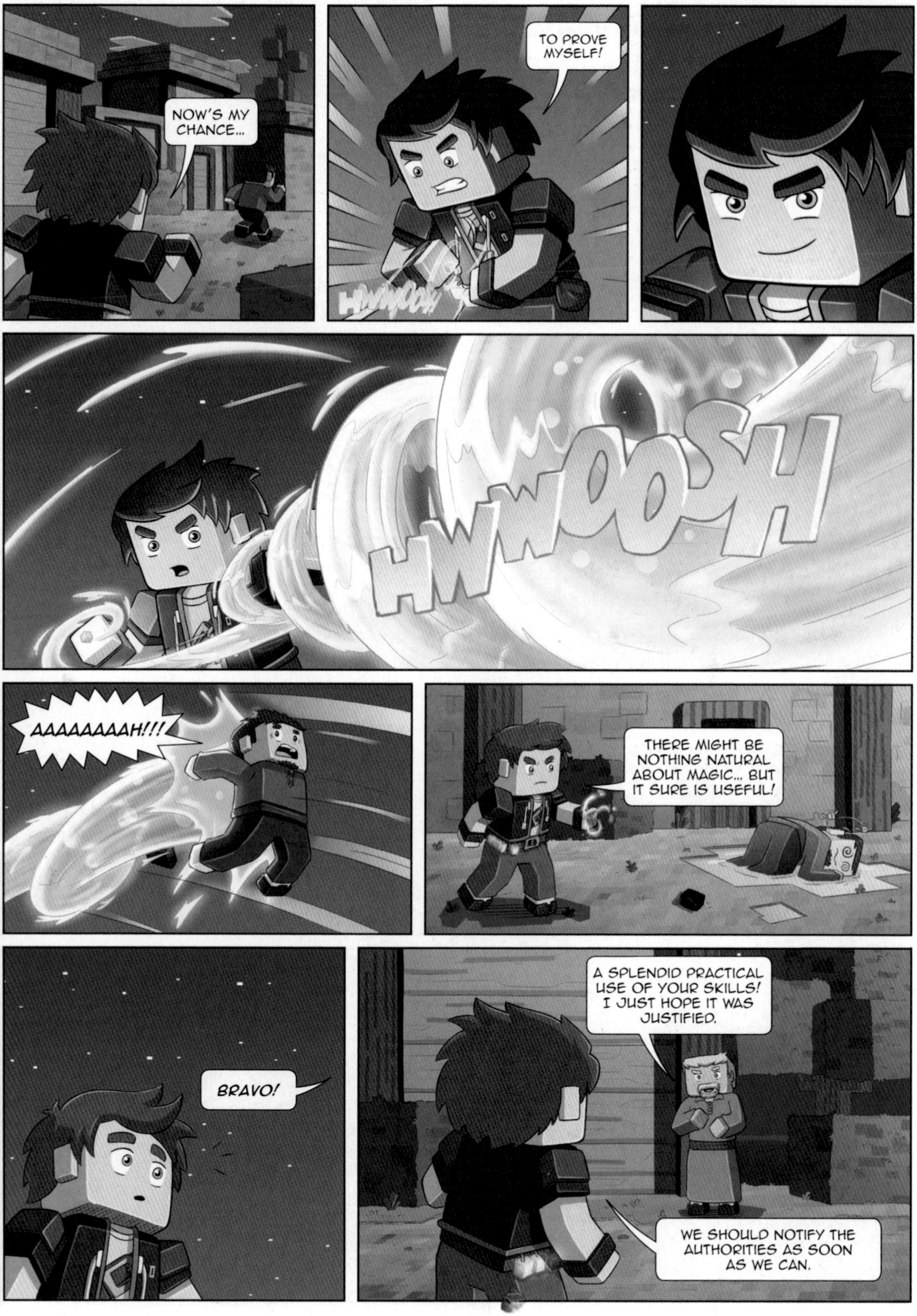
NOW'S MY CHANCE...
TO PROVE MYSELF!
HWWOOSH
HWWOOSH
AAAAAAAAH!!!
THERE MIGHT BE NOTHING NATURAL ABOUT MAGIC... BUT IT SURE IS USEFUL!
BRAVO!
A SPLENDID PRACTICAL USE OF YOUR SKILLS! I JUST HOPE IT WAS JUSTIFIED.
WE SHOULD NOTIFY THE AUTHORITIES AS SOON AS WE CAN.

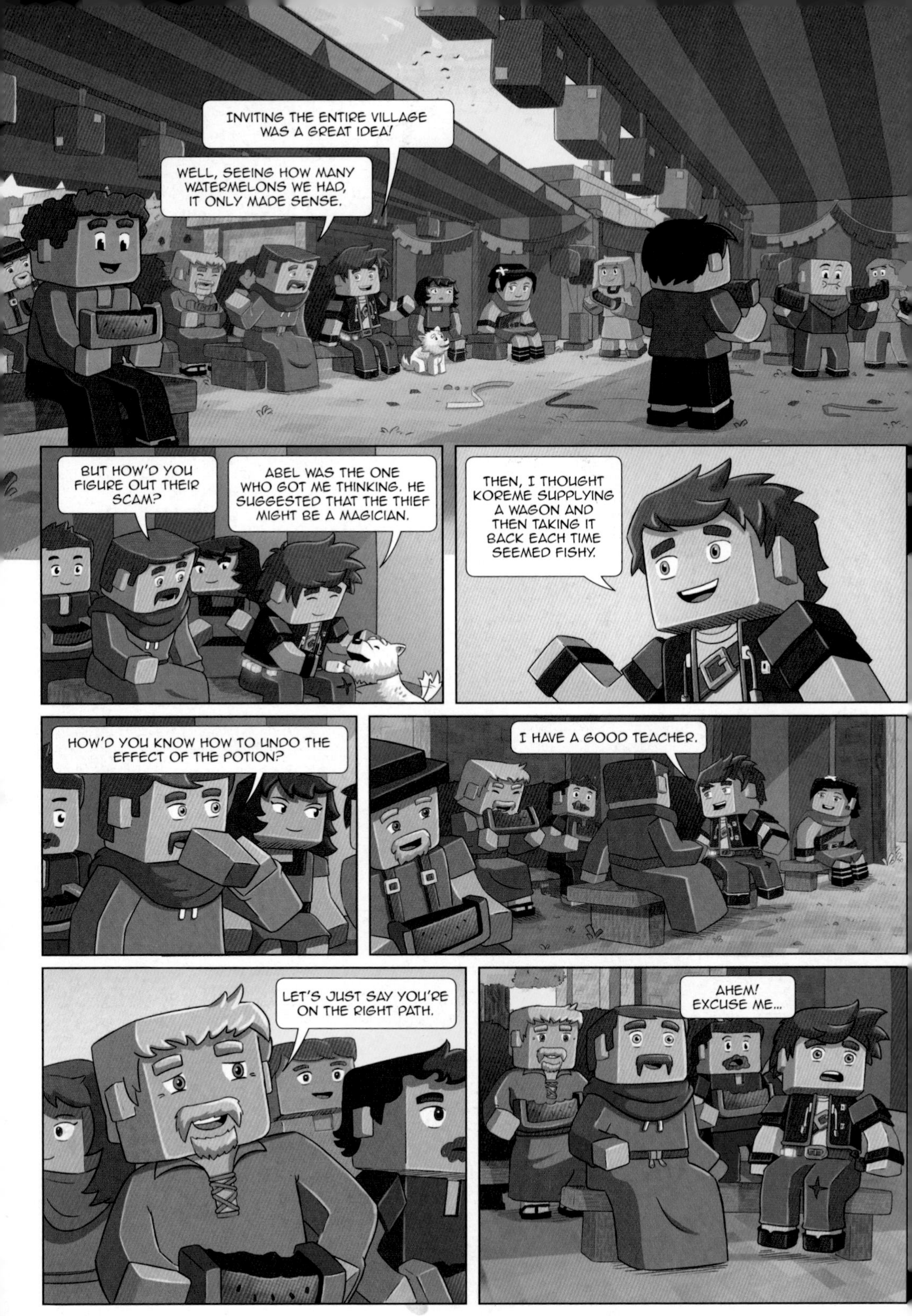
INVITING THE ENTIRE VILLAGE WAS A GREAT IDEA!
WELL, SEEING HOW MANY WATERMELONS WE HAD, IT ONLY MADE SENSE.
BUT HOW'D YOU FIGURE OUT THEIR SCAM?
ABEL WAS THE ONE WHO GOT ME THINKING. HE SUGGESTED THAT THE THIEF MIGHT BE A MAGICIAN.
THEN, I THOUGHT KOREME SUPPLYING A WAGON AND THEN TAKING IT BACK EACH TIME SEEMED FISHY.
HOW'D YOU KNOW HOW TO UNDO THE EFFECT OF THE POTION?
I HAVE A GOOD TEACHER.
LET'S JUST SAY YOU'RE ON THE RIGHT PATH.
AHEM! EXCUSE ME...

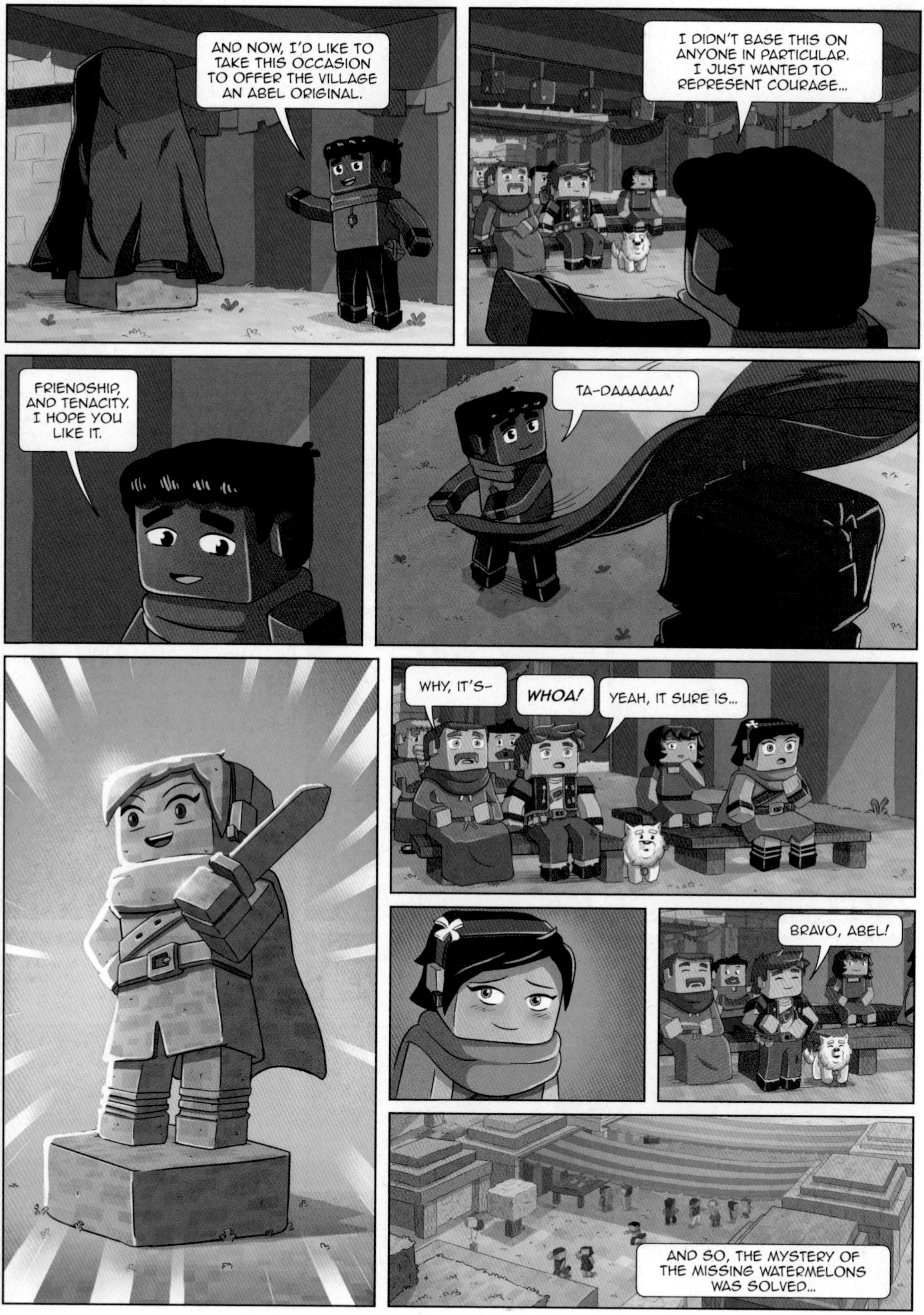
AND NOW, I'D LIKE TO TAKE THIS OCCASION TO OFFER THE VILLAGE AN ABEL ORIGINAL.
I DIDN'T BASE THIS ON ANYONE IN PARTICULAR. I JUST WANTED TO REPRESENT COURAGE...
FRIENDSHIP, AND TENACITY. I HOPE YOU LIKE IT.
TA-DAAAAAA!
WHY, IT'S-
WHOA!
YEAH, IT SURE IS...
BRAVO, ABEL!
AND SO, THE MYSTERY OF THE MISSING WATERMELONS WAS SOLVED...

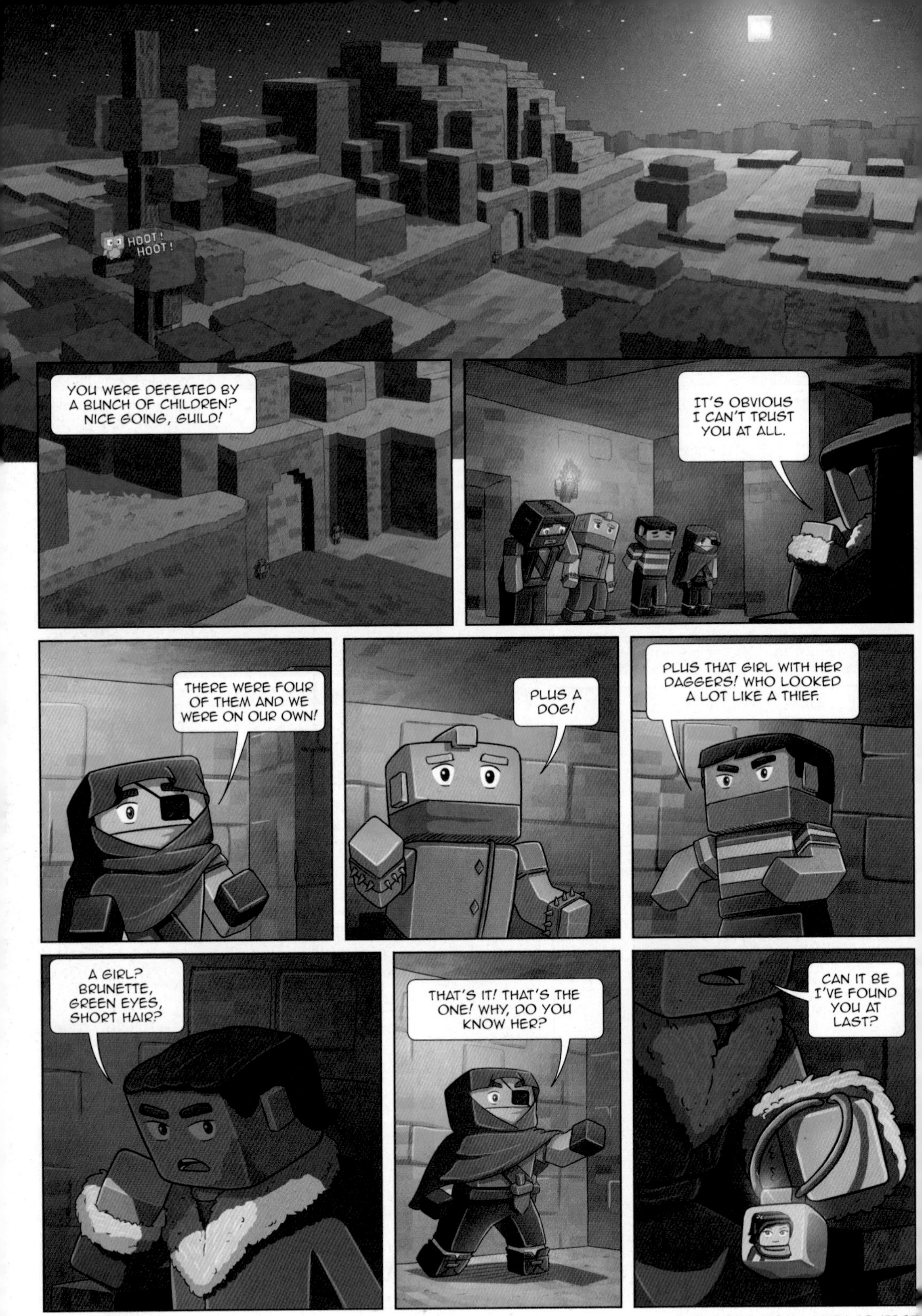
HOOT! HOOT!
YOU WERE DEFEATED BY A BUNCH OF CHILDREN? NICE GOING, GUILD!
IT'S OBVIOUS I CAN'T TRUST YOU AT ALL.
THERE WERE FOUR OF THEM AND WE WERE ON OUR OWN!
PLUS A DOG!
PLUS THAT GIRL WITH HER DAGGERS! WHO LOOKED A LOT LIKE A THIEF.
A GIRL? BRUNETTE, GREEN EYES, SHORT HAIR?
THAT'S IT! THAT'S THE ONE! WHY, DO YOU KNOW HER?
CAN IT BE I'VE FOUND YOU AT LAST?

NEXT TIME: POPULARITY CONTEST

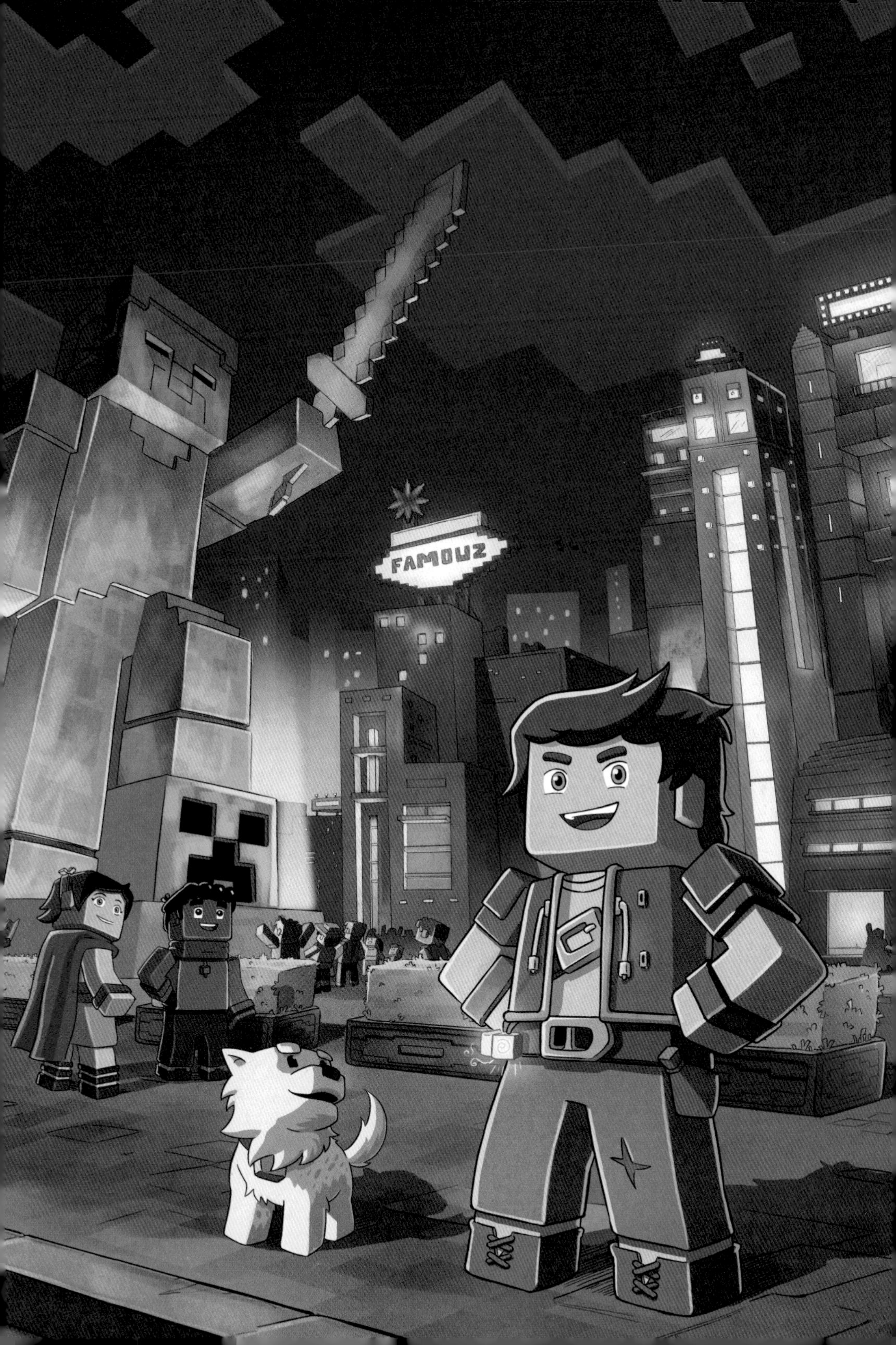
FAMOUZ

Dramatis Personae

■ Frigiel

A brave sorcerer's apprentice ever-ready to give his all for his friends. He dreams of one day becoming a true adventurer. His chance to discover the world begins today...

■ Fluffy

Frigiel's faithful canine companion, as cuddly with his master as he is bitey with the bad guys.

■ Alice

Proud and passionate, this thief-in-training keeps her secrets close to her heart...

■ Abel

A clever builder, and a somewhat mocking friend, he doesn't always see the irony of the situation.

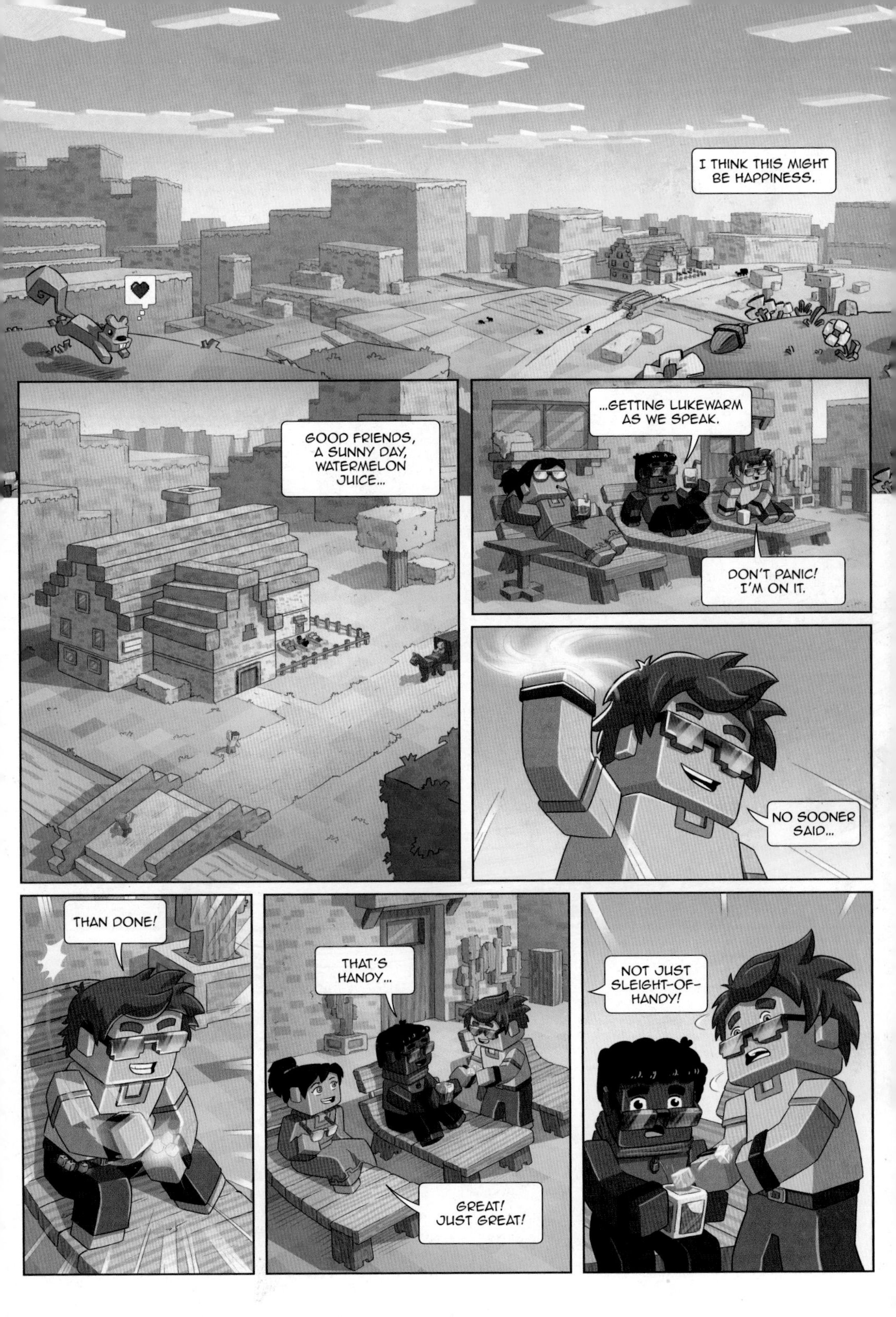
I THINK THIS MIGHT BE HAPPINESS.
GOOD FRIENDS, A SUNNY DAY, WATERMELON JUICE...
...GETTING LUKEWARM AS WE SPEAK.
DON'T PANIC! I'M ON IT.
NO SOONER SAID...
THAN DONE!
THAT'S HANDY...
GREAT! JUST GREAT!
NOT JUST SLEIGHT-OF-HANDY!

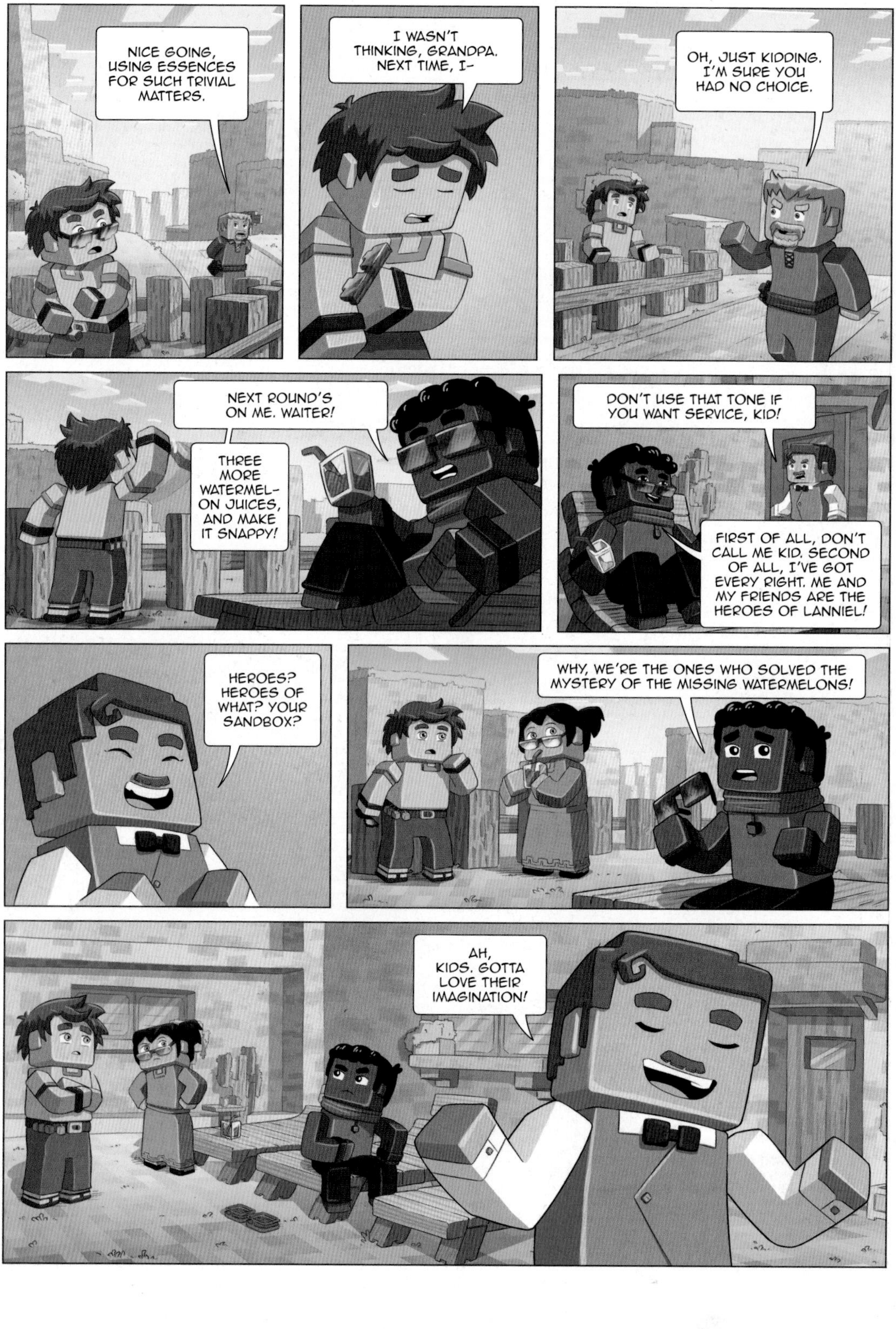
NICE GOING, USING ESSENCES FOR SUCH TRIVIAL MATTERS.
I WASN'T THINKING, GRANDPA. NEXT TIME, I-
OH, JUST KIDDING. I'M SURE YOU HAD NO CHOICE.
NEXT ROUND'S ON ME. WAITER!
THREE MORE WATERMEL-ON JUICES, AND MAKE IT SNAPPY!
DON'T USE THAT TONE IF YOU WANT SERVICE, KID!
FIRST OF ALL, DON'T CALL ME KID. SECOND OF ALL, I'VE GOT EVERY RIGHT. ME AND MY FRIENDS ARE THE HEROES OF LANNIEL!
HEROES? HEROES OF WHAT? YOUR SANDBOX?
WHY, WE'RE THE ONES WHO SOLVED THE MYSTERY OF THE MISSING WATERMELONS!
AH, KIDS. GOTTA LOVE THEIR IMAGINATION!

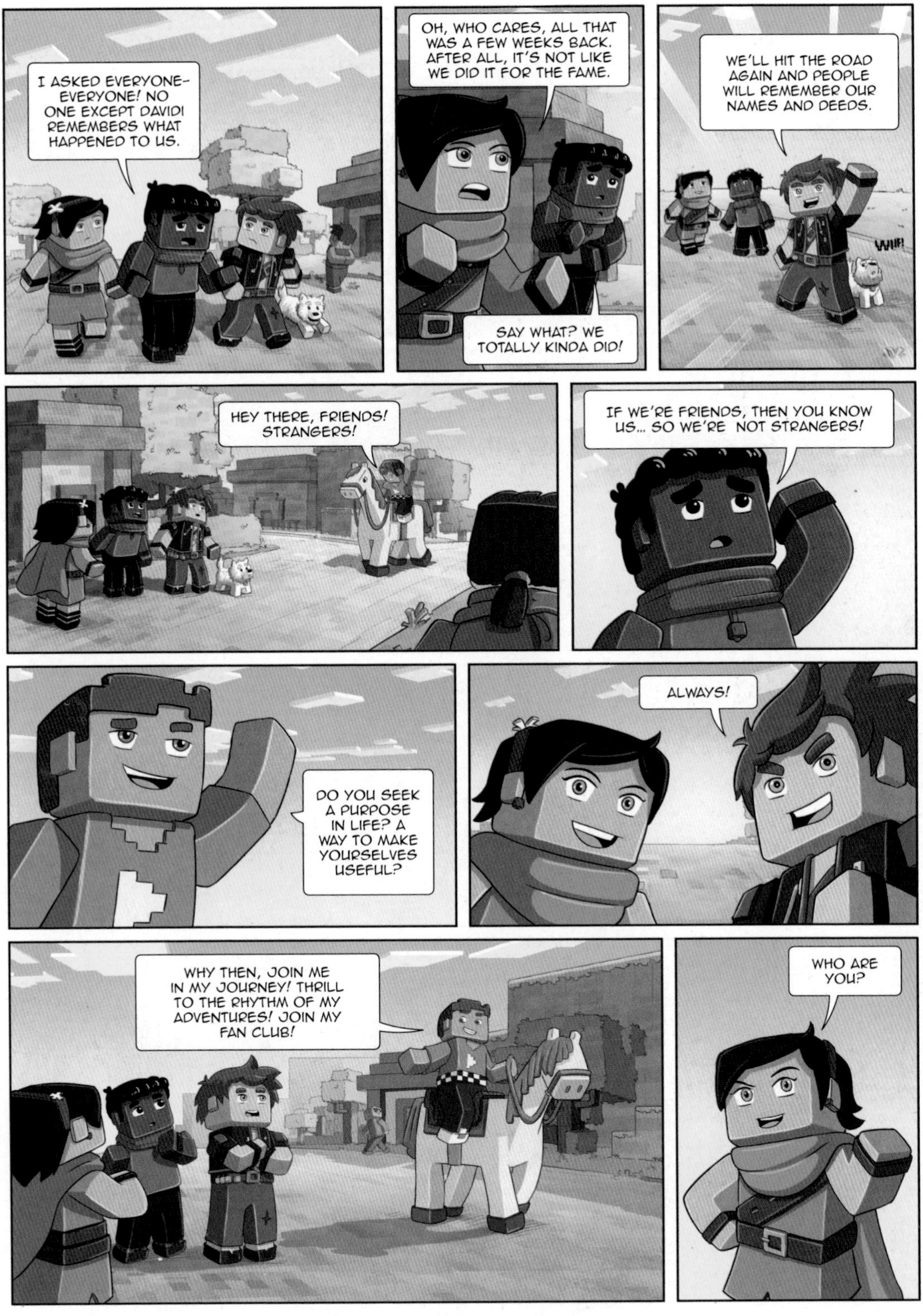
I ASKED EVERYONE—EVERYONE! NO ONE EXCEPT DAVID! REMEMBERS WHAT HAPPENED TO US.
OH, WHO CARES, ALL THAT WAS A FEW WEEKS BACK. AFTER ALL, IT'S NOT LIKE WE DID IT FOR THE FAME.
SAY WHAT? WE TOTALLY KINDA DID!
WE'LL HIT THE ROAD AGAIN AND PEOPLE WILL REMEMBER OUR NAMES AND DEEDS.
WUF!
HEY THERE, FRIENDS! STRANGERS!
IF WE'RE FRIENDS, THEN YOU KNOW US... SO WE'RE NOT STRANGERS!
DO YOU SEEK A PURPOSE IN LIFE? A WAY TO MAKE YOURSELVES USEFUL?
ALWAYS!
WHY THEN, JOIN ME IN MY JOURNEY! THRILL TO THE RHYTHM OF MY ADVENTURES! JOIN MY FAN CLUB!
WHO ARE YOU?

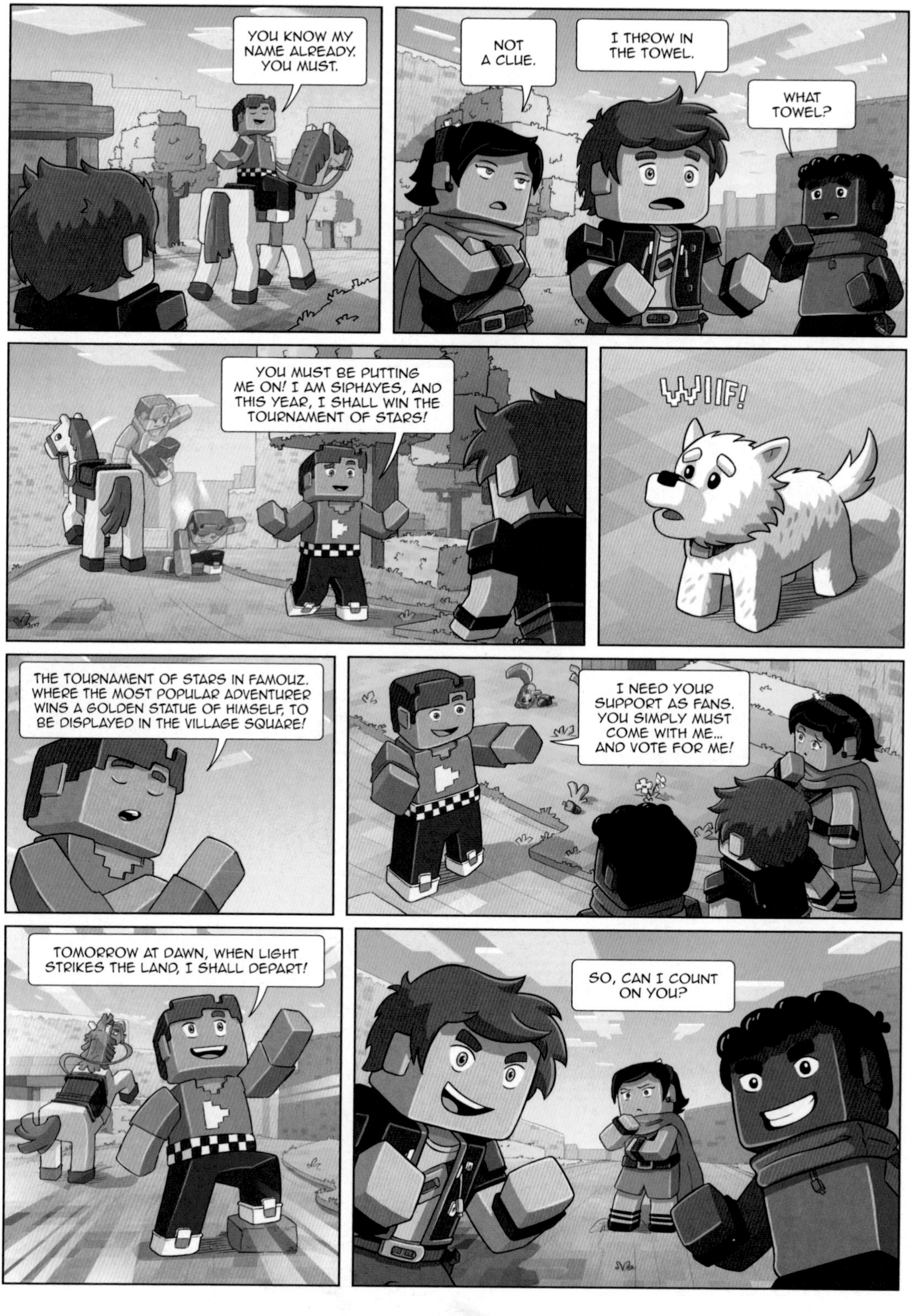
YOU KNOW MY NAME ALREADY. YOU MUST.
NOT A CLUE.
I THROW IN THE TOWEL.
WHAT TOWEL?
YOU MUST BE PUTTING ME ON! I AM SIPHAYES, AND THIS YEAR, I SHALL WIN THE TOURNAMENT OF STARS!
WIIF!
THE TOURNAMENT OF STARS IN FAMOUZ. WHERE THE MOST POPULAR ADVENTURER WINS A GOLDEN STATUE OF HIMSELF, TO BE DISPLAYED IN THE VILLAGE SQUARE!
I NEED YOUR SUPPORT AS FANS. YOU SIMPLY MUST COME WITH ME... AND VOTE FOR ME!
TOMORROW AT DAWN, WHEN LIGHT STRIKES THE LAND, I SHALL DEPART!
SO, CAN I COUNT ON YOU?

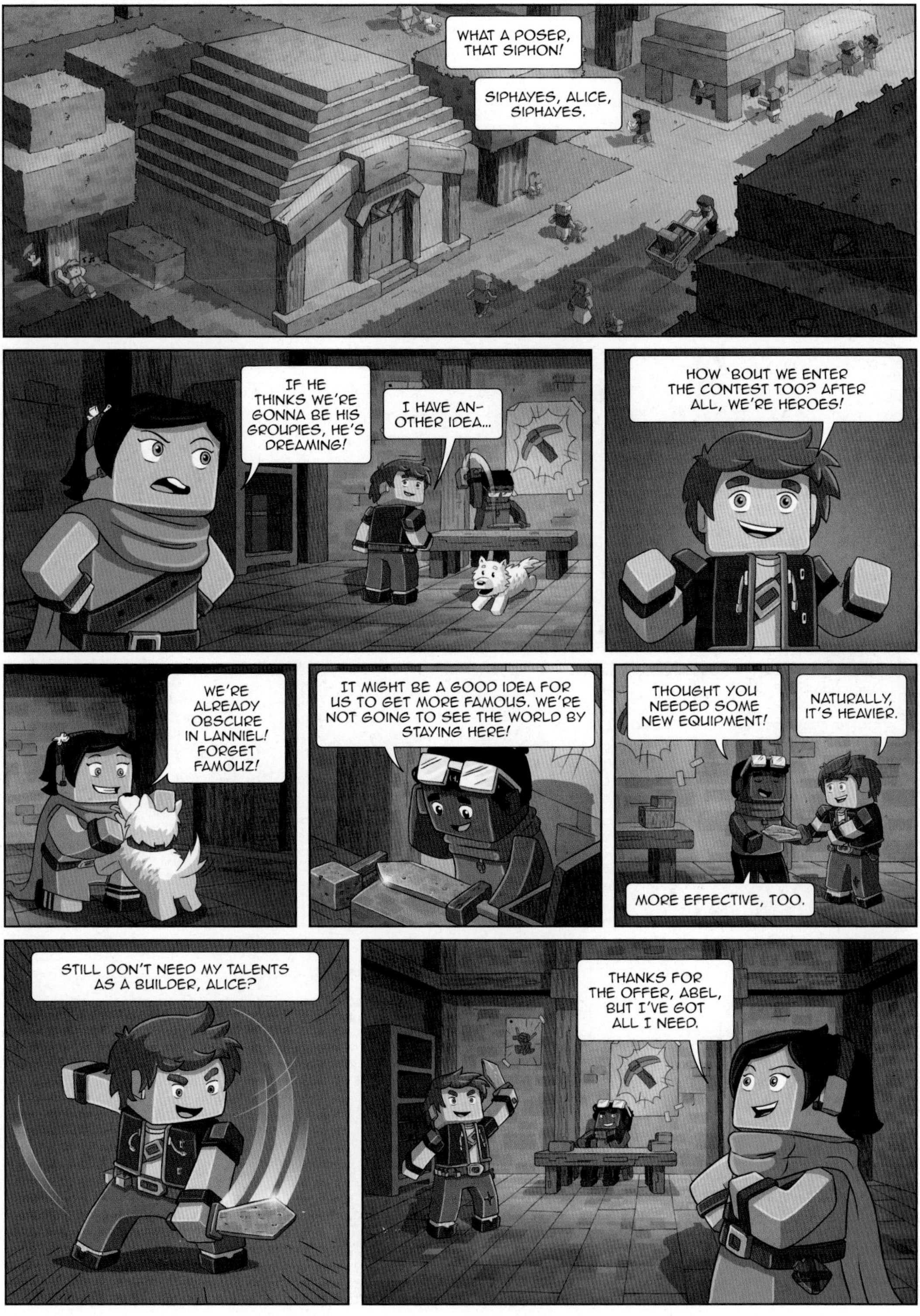

WHAT A POSER, THAT SIPHON!
SIPHAYES, ALICE, SIPHAYES.
IF HE THINKS WE'RE GONNA BE HIS GROUPIES, HE'S DREAMING!
I HAVE AN-OTHER IDEA...
HOW 'BOUT WE ENTER THE CONTEST TOO? AFTER ALL, WE'RE HEROES!
WE'RE ALREADY OBSCURE IN LANNIEL! FORGET FAMOUZ!
IT MIGHT BE A GOOD IDEA FOR US TO GET MORE FAMOUS. WE'RE NOT GOING TO SEE THE WORLD BY STAYING HERE!
THOUGHT YOU NEEDED SOME NEW EQUIPMENT!
NATURALLY, IT'S HEAVIER.
MORE EFFECTIVE, TOO.
STILL DON'T NEED MY TALENTS AS A BUILDER, ALICE?
THANKS FOR THE OFFER, ABEL, BUT I'VE GOT ALL I NEED.

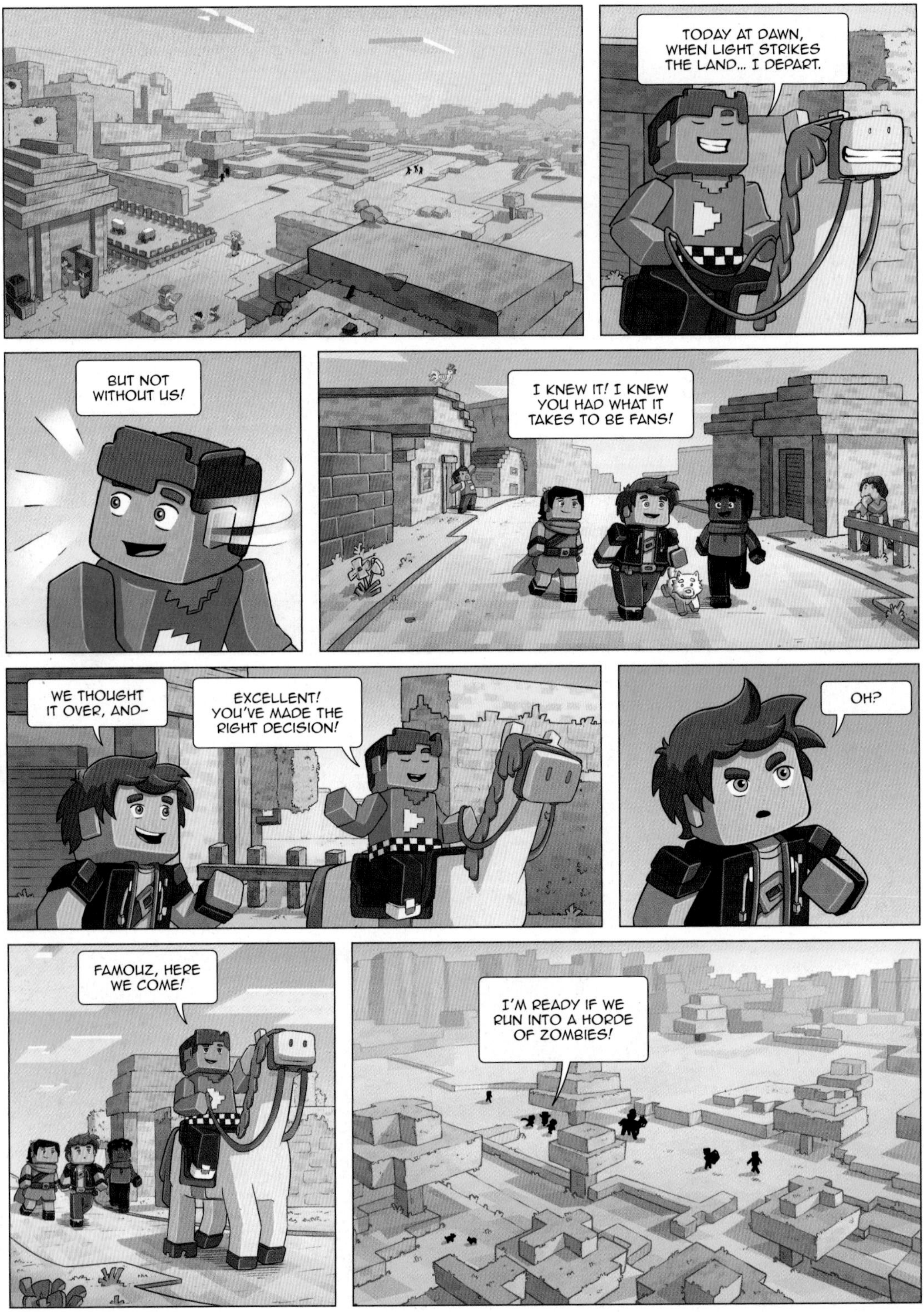
TODAY AT DAWN, WHEN LIGHT STRIKES THE LAND... I DEPART.
BUT NOT WITHOUT US!
I KNEW IT! I KNEW YOU HAD WHAT IT TAKES TO BE FANS!
WE THOUGHT IT OVER, AND-
EXCELLENT! YOU'VE MADE THE RIGHT DECISION!
OH?
FAMOUZ, HERE WE COME!
I'M READY IF WE RUN INTO A HORDE OF ZOMBIES!

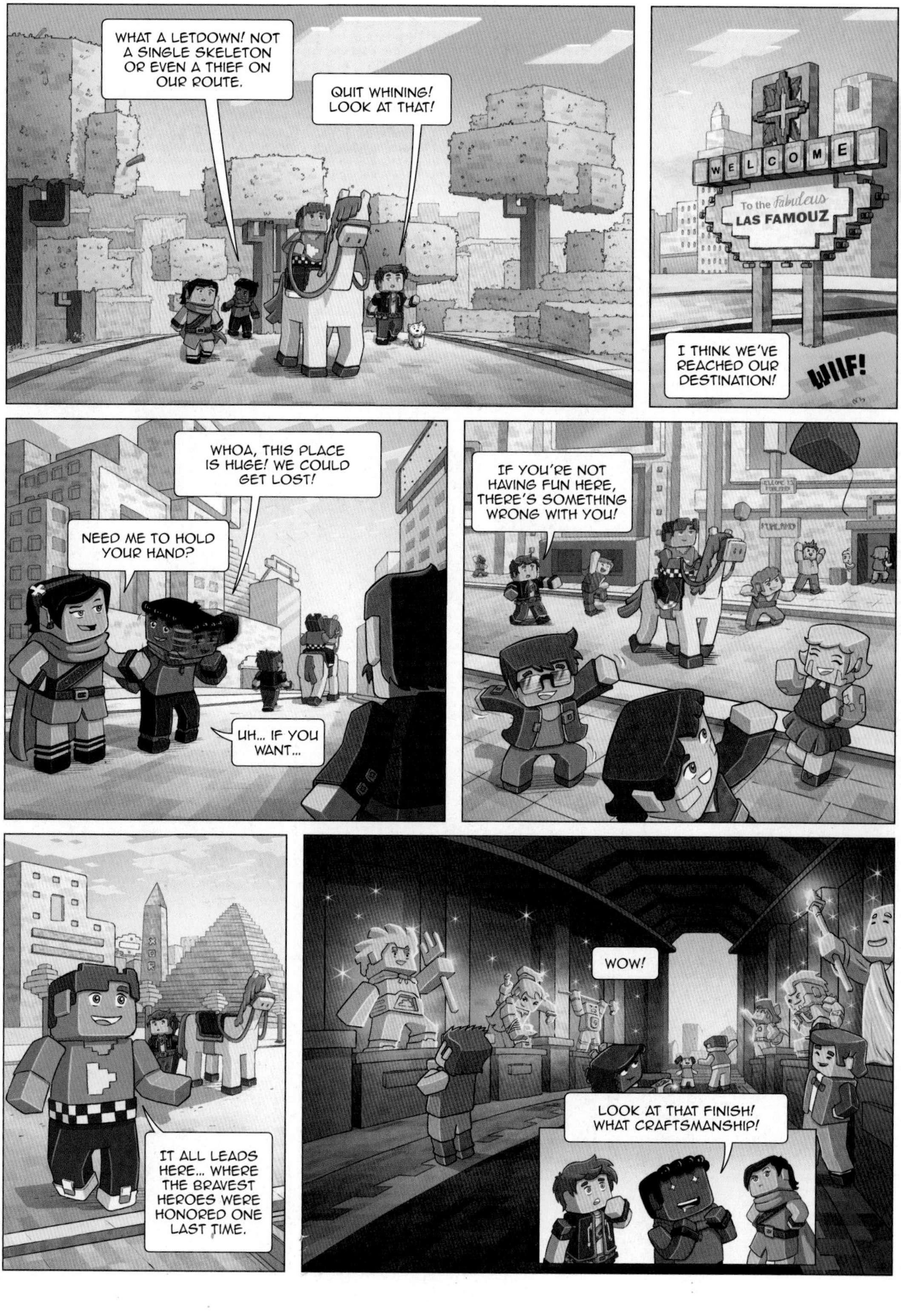
WHAT A LETDOWN! NOT A SINGLE SKELETON OR EVEN A THIEF ON OUR ROUTE.
QUIT WHINING! LOOK AT THAT!
WELCOME
To the Fabulous
LAS FAMOUZ
I THINK WE'VE REACHED OUR DESTINATION!
WIIF!
WHOA, THIS PLACE IS HUGE! WE COULD GET LOST!
NEED ME TO HOLD YOUR HAND?
UH... IF YOU WANT...
IF YOU'RE NOT HAVING FUN HERE, THERE'S SOMETHING WRONG WITH YOU!
IT ALL LEADS HERE... WHERE THE BRAVEST HEROES WERE HONORED ONE LAST TIME.
WOW!
LOOK AT THAT FINISH! WHAT CRAFTSMANSHIP!

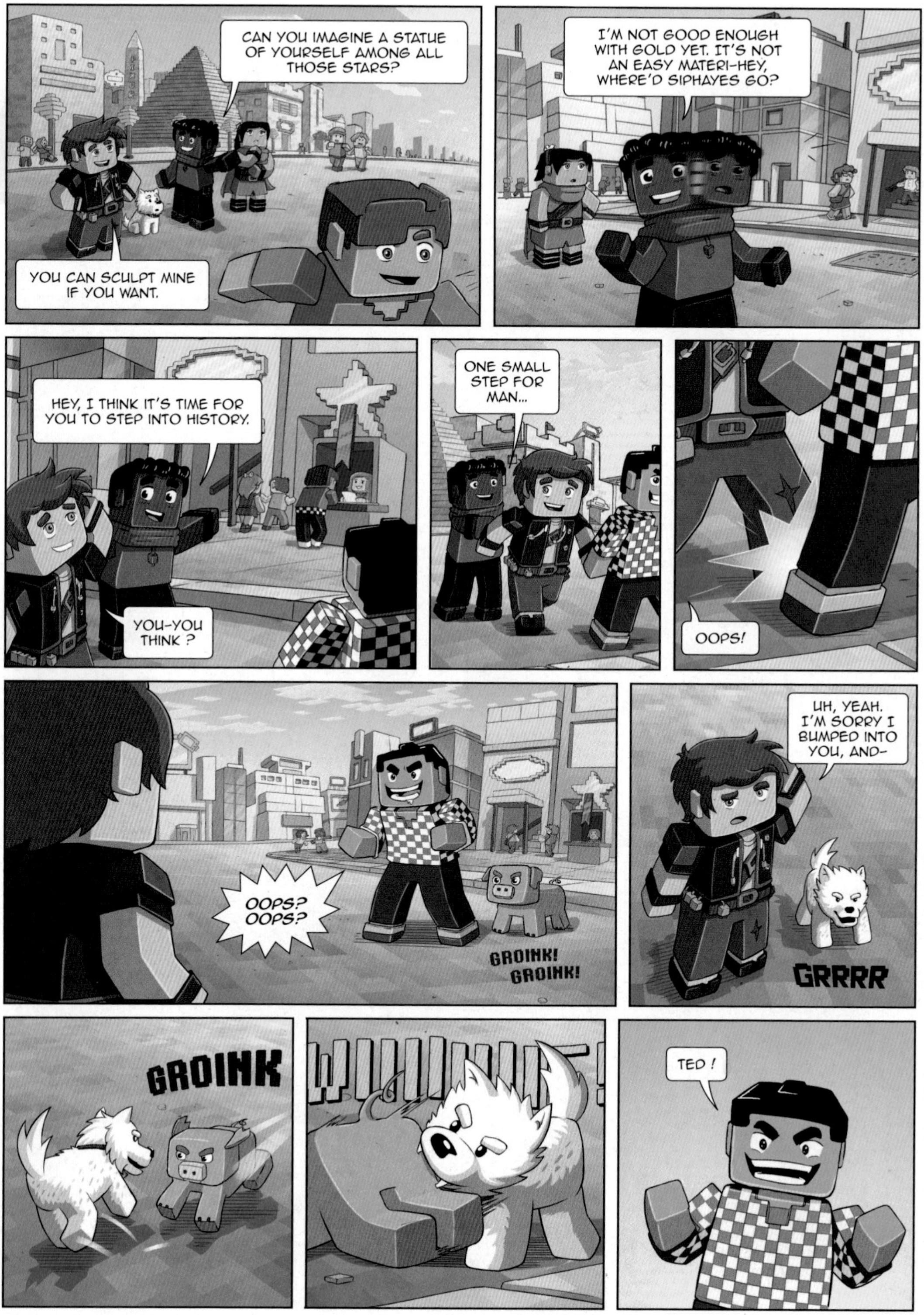
CAN YOU IMAGINE A STATUE OF YOURSELF AMONG ALL THOSE STARS?
YOU CAN SCULPT MINE IF YOU WANT.
I'M NOT GOOD ENOUGH WITH GOLD YET. IT'S NOT AN EASY MATERI–HEY, WHERE'D SIPHAYES GO?
HEY, I THINK IT'S TIME FOR YOU TO STEP INTO HISTORY.
YOU–YOU THINK ?
ONE SMALL STEP FOR MAN...
OOPS!
OOPS? OOPS?
GROINK! GROINK!
UH, YEAH. I'M SORRY I BUMPED INTO YOU, AND–
GRRRR
GROINK
TED !

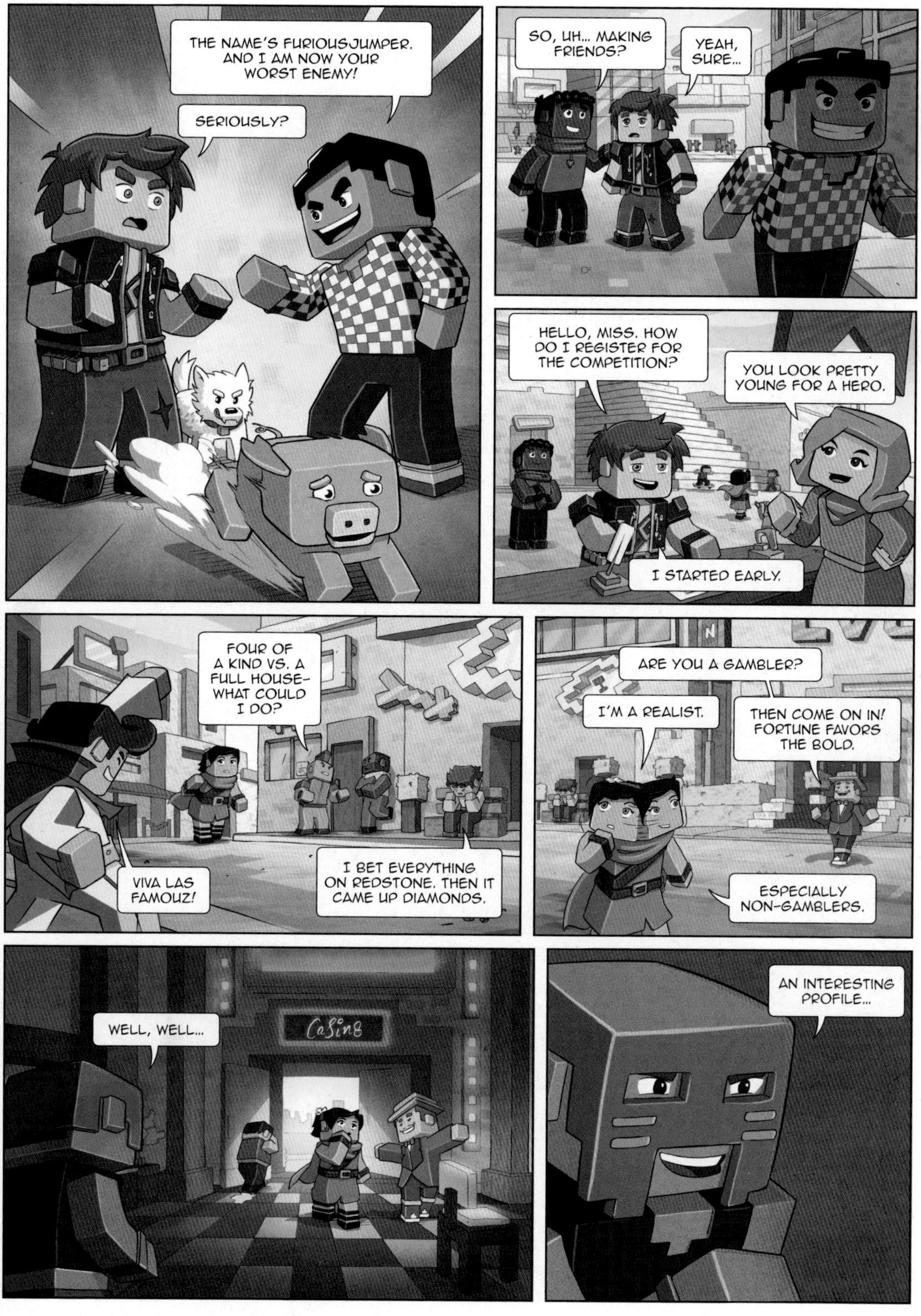
THE NAME'S FURIOUSJUMPER. AND I AM NOW YOUR WORST ENEMY!
SERIOUSLY?
SO, UH... MAKING FRIENDS?
YEAH, SURE...
HELLO, MISS. HOW DO I REGISTER FOR THE COMPETITION?
YOU LOOK PRETTY YOUNG FOR A HERO.
I STARTED EARLY.
FOUR OF A KIND VS. A FULL HOUSE- WHAT COULD I DO?
VIVA LAS FAMOUZ!
I BET EVERYTHING ON REDSTONE. THEN IT CAME UP DIAMONDS.
ARE YOU A GAMBLER?
I'M A REALIST.
THEN COME ON IN! FORTUNE FAVORS THE BOLD.
ESPECIALLY NON-GAMBLERS.
WELL, WELL...
Casino
AN INTERESTING PROFILE...

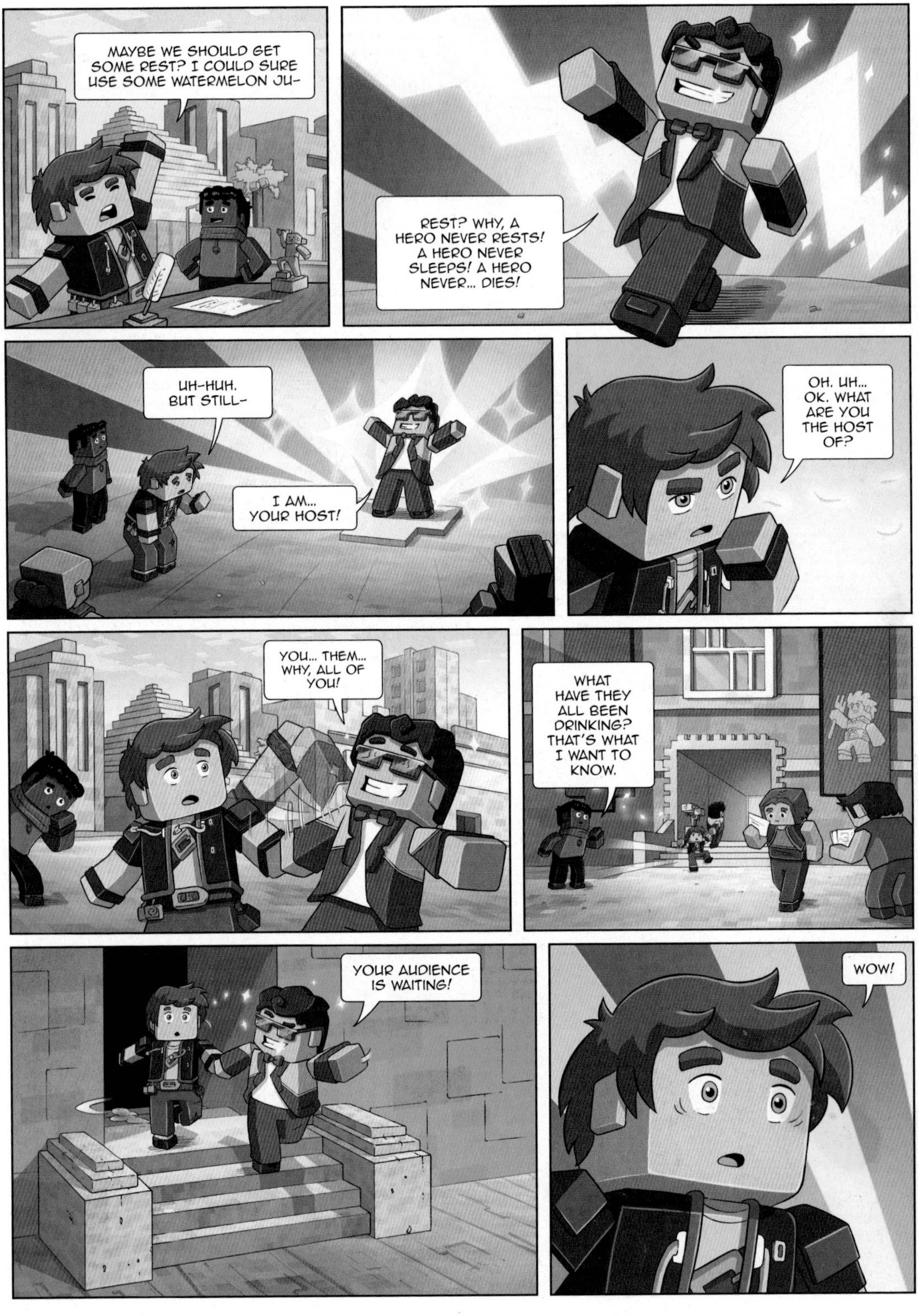
MAYBE WE SHOULD GET SOME REST? I COULD SURE USE SOME WATERMELON JU-
REST? WHY, A HERO NEVER RESTS! A HERO NEVER SLEEPS! A HERO NEVER... DIES!
UH-HUH. BUT STILL-
I AM... YOUR HOST!
OH. UH... OK. WHAT ARE YOU THE HOST OF?
YOU... THEM... WHY, ALL OF YOU!
WHAT HAVE THEY ALL BEEN DRINKING? THAT'S WHAT I WANT TO KNOW.
YOUR AUDIENCE IS WAITING!
WOW!

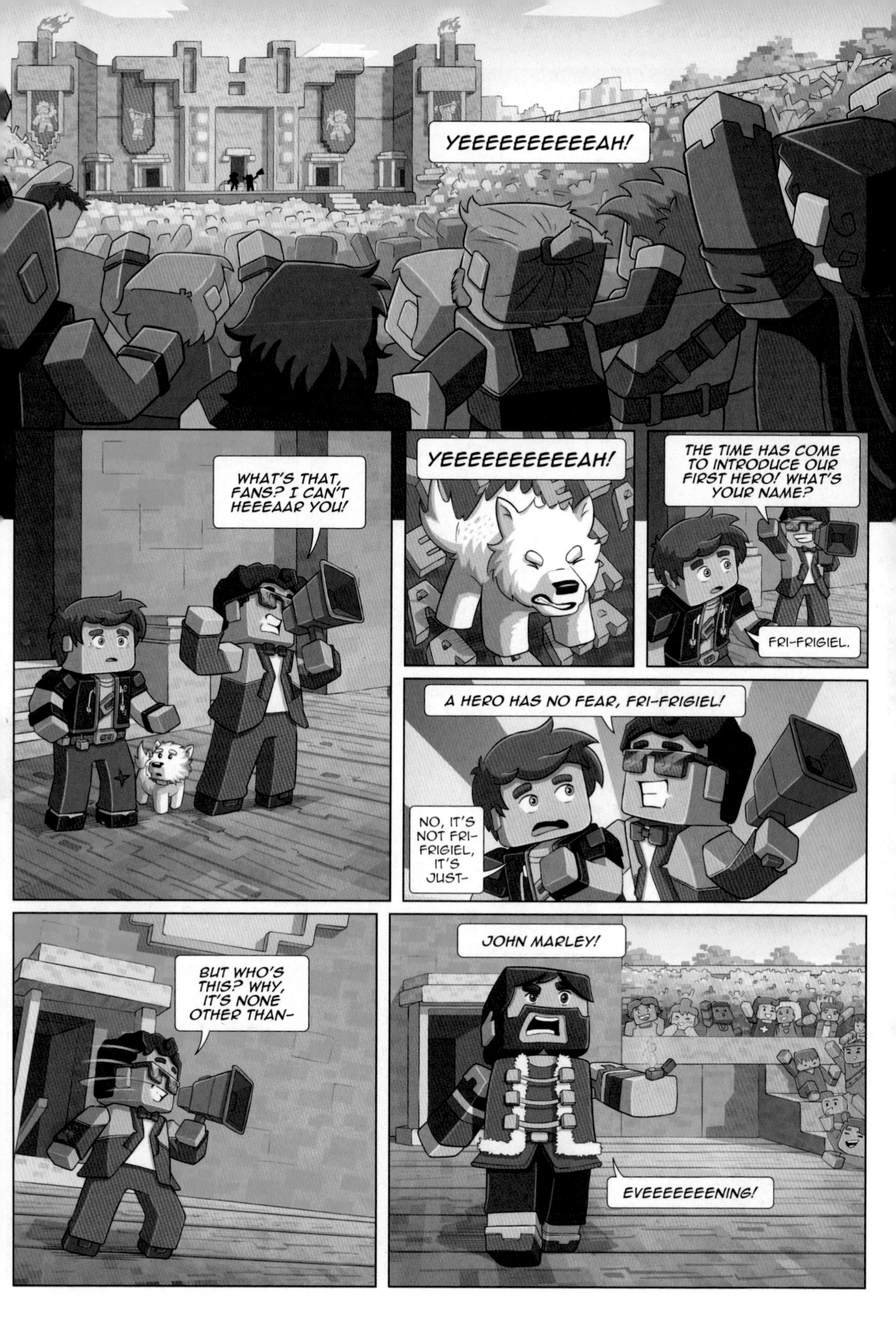
YEEEEEEEEEEAH!
WHAT'S THAT, FANS? I CAN'T HEEEAAR YOU!
YEEEEEEEEEEAH!
THE TIME HAS COME TO INTRODUCE OUR FIRST HERO! WHAT'S YOUR NAME?
FRI-FRIGIEL.
A HERO HAS NO FEAR, FRI-FRIGIEL!
NO, IT'S NOT FRI-FRIGIEL, IT'S JUST-
BUT WHO'S THIS? WHY, IT'S NONE OTHER THAN-
JOHN MARLEY!
EVEEEEEEEENING!

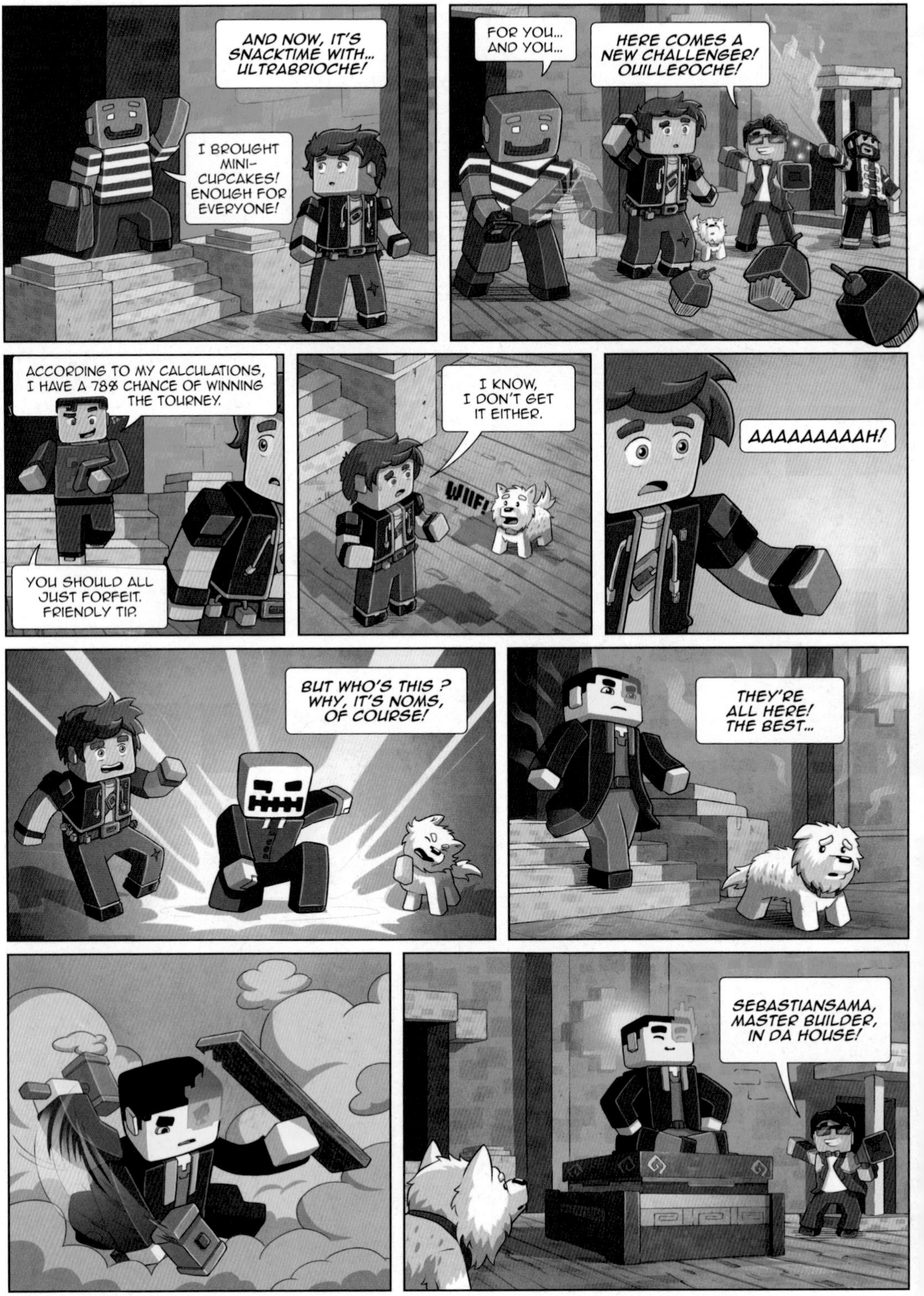
AND NOW, IT'S SNACKTIME WITH... ULTRABRIOCHE!
I BROUGHT MINI-CUPCAKES! ENOUGH FOR EVERYONE!
FOR YOU... AND YOU...
HERE COMES A NEW CHALLENGER! OUILLEROCHE!
ACCORDING TO MY CALCULATIONS, I HAVE A 78% CHANCE OF WINNING THE TOURNEY.
YOU SHOULD ALL JUST FORFEIT. FRIENDLY TIP.
I KNOW, I DON'T GET IT EITHER.
WIIF!
AAAAAAAAAH!
BUT WHO'S THIS ? WHY, IT'S NOMS, OF COURSE!
THEY'RE ALL HERE! THE BEST...
SEBASTIANSAMA, MASTER BUILDER, IN DA HOUSE!

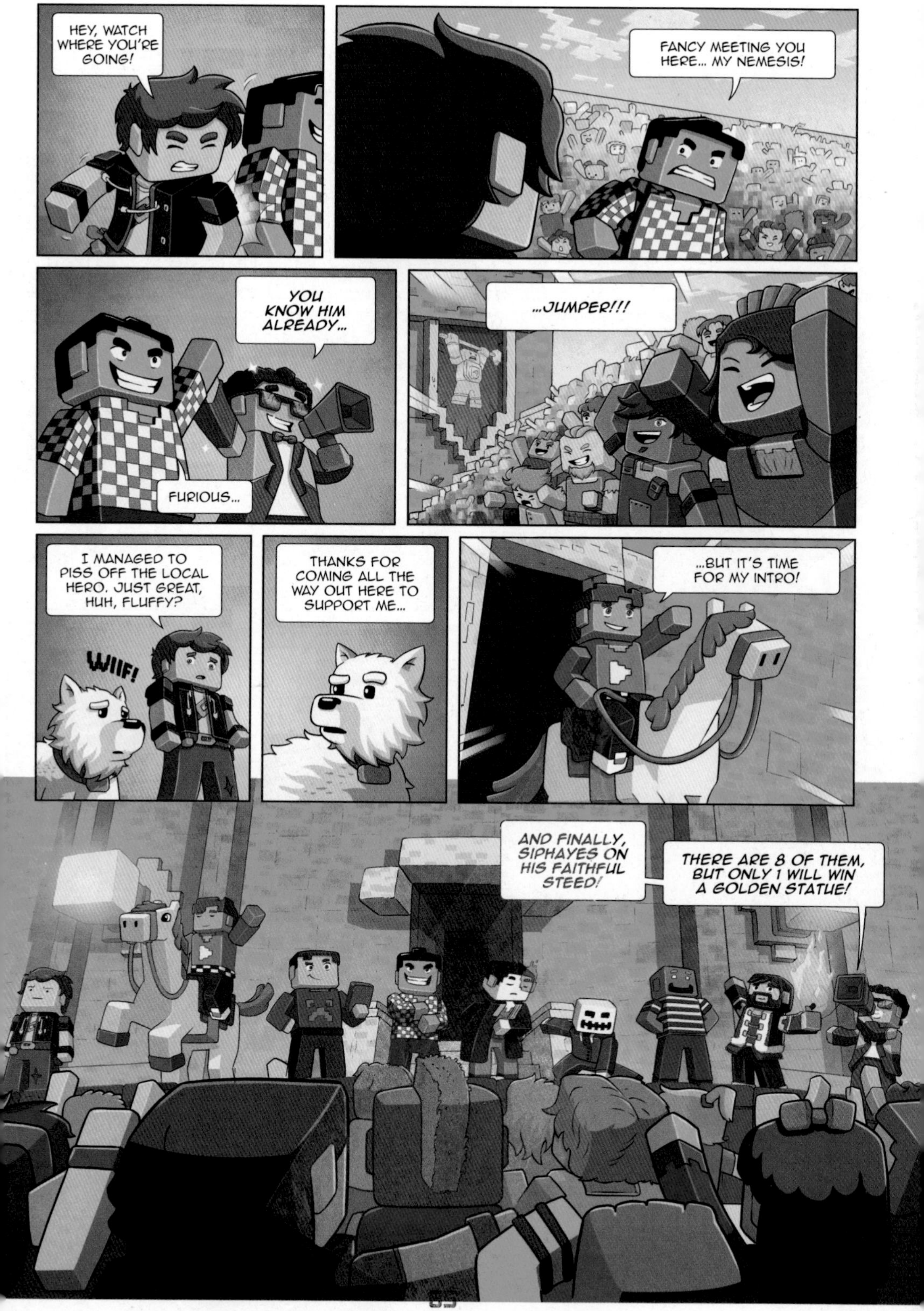
HEY, WATCH WHERE YOU'RE GOING!
FANCY MEETING YOU HERE... MY NEMESIS!
YOU KNOW HIM ALREADY...
FURIOUS...
...JUMPER!!!
I MANAGED TO PISS OFF THE LOCAL HERO. JUST GREAT, HUH, FLUFFY?
WIIF!
THANKS FOR COMING ALL THE WAY OUT HERE TO SUPPORT ME...
...BUT IT'S TIME FOR MY INTRO!
AND FINALLY, SIPHAYES ON HIS FAITHFUL STEED!
THERE ARE 8 OF THEM, BUT ONLY 1 WILL WIN A GOLDEN STATUE!

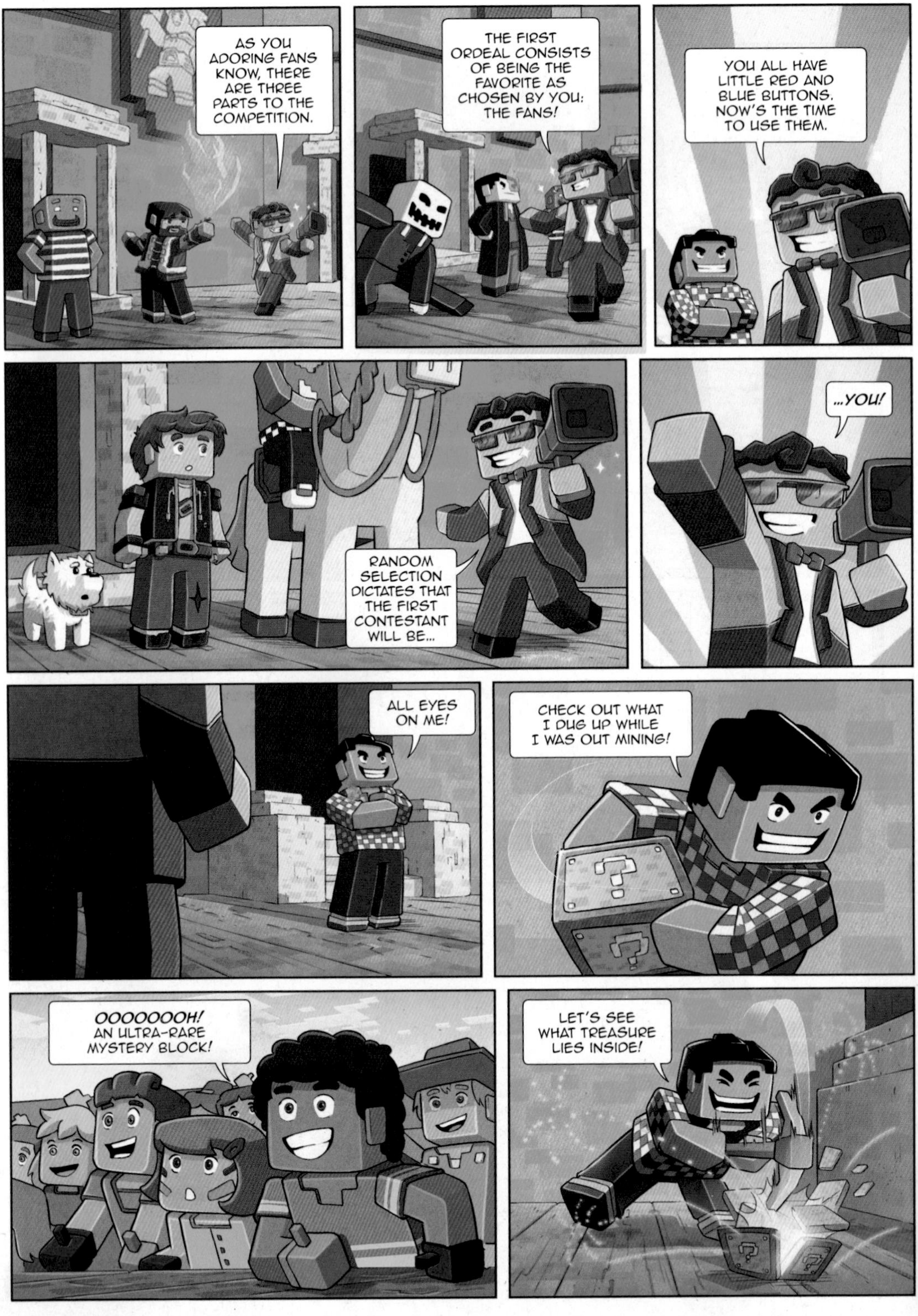
AS YOU ADORING FANS KNOW, THERE ARE THREE PARTS TO THE COMPETITION.
THE FIRST ORDEAL CONSISTS OF BEING THE FAVORITE AS CHOSEN BY YOU: THE FANS!
YOU ALL HAVE LITTLE RED AND BLUE BUTTONS. NOW'S THE TIME TO USE THEM.
RANDOM SELECTION DICTATES THAT THE FIRST CONTESTANT WILL BE...
...YOU!
ALL EYES ON ME!
CHECK OUT WHAT I DUG UP WHILE I WAS OUT MINING!
OOOOOOOH! AN ULTRA-RARE MYSTERY BLOCK!
LET'S SEE WHAT TREASURE LIES INSIDE!

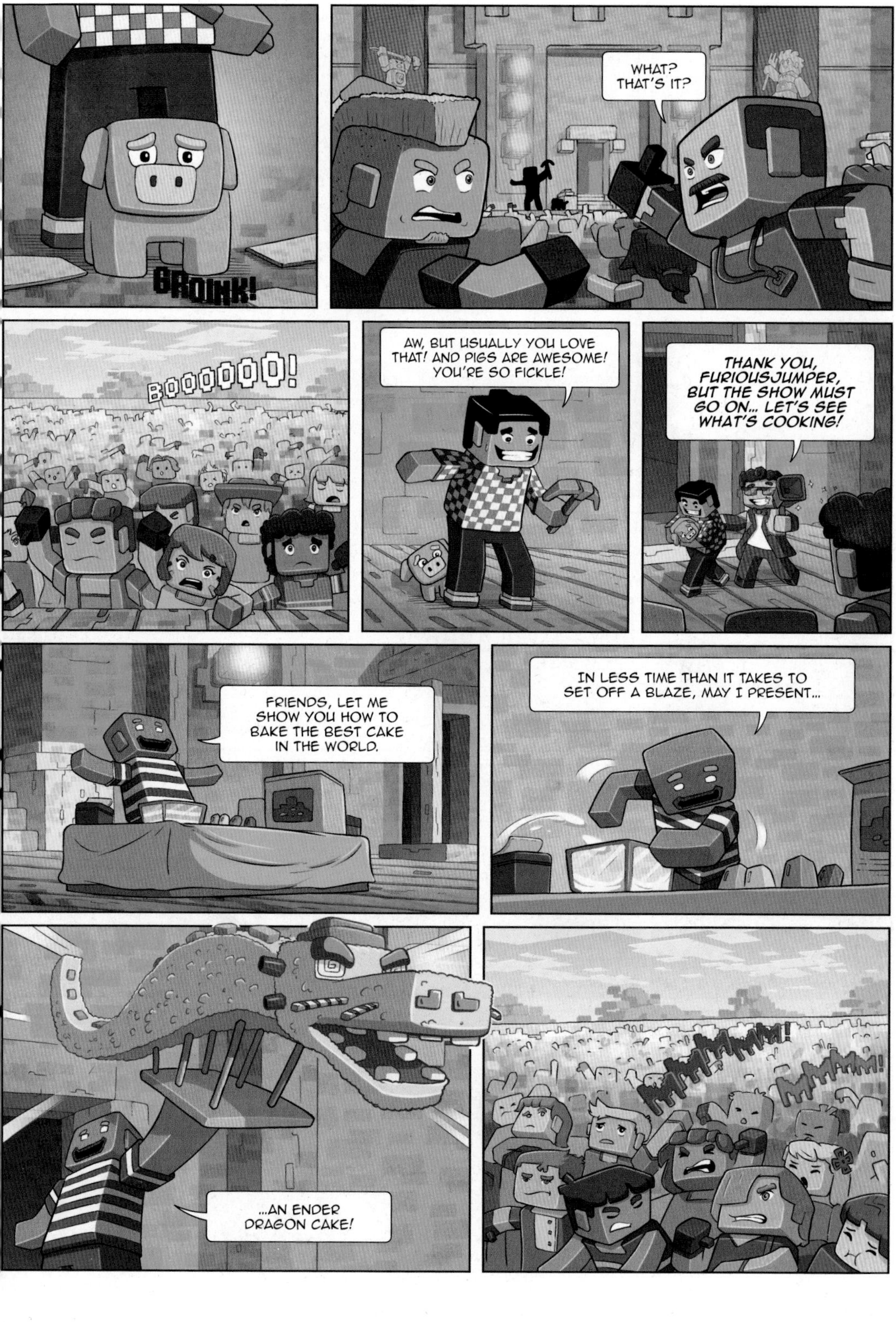
GROINK!
WHAT? THAT'S IT?
BOOOOOOO!
AW, BUT USUALLY YOU LOVE THAT! AND PIGS ARE AWESOME! YOU'RE SO FICKLE!
THANK YOU, FURIOUSJUMPER, BUT THE SHOW MUST GO ON... LET'S SEE WHAT'S COOKING!
FRIENDS, LET ME SHOW YOU HOW TO BAKE THE BEST CAKE IN THE WORLD.
IN LESS TIME THAN IT TAKES TO SET OFF A BLAZE, MAY I PRESENT...
...AN ENDER DRAGON CAKE!

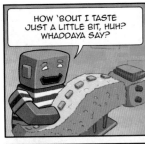

HOW 'BOUT I TASTE JUST A LITTLE BIT, HUH? WHADDAYA SAY?

I DON'T THINK I'M HUNGRY...

...NOW.

WE NEED A DOCTOR! STAT!

LOOK CLOSELY. DON'T TAKE YOUR EYES OFF THE CUBE.

ABRACA-DABRA!

WELL? WELL, WHERE IS IT NOW? 10 EMERALDS TO PLAY. DIRT CHEAP!

THE CUP ON THE LEFT. I JUST KNOW IT!

OH, TOO BAD! NOPE! WHO KNOWS, MAYBE NEXT TIME!

HMPH! WHAT A SCAM!

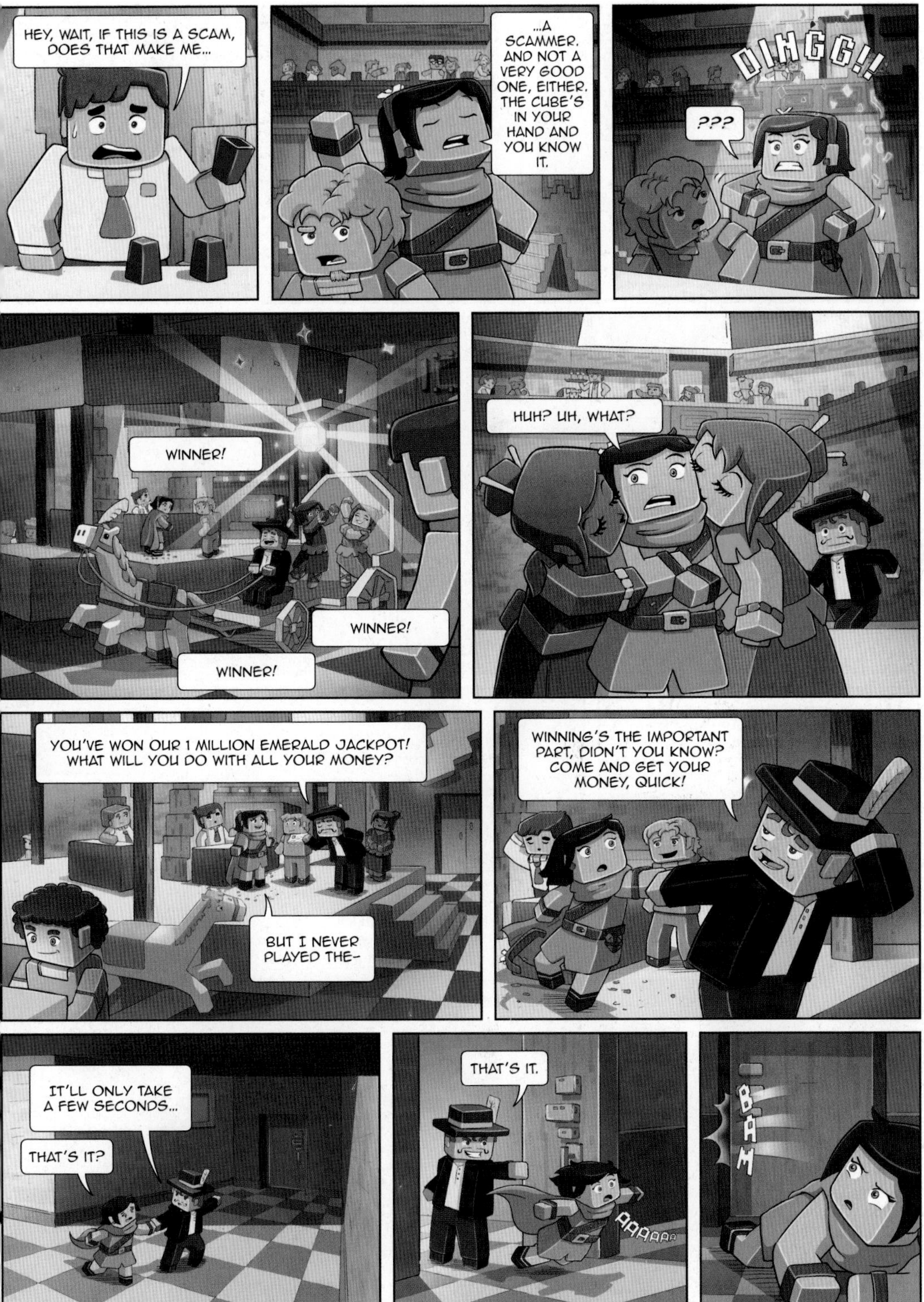
HEY, WAIT, IF THIS IS A SCAM, DOES THAT MAKE ME...
...A SCAMMER. AND NOT A VERY GOOD ONE, EITHER. THE CUBE'S IN YOUR HAND AND YOU KNOW IT.
DINGG!!
???
WINNER!
WINNER!
WINNER!
HUH? UH, WHAT?
YOU'VE WON OUR 1 MILLION EMERALD JACKPOT! WHAT WILL YOU DO WITH ALL YOUR MONEY?
BUT I NEVER PLAYED THE-
WINNING'S THE IMPORTANT PART, DIDN'T YOU KNOW? COME AND GET YOUR MONEY, QUICK!
IT'LL ONLY TAKE A FEW SECONDS...
THAT'S IT?
THAT'S IT.
AAAAAA
BAM

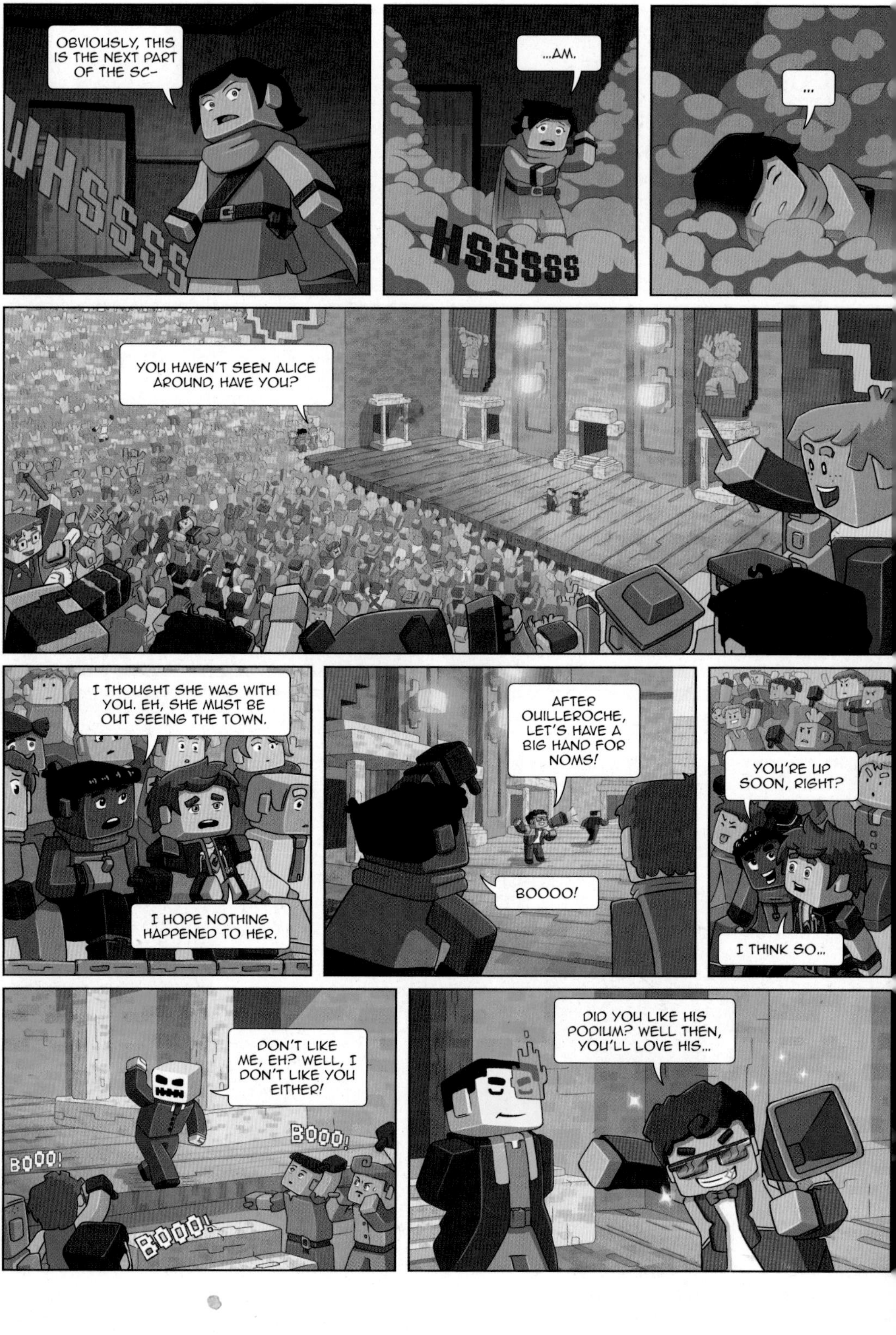

OBVIOUSLY, THIS IS THE NEXT PART OF THE SC-
WHSSSSSS
...AM.
HSSSSS
...
YOU HAVEN'T SEEN ALICE AROUND, HAVE YOU?
I THOUGHT SHE WAS WITH YOU. EH, SHE MUST BE OUT SEEING THE TOWN.
I HOPE NOTHING HAPPENED TO HER.
AFTER OUILLEROCHE, LET'S HAVE A BIG HAND FOR NOMS!
BOOOO!
YOU'RE UP SOON, RIGHT?
I THINK SO...
DON'T LIKE ME, EH? WELL, I DON'T LIKE YOU EITHER!
BOOO!
BOOO!
BOOO!
DID YOU LIKE HIS PODIUM? WELL THEN, YOU'LL LOVE HIS...

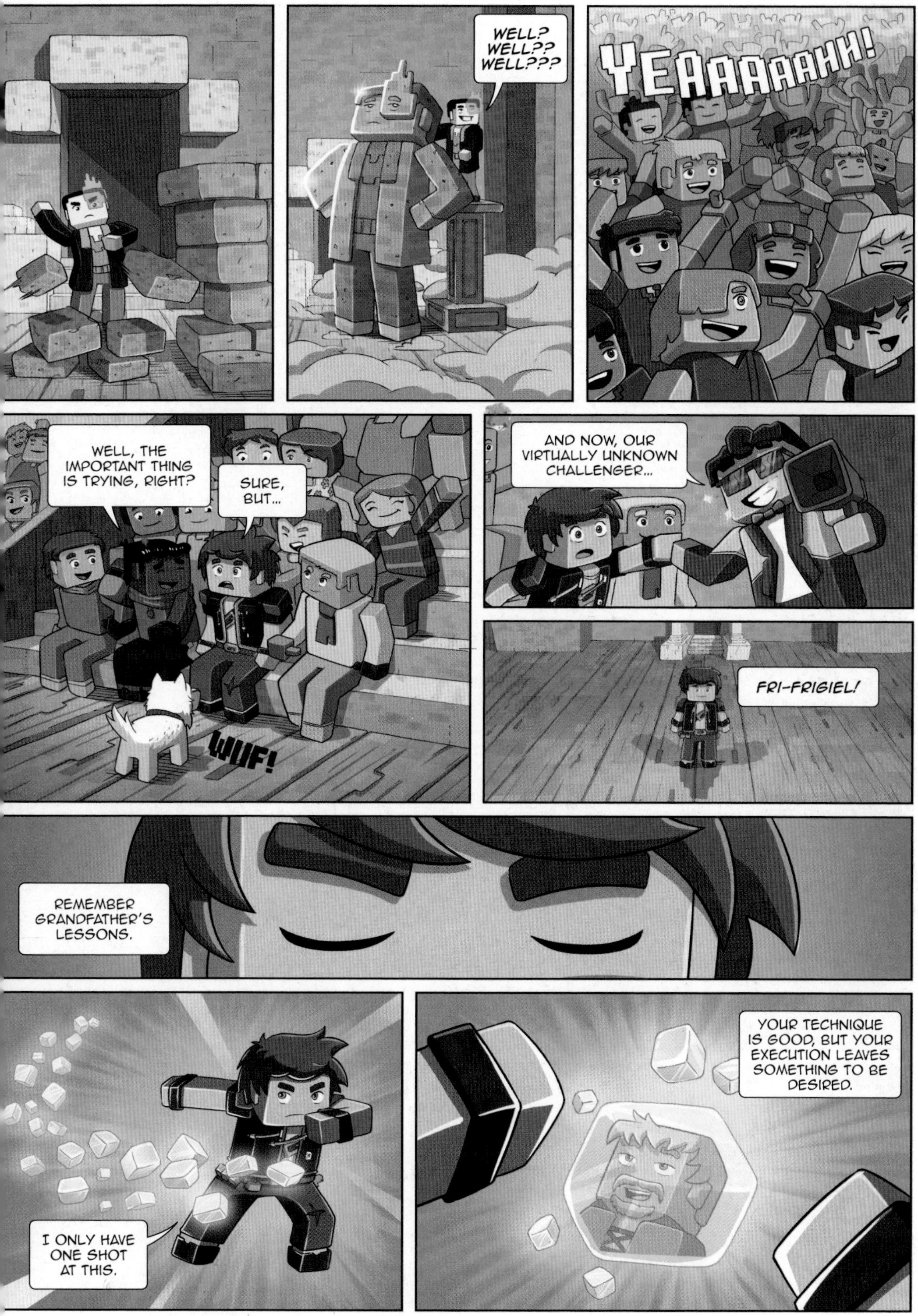

WELL?
WELL??
WELL???
YEAAAAAAHH!
WELL, THE IMPORTANT THING IS TRYING, RIGHT?
SURE, BUT...
WUF!
AND NOW, OUR VIRTUALLY UNKNOWN CHALLENGER...
FRI-FRIGIEL!
REMEMBER GRANDFATHER'S LESSONS.
I ONLY HAVE ONE SHOT AT THIS.
YOUR TECHNIQUE IS GOOD, BUT YOUR EXECUTION LEAVES SOMETHING TO BE DESIRED.

OOOOOH!

TA-DAA!

HE'S MY FRIEND! HE'S MY FRIEND!

YAAAAHOOOOOO!

NOT BAD, KID, NOT BAD...

BUT DON'T GO YET, 'CAUSE HERE COMES SIPHAYES!

YEEHAAAH!

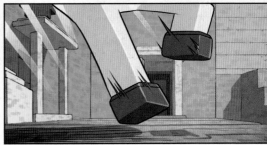

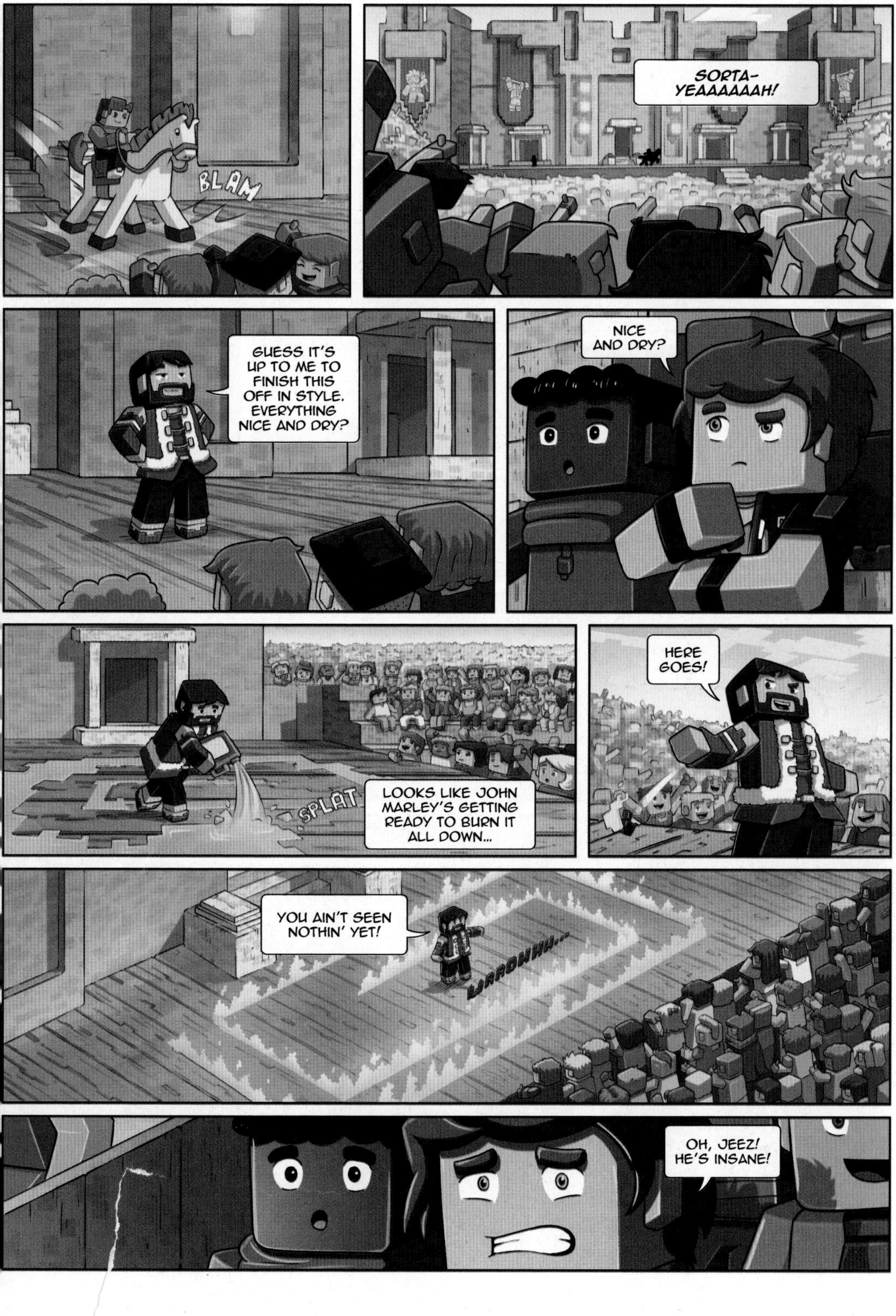
BLAM
SORTA-YEAAAAAAH!
GUESS IT'S UP TO ME TO FINISH THIS OFF IN STYLE. EVERYTHING NICE AND DRY?
NICE AND DRY?
SPLAT
LOOKS LIKE JOHN MARLEY'S GETTING READY TO BURN IT ALL DOWN...
HERE GOES!
YOU AIN'T SEEN NOTHIN' YET!
WROOHHH...
OH, JEEZ! HE'S INSANE!

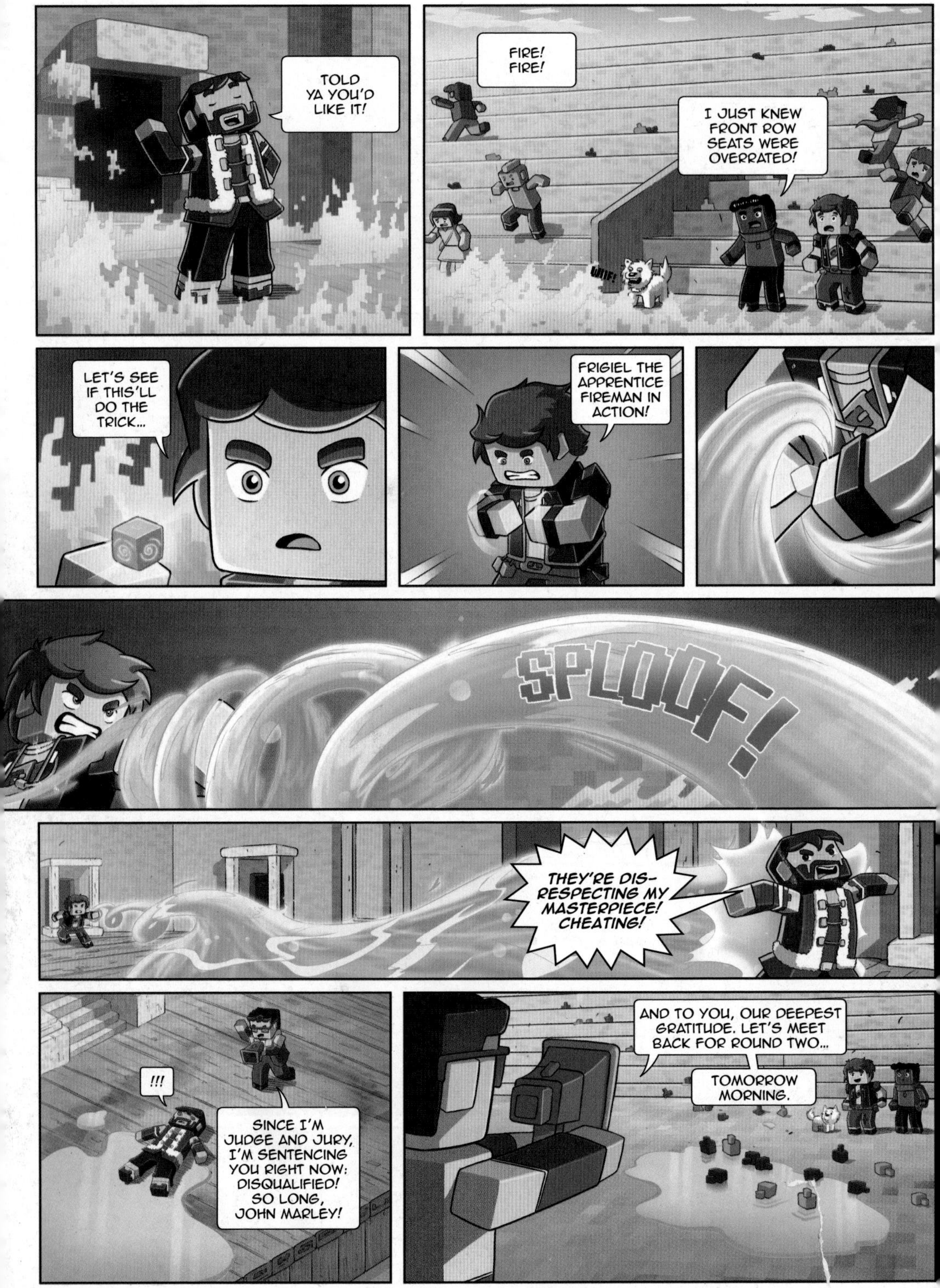

TOLD YA YOU'D LIKE IT!
FIRE! FIRE!
I JUST KNEW FRONT ROW SEATS WERE OVERRATED!
WUF!
LET'S SEE IF THIS'LL DO THE TRICK...
FRIGIEL THE APPRENTICE FIREMAN IN ACTION!
SPLOOF!
THEY'RE DIS-RESPECTING MY MASTERPIECE! CHEATING!
!!!
SINCE I'M JUDGE AND JURY, I'M SENTENCING YOU RIGHT NOW: DISQUALIFIED! SO LONG, JOHN MARLEY!
AND TO YOU, OUR DEEPEST GRATITUDE. LET'S MEET BACK FOR ROUND TWO...
TOMORROW MORNING.

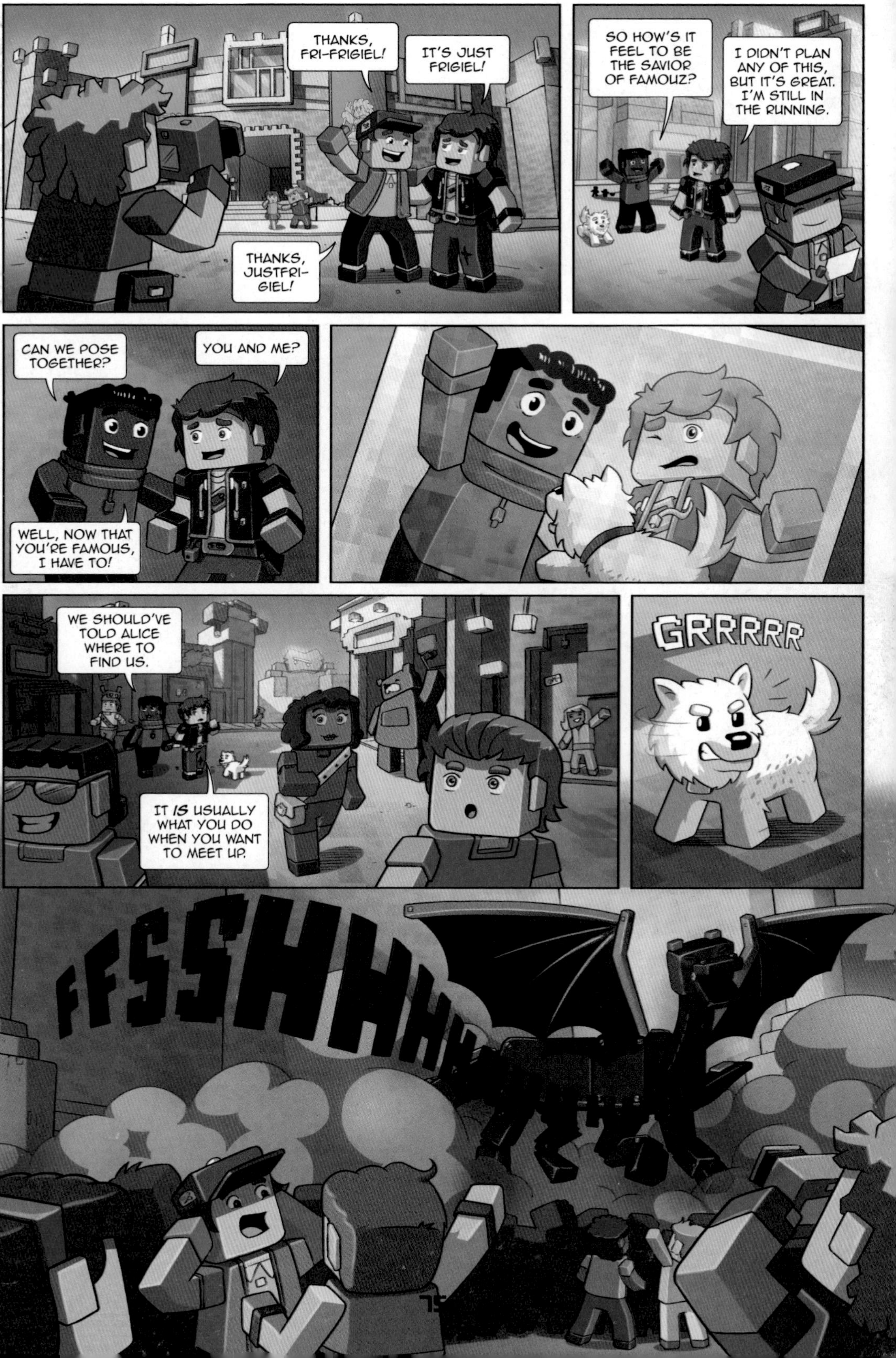
THANKS, FRI-FRIGIEL!
IT'S JUST FRIGIEL!
THANKS, JUSTFRI-GIEL!
SO HOW'S IT FEEL TO BE THE SAVIOR OF FAMOUZ?
I DIDN'T PLAN ANY OF THIS, BUT IT'S GREAT. I'M STILL IN THE RUNNING.
CAN WE POSE TOGETHER?
YOU AND ME?
WELL, NOW THAT YOU'RE FAMOUS, I HAVE TO!
WE SHOULD'VE TOLD ALICE WHERE TO FIND US.
IT *IS* USUALLY WHAT YOU DO WHEN YOU WANT TO MEET UP.
GRRRRR
FFSSHHHH

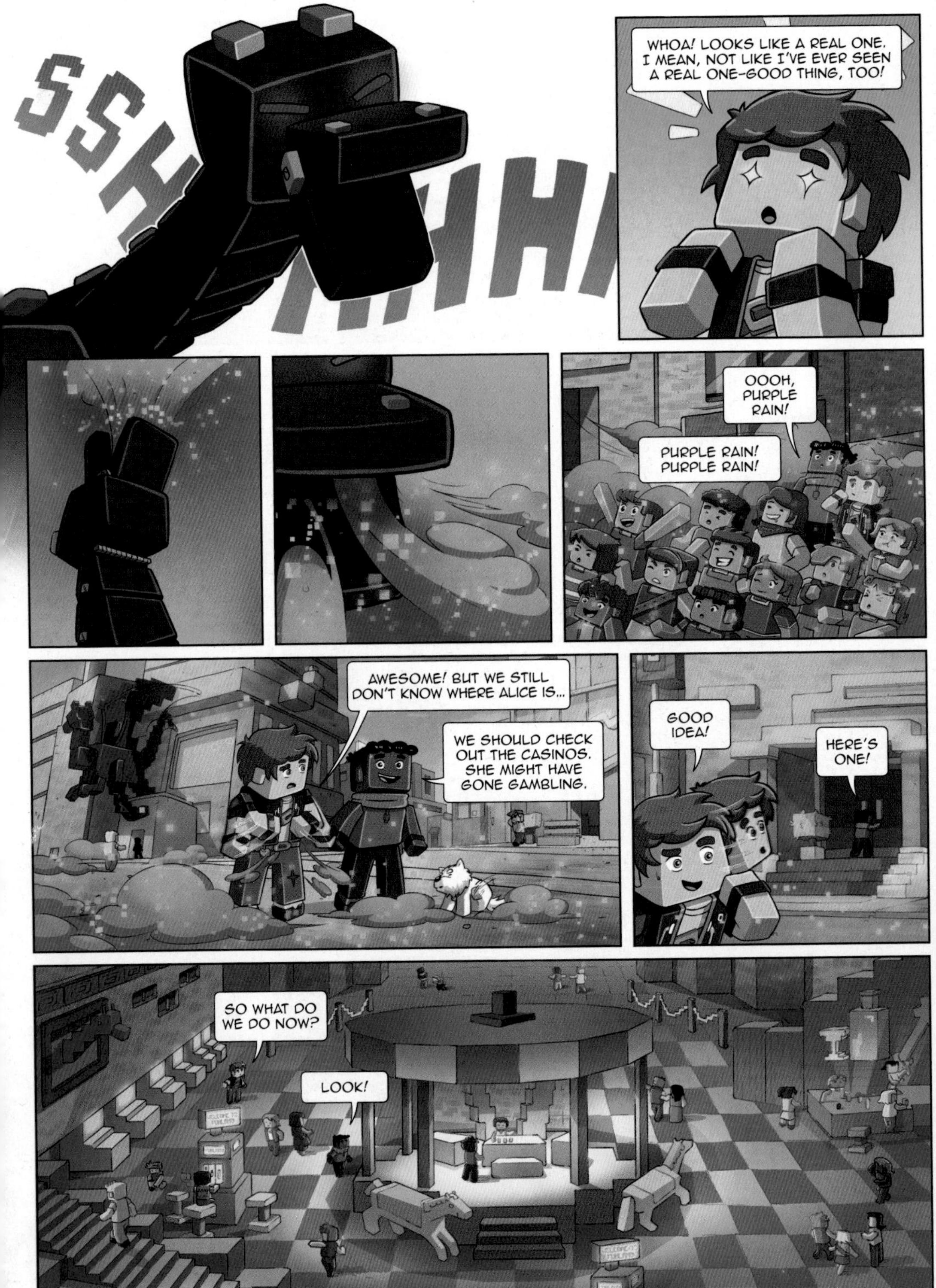
SSHHHHH
WHOA! LOOKS LIKE A REAL ONE. I MEAN, NOT LIKE I'VE EVER SEEN A REAL ONE–GOOD THING, TOO!
OOOH, PURPLE RAIN!
PURPLE RAIN! PURPLE RAIN!
AWESOME! BUT WE STILL DON'T KNOW WHERE ALICE IS...
WE SHOULD CHECK OUT THE CASINOS. SHE MIGHT HAVE GONE GAMBLING.
GOOD IDEA!
HERE'S ONE!
SO WHAT DO WE DO NOW?
LOOK!

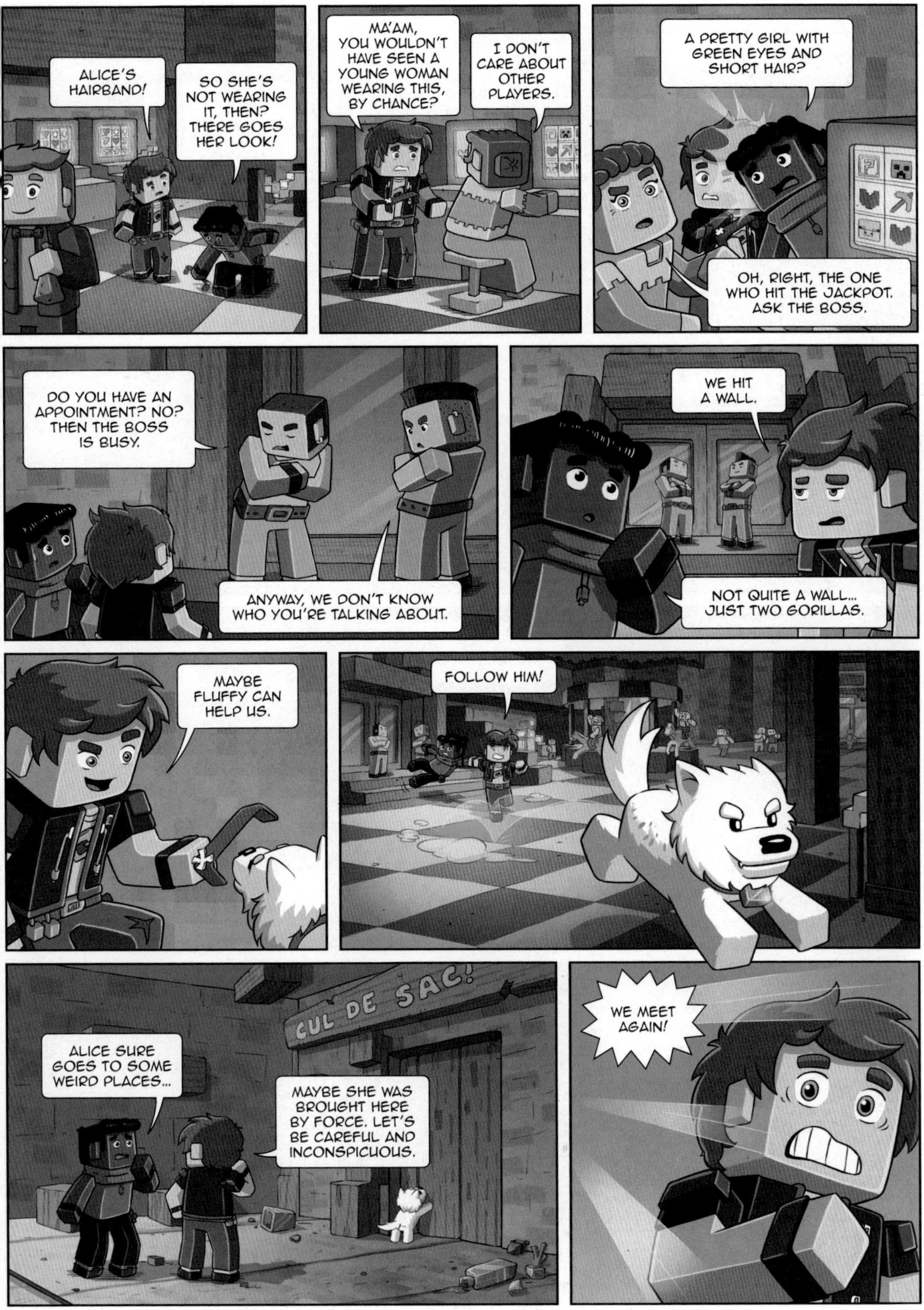
ALICE'S HAIRBAND!
SO SHE'S NOT WEARING IT, THEN? THERE GOES HER LOOK!
MA'AM, YOU WOULDN'T HAVE SEEN A YOUNG WOMAN WEARING THIS, BY CHANCE?
I DON'T CARE ABOUT OTHER PLAYERS.
A PRETTY GIRL WITH GREEN EYES AND SHORT HAIR?
OH, RIGHT, THE ONE WHO HIT THE JACKPOT. ASK THE BOSS.
DO YOU HAVE AN APPOINTMENT? NO? THEN THE BOSS IS BUSY.
ANYWAY, WE DON'T KNOW WHO YOU'RE TALKING ABOUT.
WE HIT A WALL.
NOT QUITE A WALL... JUST TWO GORILLAS.
MAYBE FLUFFY CAN HELP US.
FOLLOW HIM!
CUL DE SAC!
ALICE SURE GOES TO SOME WEIRD PLACES...
MAYBE SHE WAS BROUGHT HERE BY FORCE. LET'S BE CAREFUL AND INCONSPICUOUS.
WE MEET AGAIN!

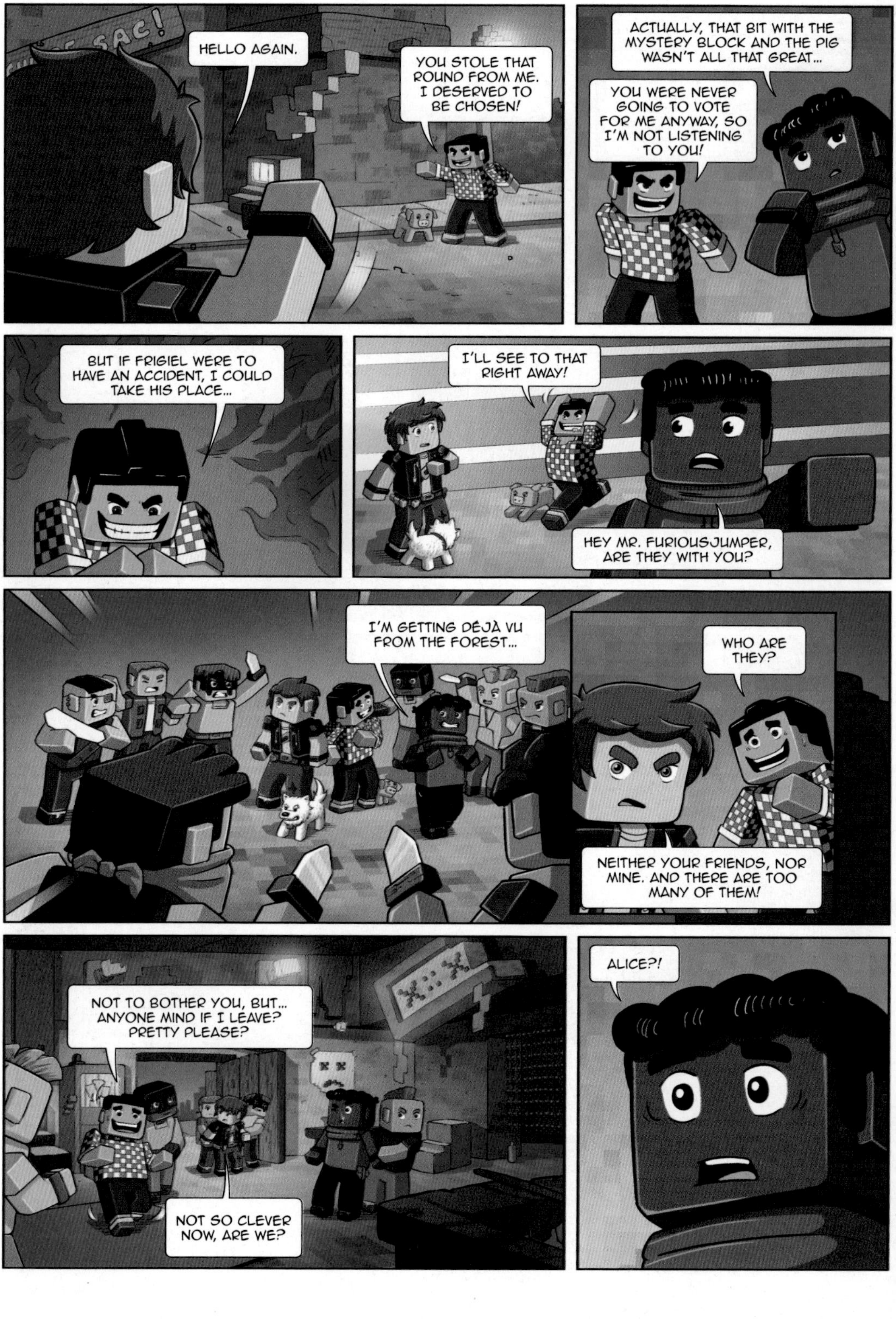

HELLO AGAIN.
YOU STOLE THAT ROUND FROM ME. I DESERVED TO BE CHOSEN!
ACTUALLY, THAT BIT WITH THE MYSTERY BLOCK AND THE PIG WASN'T ALL THAT GREAT...
YOU WERE NEVER GOING TO VOTE FOR ME ANYWAY, SO I'M NOT LISTENING TO YOU!
BUT IF FRIGIEL WERE TO HAVE AN ACCIDENT, I COULD TAKE HIS PLACE...
I'LL SEE TO THAT RIGHT AWAY!
HEY MR. FURIOUSJUMPER, ARE THEY WITH YOU?
I'M GETTING DÉJÀ VU FROM THE FOREST...
WHO ARE THEY?
NEITHER YOUR FRIENDS, NOR MINE. AND THERE ARE TOO MANY OF THEM!
NOT TO BOTHER YOU, BUT... ANYONE MIND IF I LEAVE? PRETTY PLEASE?
NOT SO CLEVER NOW, ARE WE?
ALICE?!

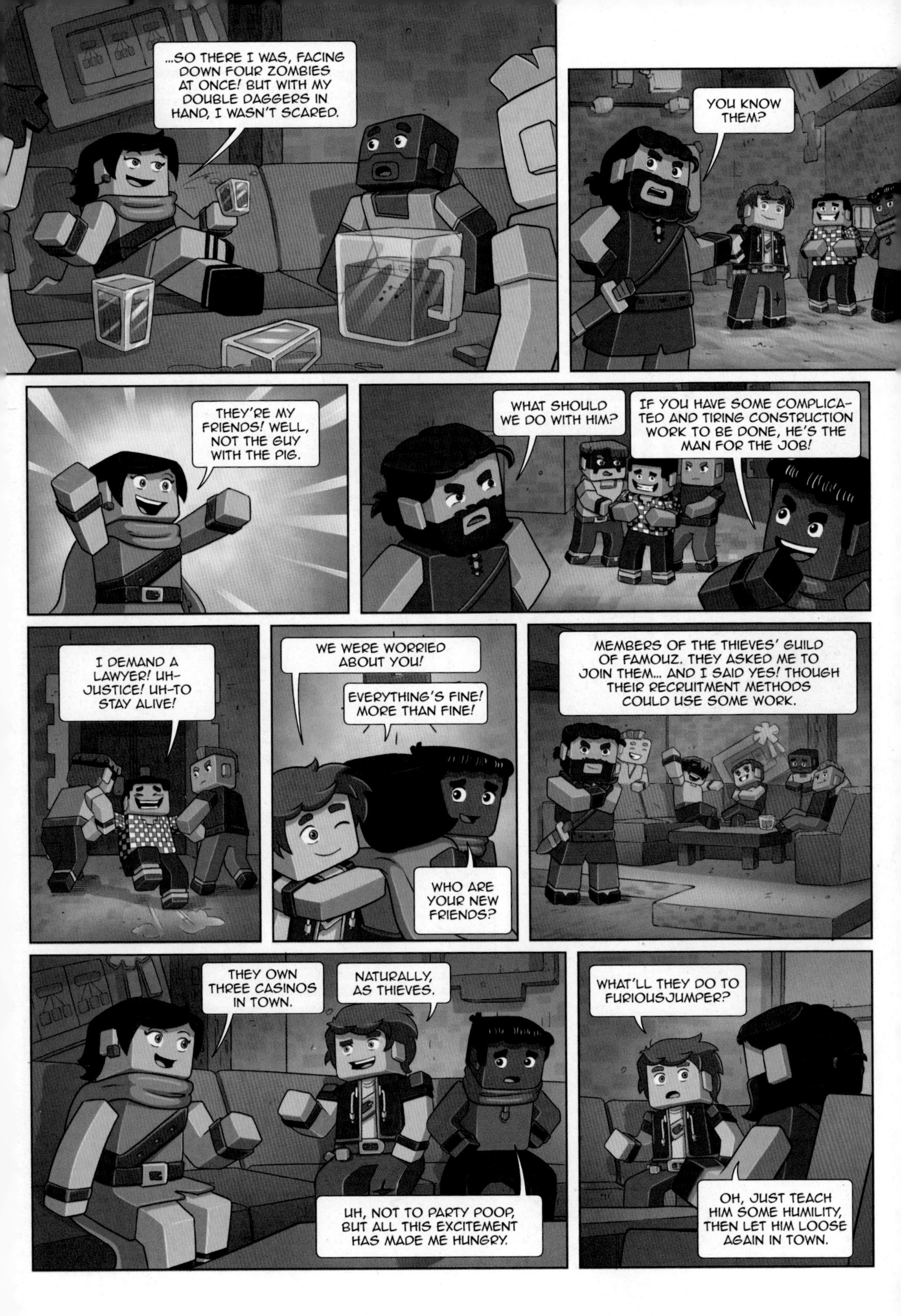
...SO THERE I WAS, FACING DOWN FOUR ZOMBIES AT ONCE! BUT WITH MY DOUBLE DAGGERS IN HAND, I WASN'T SCARED.
YOU KNOW THEM?
THEY'RE MY FRIENDS! WELL, NOT THE GUY WITH THE PIG.
WHAT SHOULD WE DO WITH HIM?
IF YOU HAVE SOME COMPLICA-TED AND TIRING CONSTRUCTION WORK TO BE DONE, HE'S THE MAN FOR THE JOB!
I DEMAND A LAWYER! UH-JUSTICE! UH-TO STAY ALIVE!
WE WERE WORRIED ABOUT YOU!
EVERYTHING'S FINE! MORE THAN FINE!
WHO ARE YOUR NEW FRIENDS?
MEMBERS OF THE THIEVES' GUILD OF FAMOUZ. THEY ASKED ME TO JOIN THEM... AND I SAID YES! THOUGH THEIR RECRUITMENT METHODS COULD USE SOME WORK.
THEY OWN THREE CASINOS IN TOWN.
NATURALLY, AS THIEVES.
UH, NOT TO PARTY POOP, BUT ALL THIS EXCITEMENT HAS MADE ME HUNGRY.
WHAT'LL THEY DO TO FURIOUSJUMPER?
OH, JUST TEACH HIM SOME HUMILITY, THEN LET HIM LOOSE AGAIN IN TOWN.

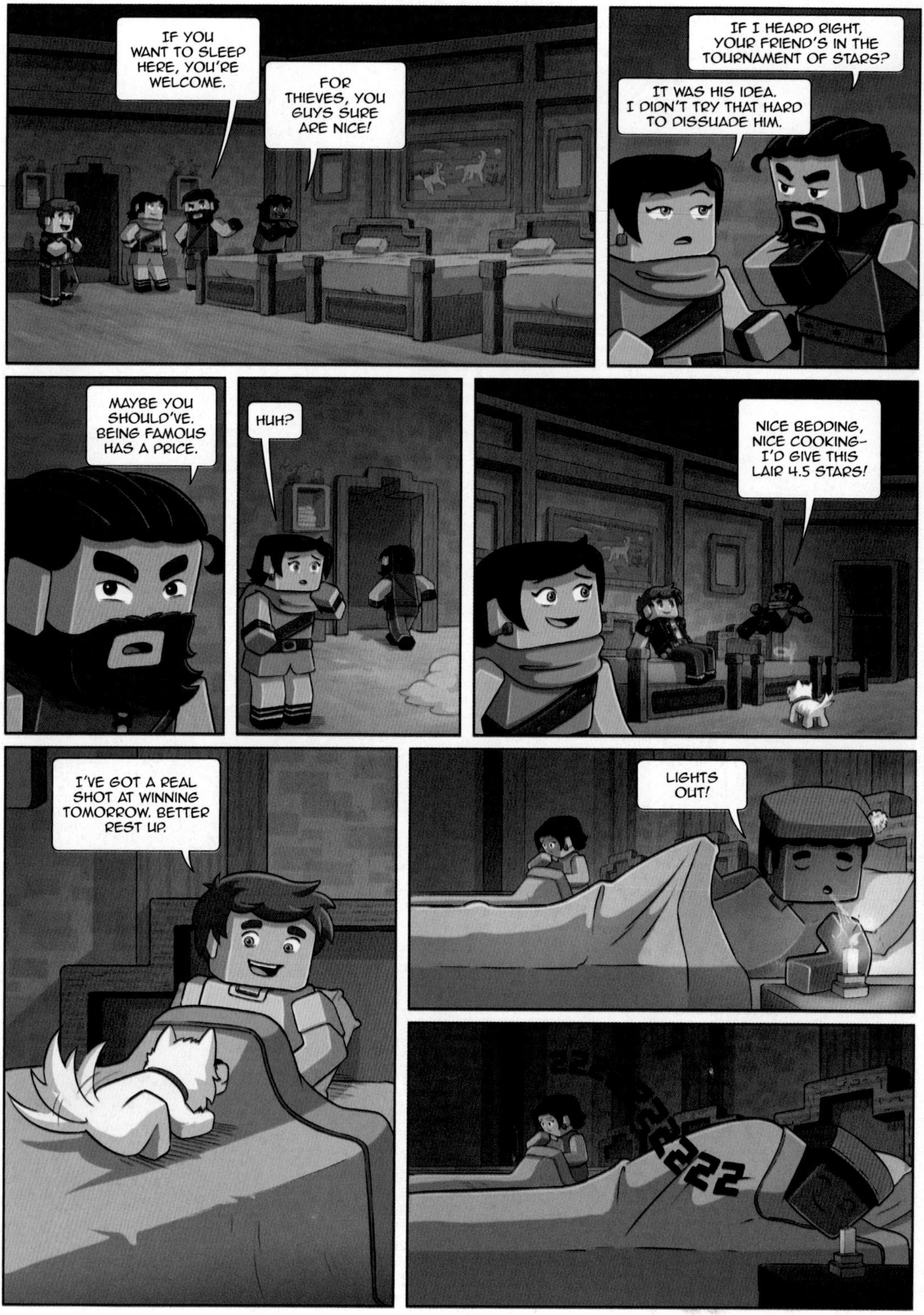
IF YOU WANT TO SLEEP HERE, YOU'RE WELCOME.
FOR THIEVES, YOU GUYS SURE ARE NICE!
IF I HEARD RIGHT, YOUR FRIEND'S IN THE TOURNAMENT OF STARS?
IT WAS HIS IDEA. I DIDN'T TRY THAT HARD TO DISSUADE HIM.
MAYBE YOU SHOULD'VE. BEING FAMOUS HAS A PRICE.
HUH?
NICE BEDDING, NICE COOKING– I'D GIVE THIS LAIR 4.5 STARS!
I'VE GOT A REAL SHOT AT WINNING TOMORROW. BETTER REST UP.
LIGHTS OUT!

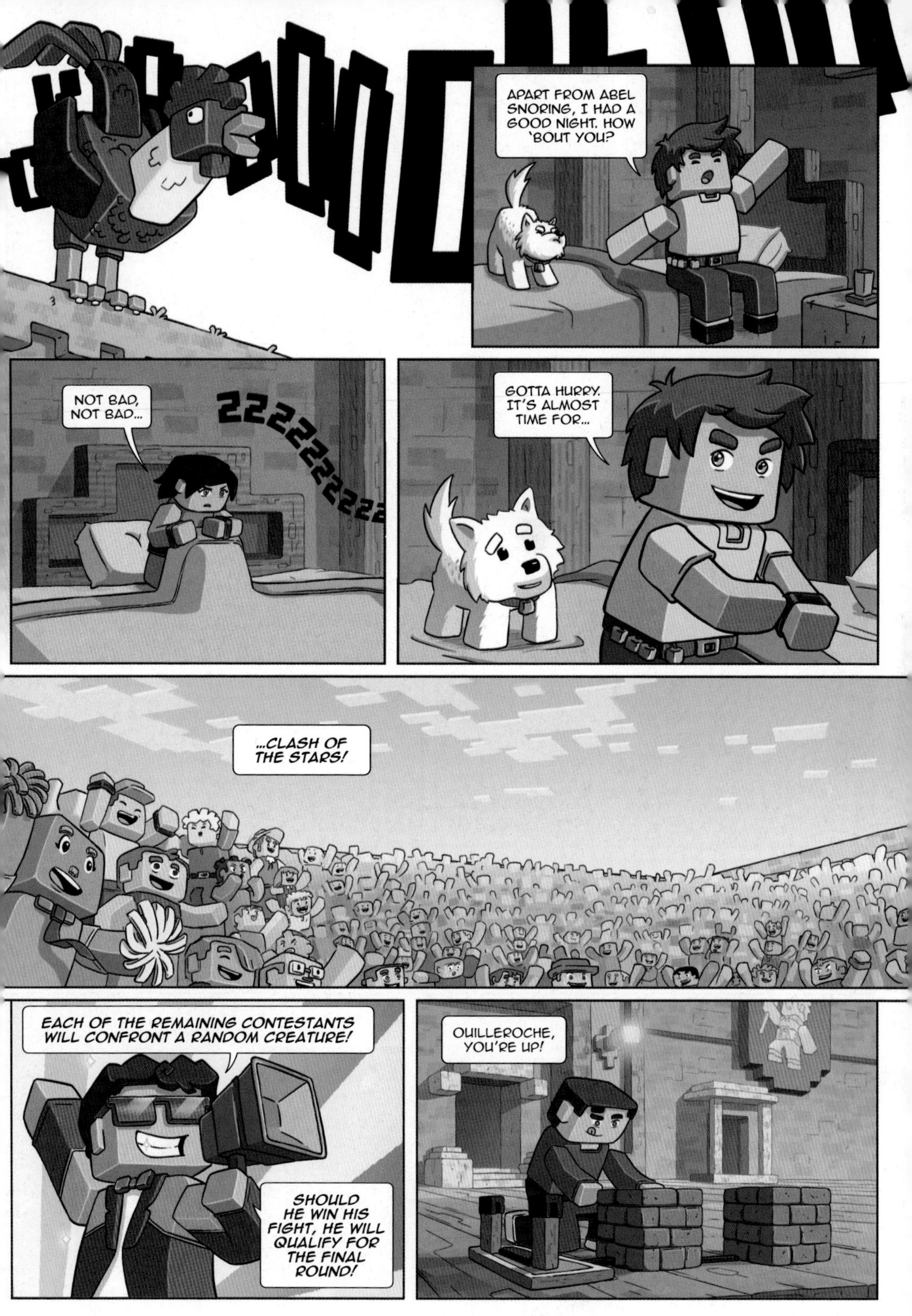
KOKOROOOO!
APART FROM ABEL SNORING, I HAD A GOOD NIGHT. HOW 'BOUT YOU?
NOT BAD, NOT BAD...
ZZZZZZZZZZZ
GOTTA HURRY. IT'S ALMOST TIME FOR...
...CLASH OF THE STARS!
EACH OF THE REMAINING CONTESTANTS WILL CONFRONT A RANDOM CREATURE!
SHOULD HE WIN HIS FIGHT, HE WILL QUALIFY FOR THE FINAL ROUND!
OUILLEROCHE, YOU'RE UP!

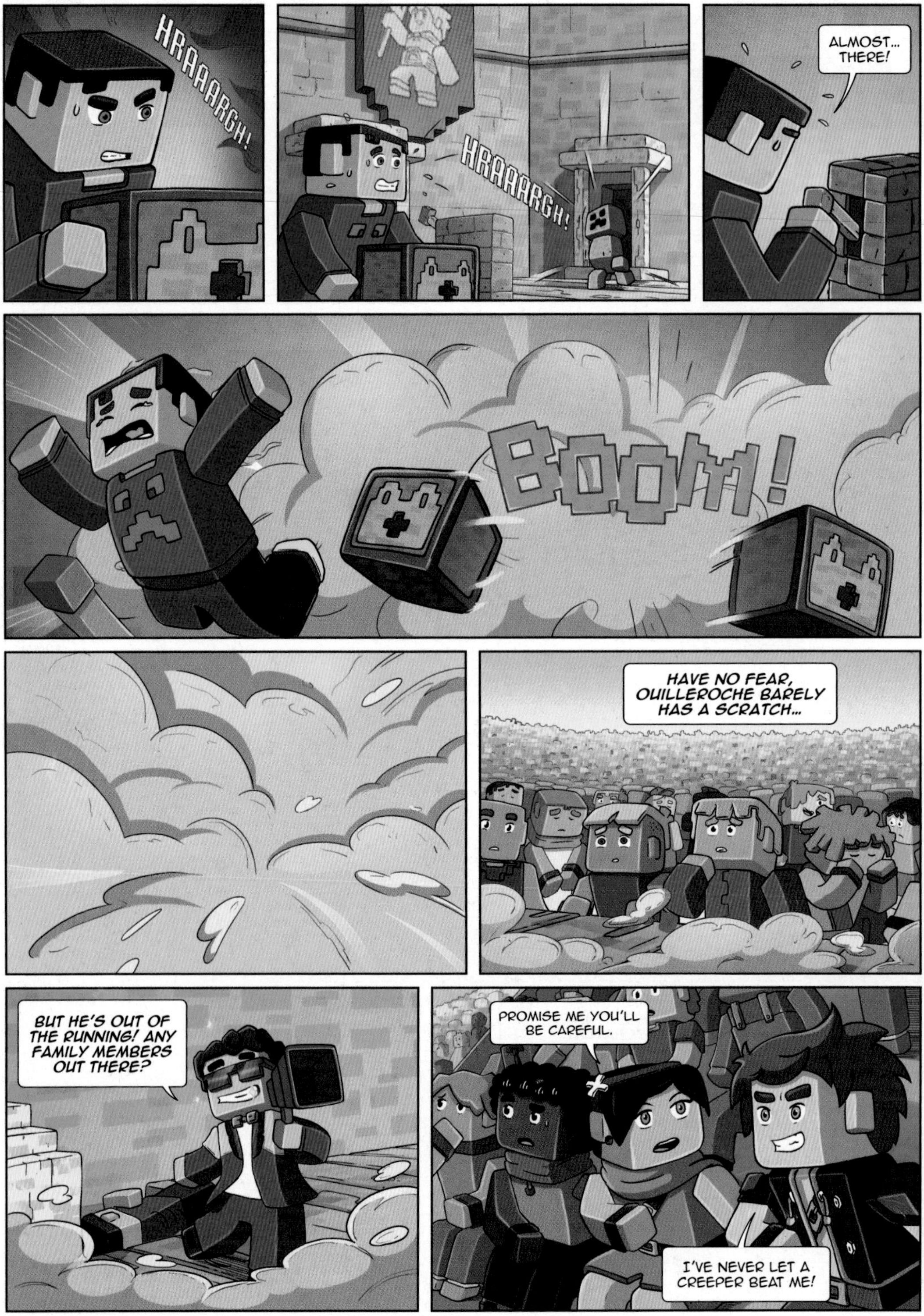
HRAAAARGH!
HRAAAARGH!
ALMOST... THERE!
BOOM!
HAVE NO FEAR, OUILLEROCHE BARELY HAS A SCRATCH...
BUT HE'S OUT OF THE RUNNING! ANY FAMILY MEMBERS OUT THERE?
PROMISE ME YOU'LL BE CAREFUL.
I'VE NEVER LET A CREEPER BEAT ME!

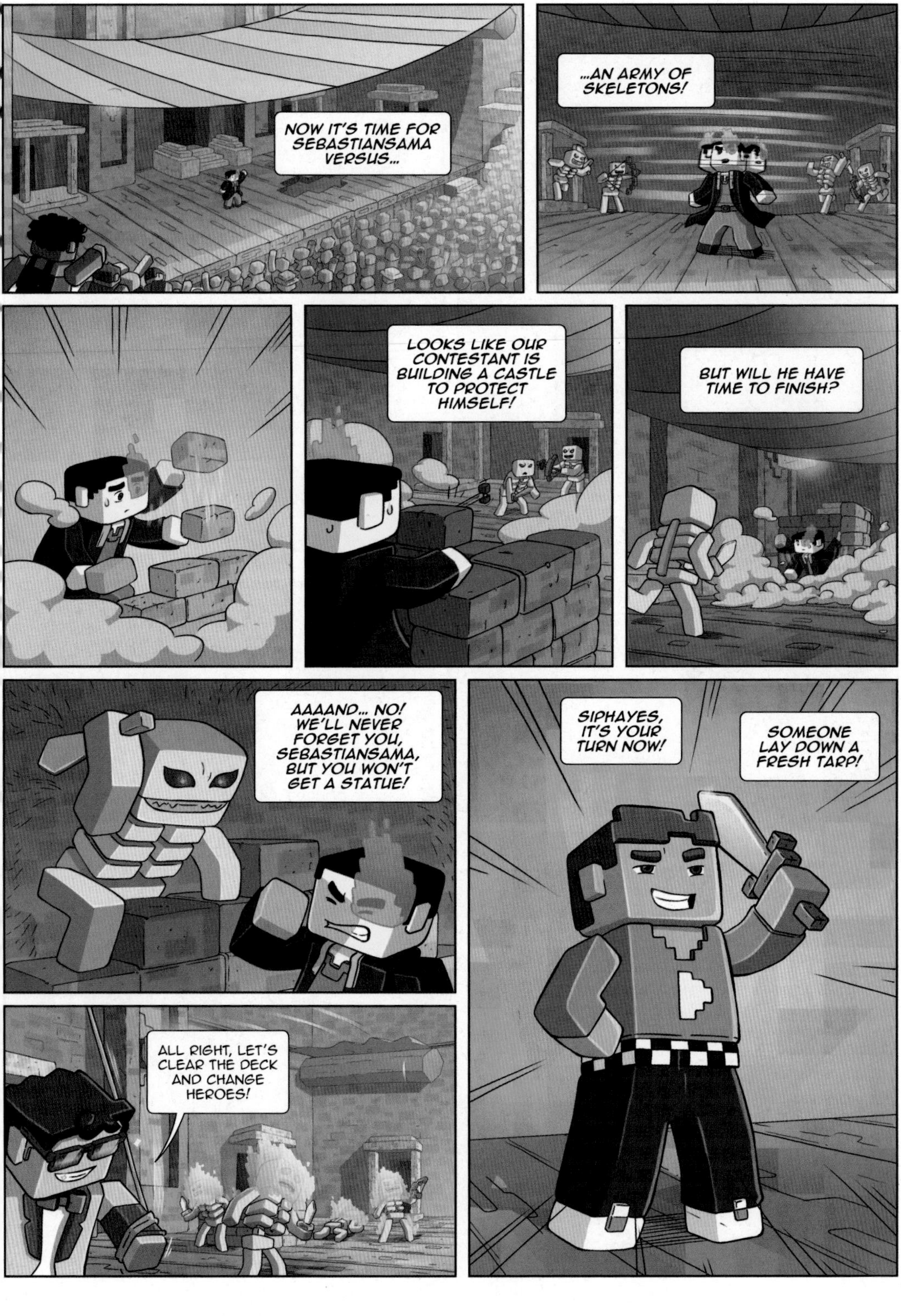
NOW IT'S TIME FOR SEBASTIANSAMA VERSUS...
...AN ARMY OF SKELETONS!
LOOKS LIKE OUR CONTESTANT IS BUILDING A CASTLE TO PROTECT HIMSELF!
BUT WILL HE HAVE TIME TO FINISH?
AAAAND... NO! WE'LL NEVER FORGET YOU, SEBASTIANSAMA, BUT YOU WON'T GET A STATUE!
ALL RIGHT, LET'S CLEAR THE DECK AND CHANGE HEROES!
SIPHAYES, IT'S YOUR TURN NOW!
SOMEONE LAY DOWN A FRESH TARP!

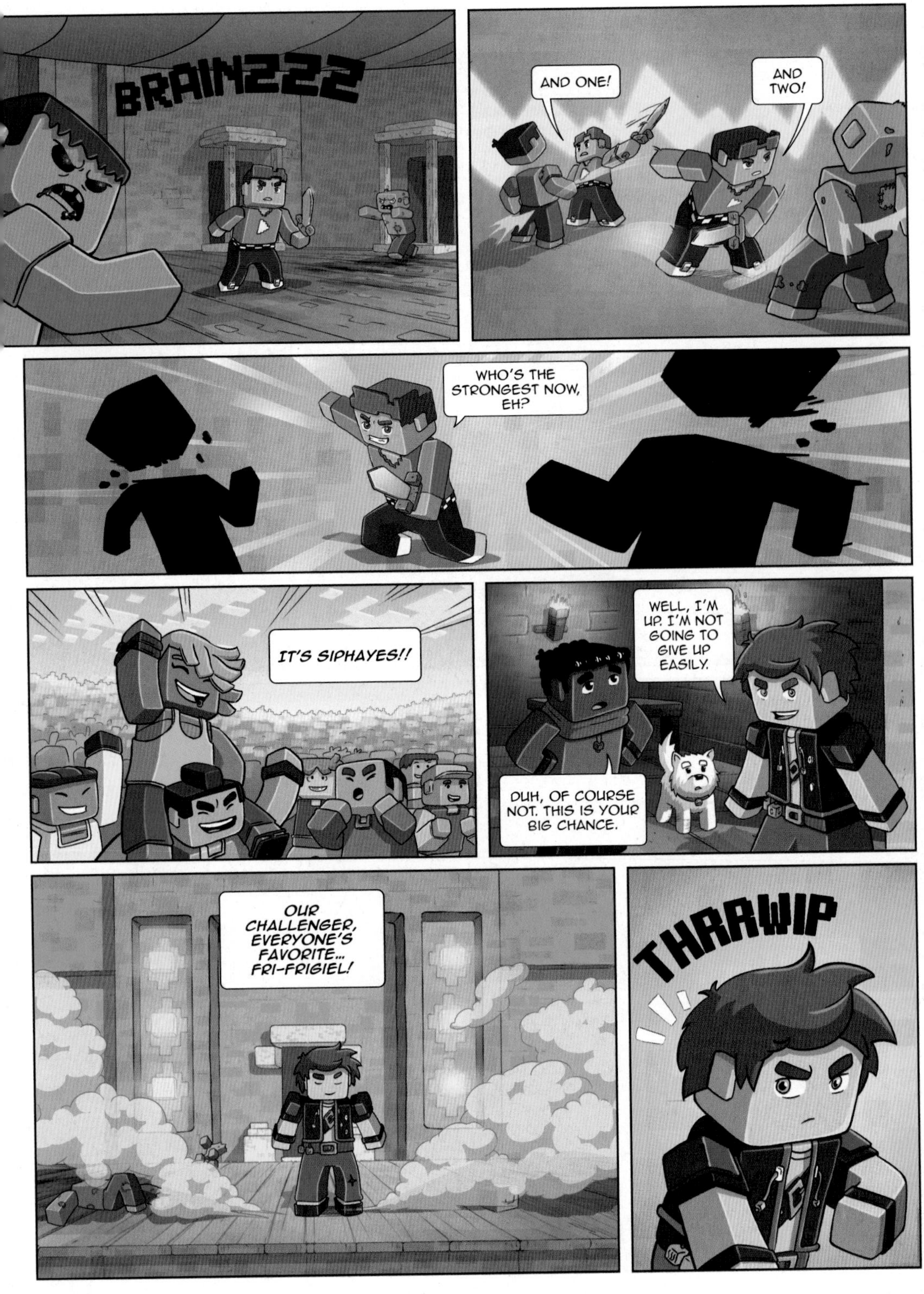
BRAINZZZ
AND ONE!
AND TWO!
WHO'S THE STRONGEST NOW, EH?
IT'S SIPHAYES!!
WELL, I'M UP. I'M NOT GOING TO GIVE UP EASILY.
DUH, OF COURSE NOT. THIS IS YOUR BIG CHANCE.
OUR CHALLENGER, EVERYONE'S FAVORITE... FRI-FRIGIEL!
THRRWIP

THAT'S RIGHT! AFTER CREEPERS, ZOMBIES, AND SKELETONS COME OUR FRIENDS THE SPIDERS!

WILL FRI-FRIGIEL ASTONISH US ALL WITH HIS MAGIC TRICKS?

THRWP

DON'T WORRY, HE'LL BE JUST FINE. I MEAN—I HOPE SO!

FIGURE SKATING!

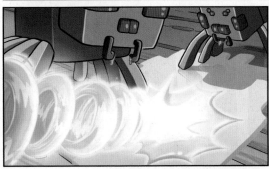

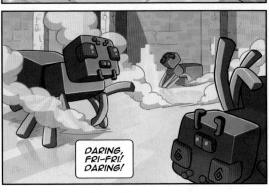

DARING, FRI-FRI! DARING!

A JOB WELL DONE!

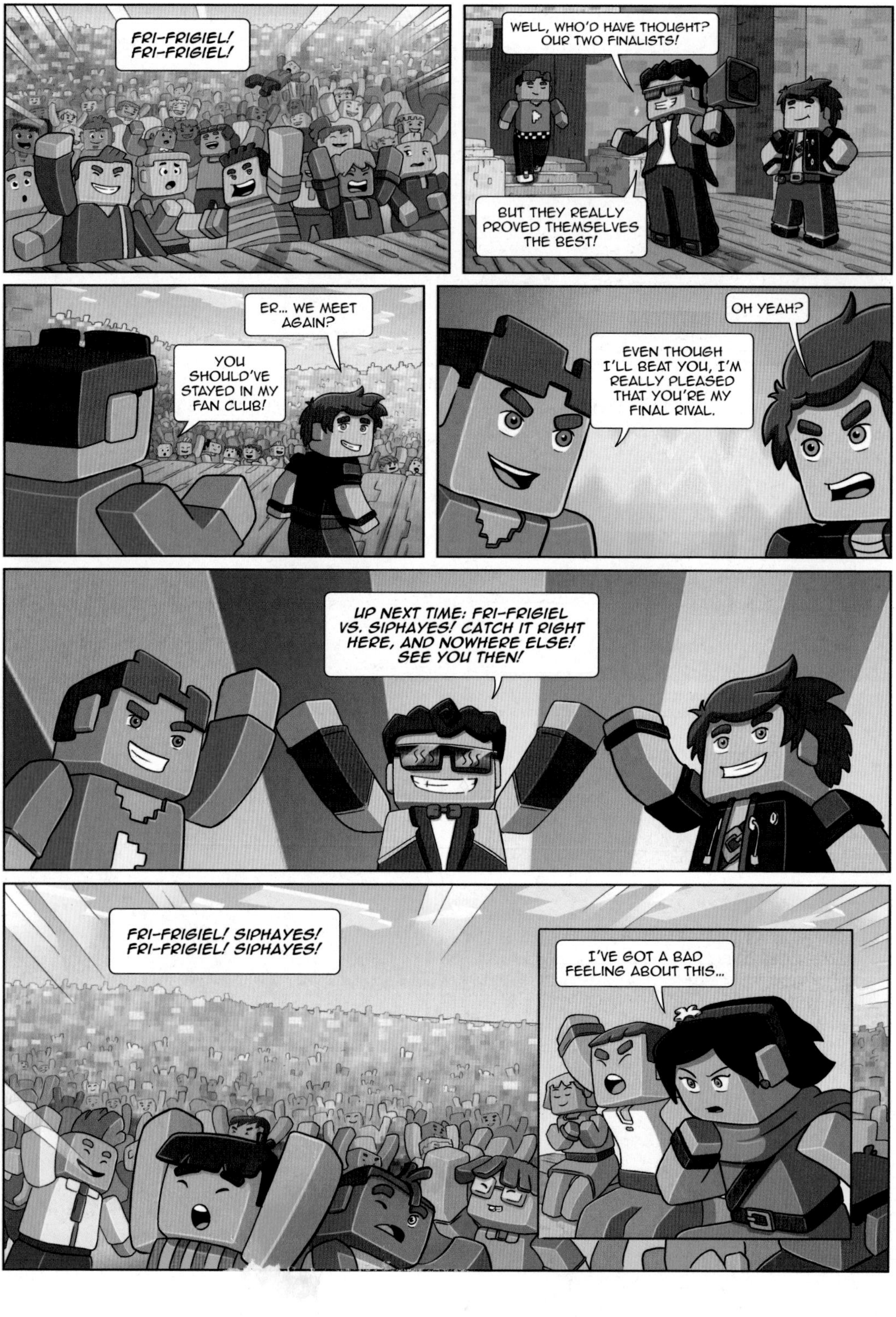
FRI-FRIGIEL!
FRI-FRIGIEL!
WELL, WHO'D HAVE THOUGHT? OUR TWO FINALISTS!
BUT THEY REALLY PROVED THEMSELVES THE BEST!
ER... WE MEET AGAIN?
YOU SHOULD'VE STAYED IN MY FAN CLUB!
OH YEAH?
EVEN THOUGH I'LL BEAT YOU, I'M REALLY PLEASED THAT YOU'RE MY FINAL RIVAL.
UP NEXT TIME: FRI-FRIGIEL VS. SIPHAYES! CATCH IT RIGHT HERE, AND NOWHERE ELSE! SEE YOU THEN!
FRI-FRIGIEL! SIPHAYES! FRI-FRIGIEL! SIPHAYES!
I'VE GOT A BAD FEELING ABOUT THIS...

ZELVAC, LEOGZANDAR, POPIGAMES...

SO WHAT HAPPENED AFTER? DID YOU ALL RETIRE?

AFTER THEY WON, THEY WERE NEVER SEEN AGAIN.

WEIRD... FIRST THEY WIN, AND THEN... POOF!

YOU NEVER HEAR FROM THEM AGAIN.

IF YOU ASK ME, THEY MOVED TO A HERO RETIREMENT VILLAGE. WHAT DO YOU THINK?

WELL, GOTTA RUN. IT'S HAPPY HOUR FOR HALF-PRICE WATERMELON JUICE. CAN'T MISS THAT!

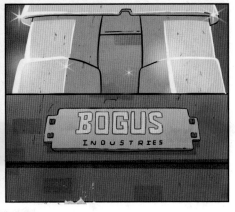

BOGUS
INDUSTRIES

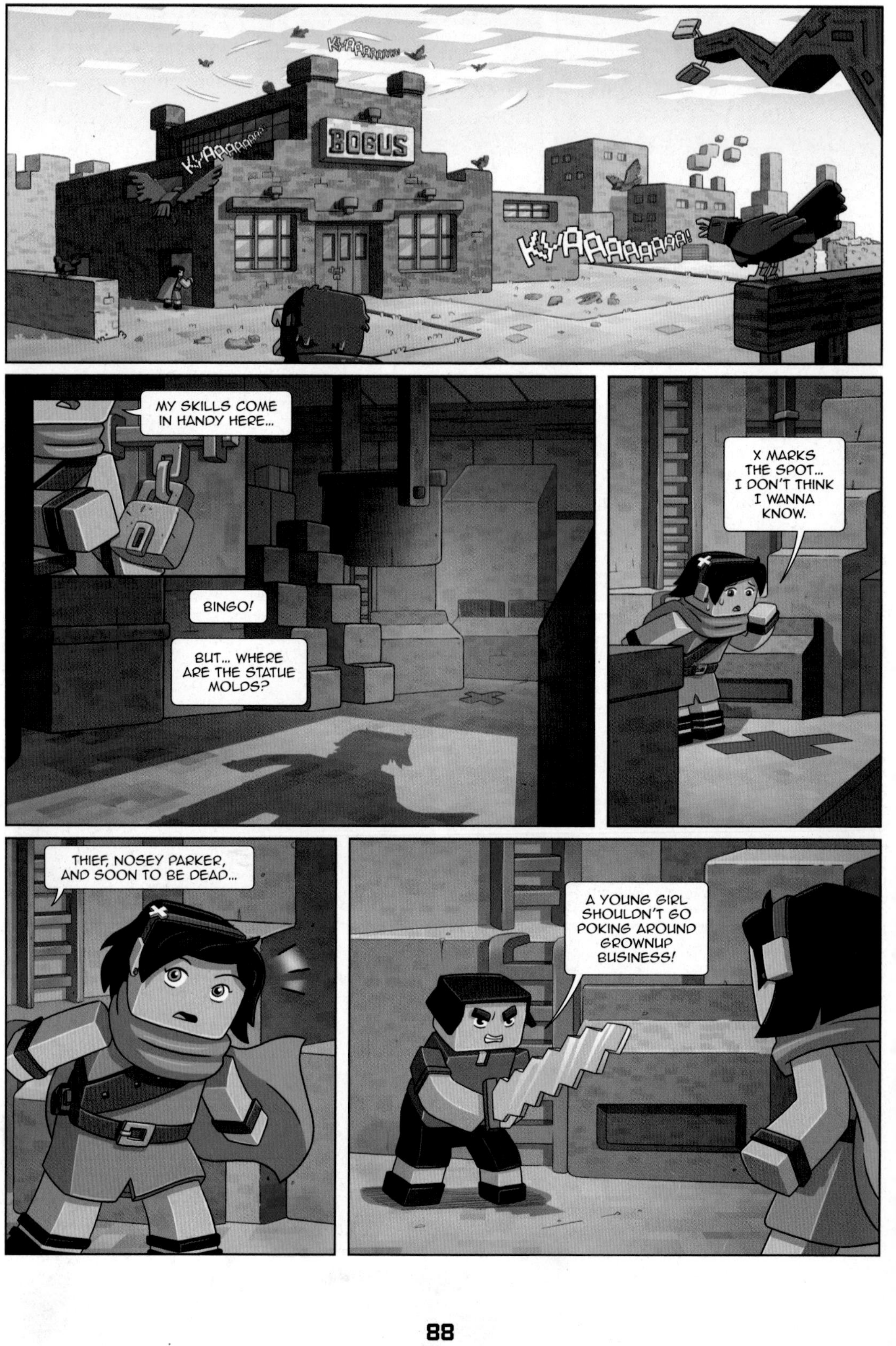
BOBUS
MY SKILLS COME IN HANDY HERE...
BINGO!
BUT... WHERE ARE THE STATUE MOLDS?
X MARKS THE SPOT... I DON'T THINK I WANNA KNOW.
THIEF, NOSEY PARKER, AND SOON TO BE DEAD...
A YOUNG GIRL SHOULDN'T GO POKING AROUND GROWNUP BUSINESS!

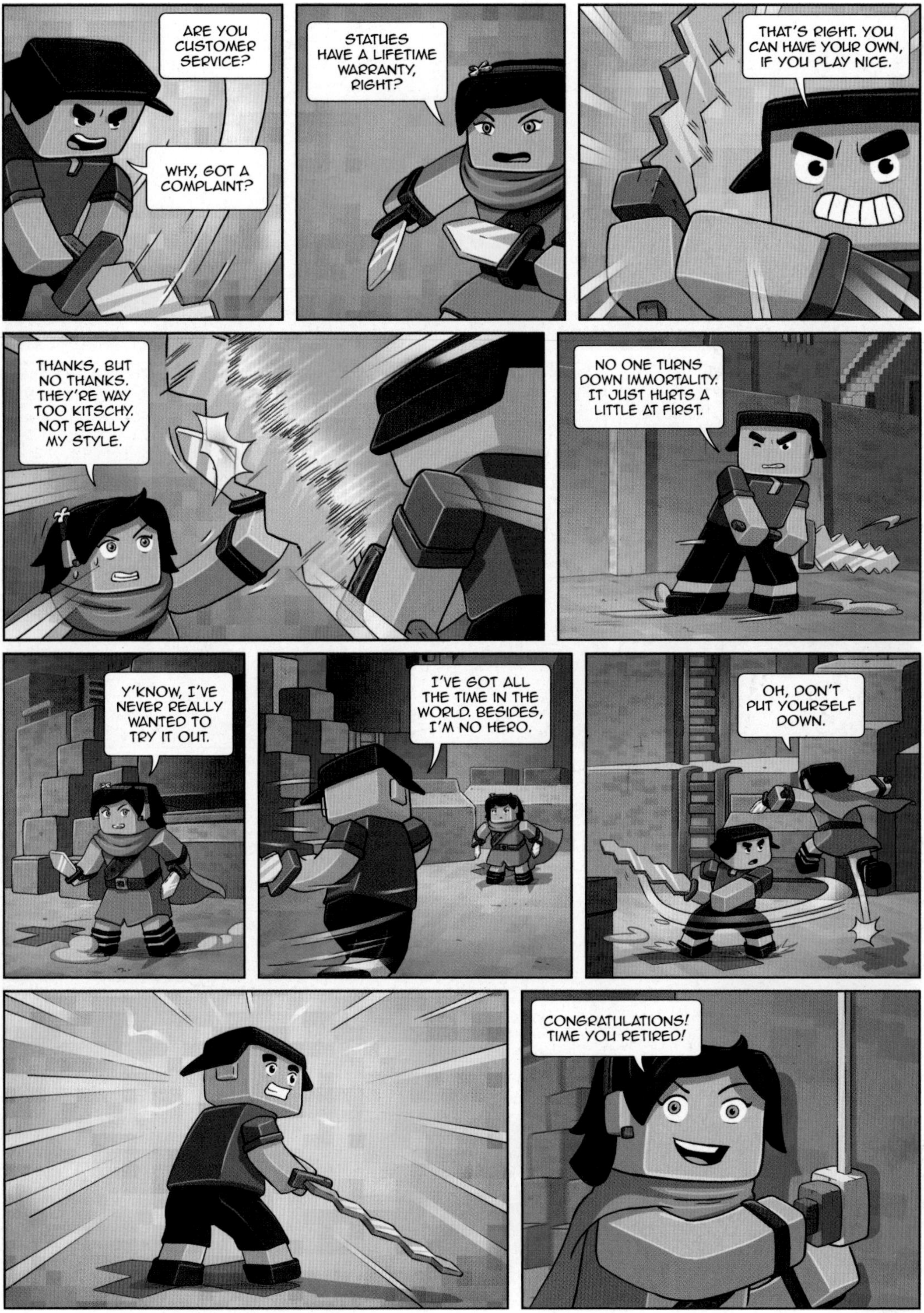
ARE YOU CUSTOMER SERVICE?
WHY, GOT A COMPLAINT?
STATUES HAVE A LIFETIME WARRANTY, RIGHT?
THAT'S RIGHT. YOU CAN HAVE YOUR OWN, IF YOU PLAY NICE.
THANKS, BUT NO THANKS. THEY'RE WAY TOO KITSCHY. NOT REALLY MY STYLE.
NO ONE TURNS DOWN IMMORTALITY. IT JUST HURTS A LITTLE AT FIRST.
Y'KNOW, I'VE NEVER REALLY WANTED TO TRY IT OUT.
I'VE GOT ALL THE TIME IN THE WORLD. BESIDES, I'M NO HERO.
OH, DON'T PUT YOURSELF DOWN.
CONGRATULATIONS! TIME YOU RETIRED!

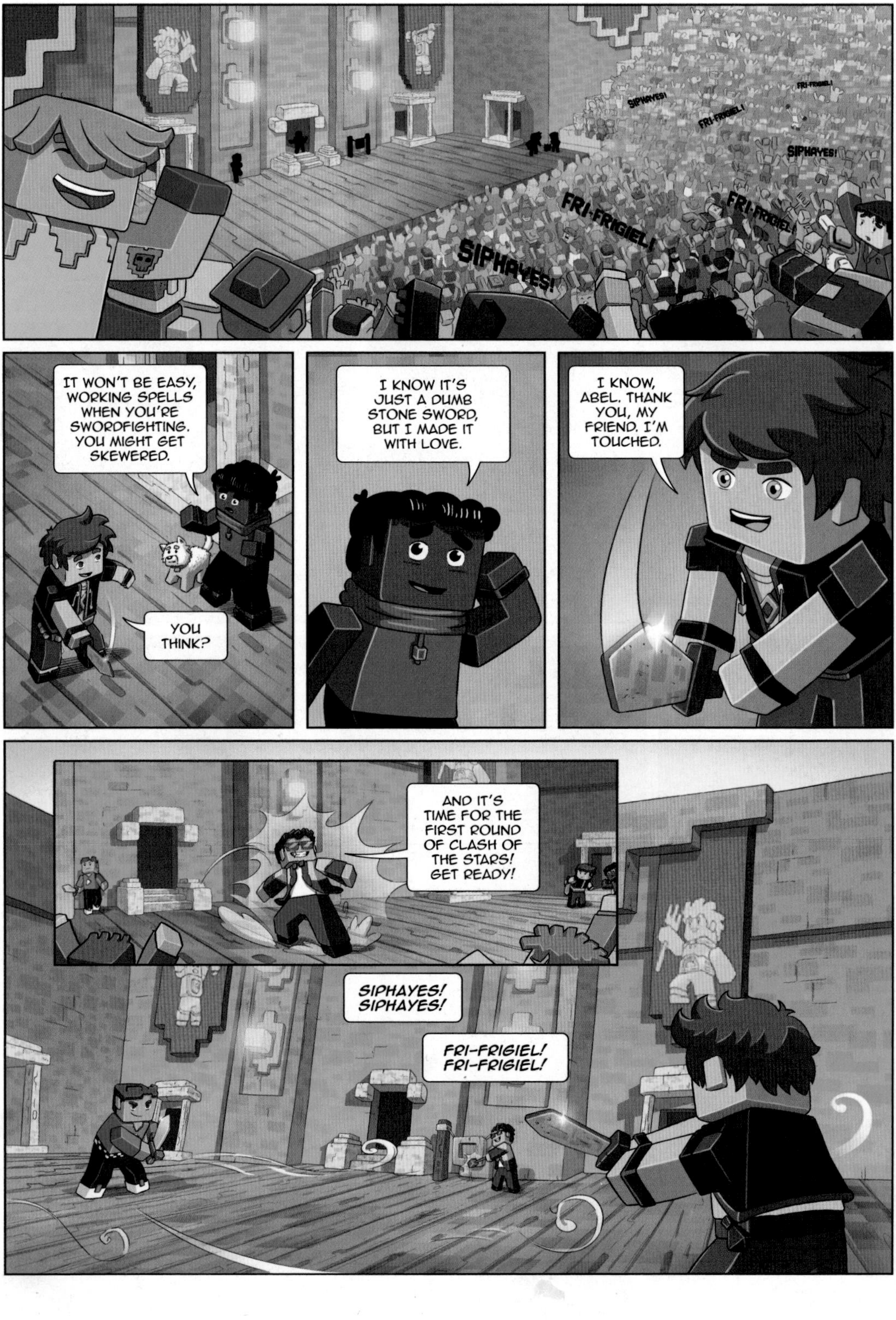
SIPHAYES!
FRI-FRIGIEL!
SIPHAYES!
FRI-FRIGIEL!
SIPHAYES!
FRI-FRIGIEL!
SIPHAYES!
IT WON'T BE EASY, WORKING SPELLS WHEN YOU'RE SWORDFIGHTING. YOU MIGHT GET SKEWERED.
YOU THINK?
I KNOW IT'S JUST A DUMB STONE SWORD, BUT I MADE IT WITH LOVE.
I KNOW, ABEL. THANK YOU, MY FRIEND. I'M TOUCHED.
AND IT'S TIME FOR THE FIRST ROUND OF CLASH OF THE STARS! GET READY!
SIPHAYES! SIPHAYES!
FRI-FRIGIEL! FRI-FRIGIEL!

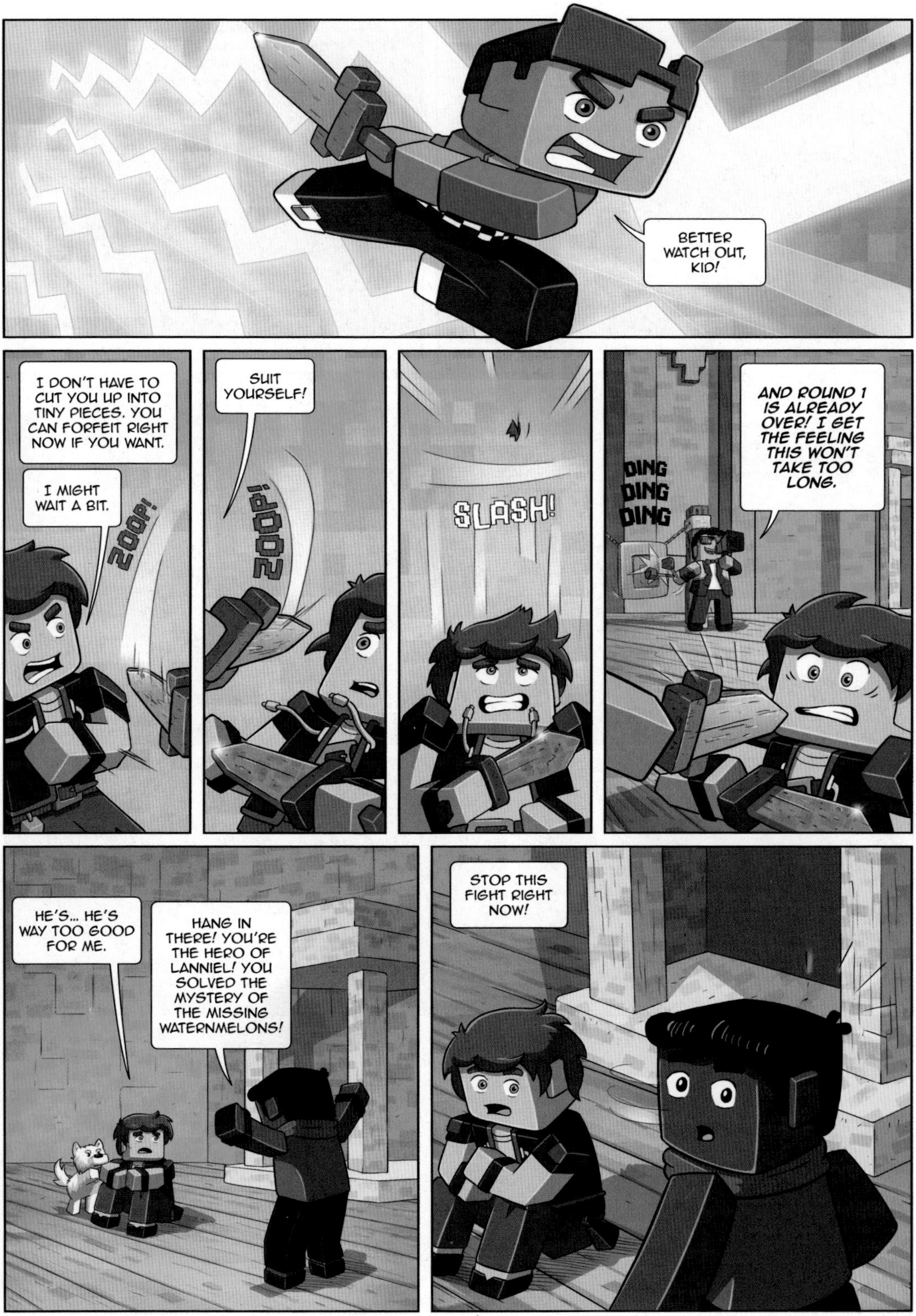
BETTER WATCH OUT, KID!
I DON'T HAVE TO CUT YOU UP INTO TINY PIECES. YOU CAN FORFEIT RIGHT NOW IF YOU WANT.
I MIGHT WAIT A BIT.
ZOOP!
SUIT YOURSELF!
ZOOP!
SLASH!
DING
DING
DING
AND ROUND 1 IS ALREADY OVER! I GET THE FEELING THIS WON'T TAKE TOO LONG.
HE'S... HE'S WAY TOO GOOD FOR ME.
HANG IN THERE! YOU'RE THE HERO OF LANNIEL! YOU SOLVED THE MYSTERY OF THE MISSING WATERNMELONS!
STOP THIS FIGHT RIGHT NOW!

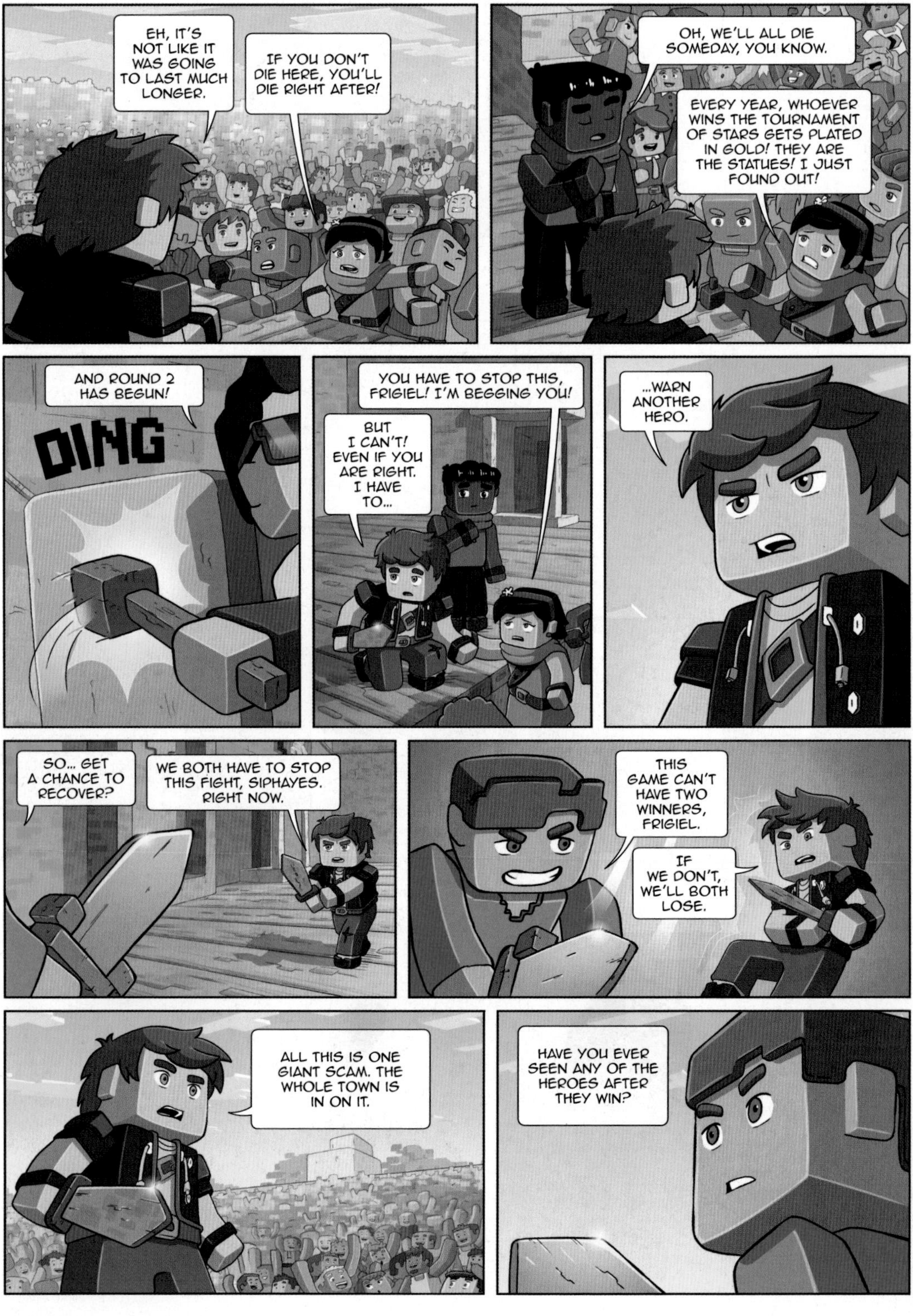
EH, IT'S NOT LIKE IT WAS GOING TO LAST MUCH LONGER.
IF YOU DON'T DIE HERE, YOU'LL DIE RIGHT AFTER!
OH, WE'LL ALL DIE SOMEDAY, YOU KNOW.
EVERY YEAR, WHOEVER WINS THE TOURNAMENT OF STARS GETS PLATED IN GOLD! THEY ARE THE STATUES! I JUST FOUND OUT!
AND ROUND 2 HAS BEGUN!
DING
YOU HAVE TO STOP THIS, FRIGIEL! I'M BEGGING YOU!
BUT I CAN'T! EVEN IF YOU ARE RIGHT. I HAVE TO...
...WARN ANOTHER HERO.
SO... GET A CHANCE TO RECOVER?
WE BOTH HAVE TO STOP THIS FIGHT, SIPHAYES. RIGHT NOW.
THIS GAME CAN'T HAVE TWO WINNERS, FRIGIEL.
IF WE DON'T, WE'LL BOTH LOSE.
ALL THIS IS ONE GIANT SCAM. THE WHOLE TOWN IS IN ON IT.
HAVE YOU EVER SEEN ANY OF THE HEROES AFTER THEY WIN?

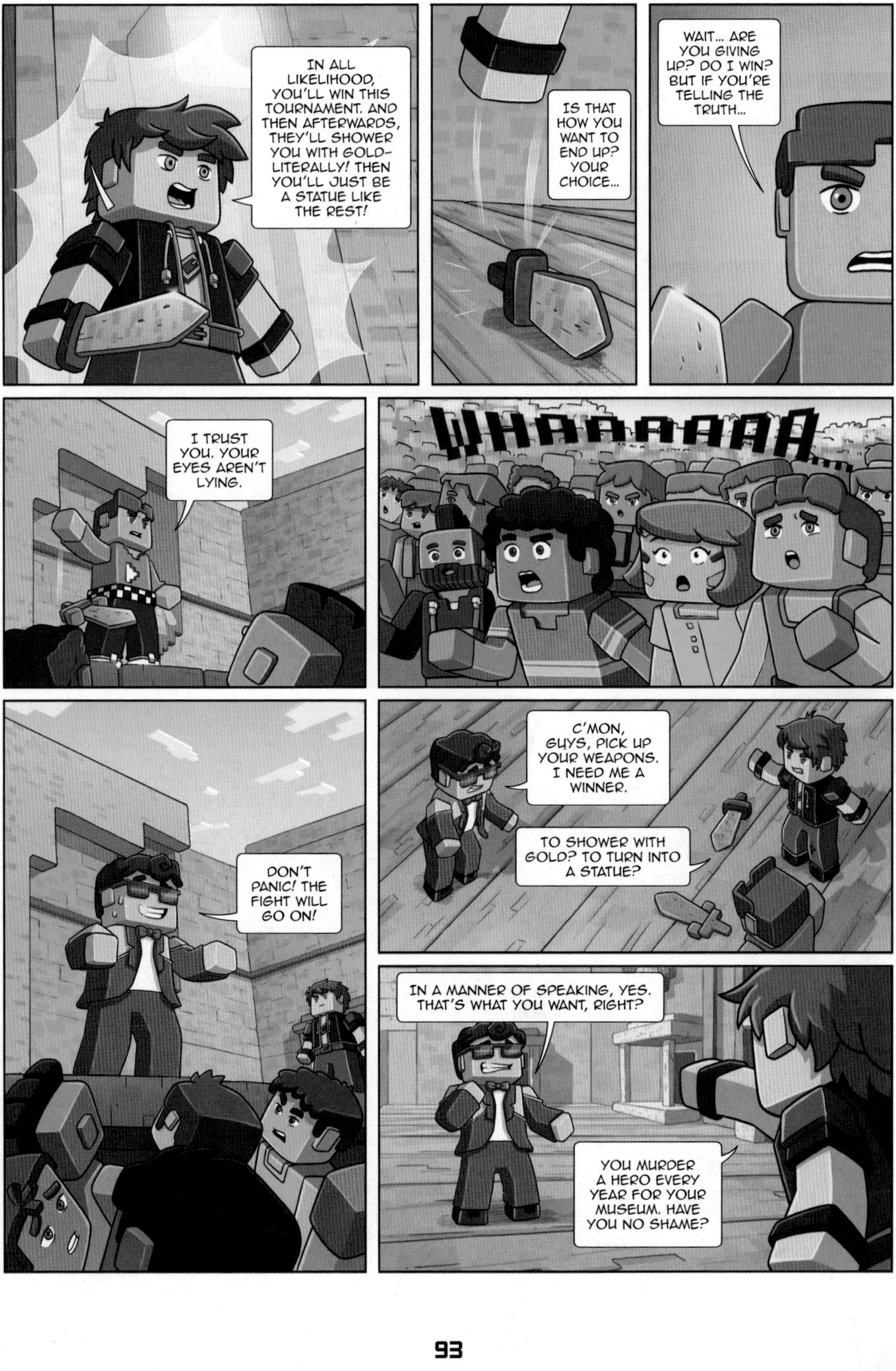
IN ALL LIKELIHOOD, YOU'LL WIN THIS TOURNAMENT. AND THEN AFTERWARDS, THEY'LL SHOWER YOU WITH GOLD-LITERALLY! THEN YOU'LL JUST BE A STATUE LIKE THE REST!
IS THAT HOW YOU WANT TO END UP? YOUR CHOICE...
WAIT... ARE YOU GIVING UP? DO I WIN? BUT IF YOU'RE TELLING THE TRUTH...
I TRUST YOU. YOUR EYES AREN'T LYING.
WHAAAAAAA...
DON'T PANIC! THE FIGHT WILL GO ON!
C'MON, GUYS, PICK UP YOUR WEAPONS. I NEED ME A WINNER.
TO SHOWER WITH GOLD? TO TURN INTO A STATUE?
IN A MANNER OF SPEAKING, YES. THAT'S WHAT YOU WANT, RIGHT?
YOU MURDER A HERO EVERY YEAR FOR YOUR MUSEUM. HAVE YOU NO SHAME?

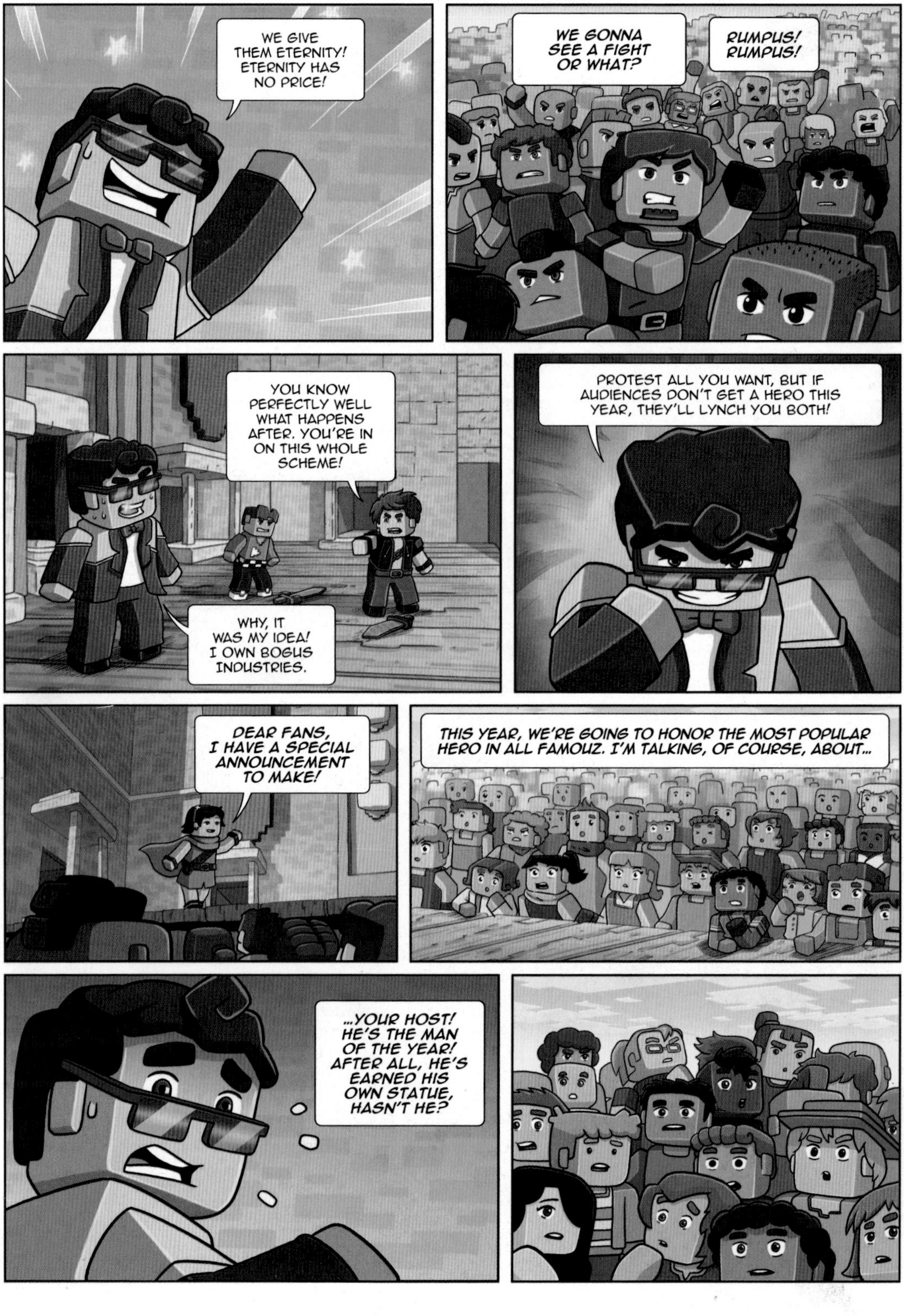
WE GIVE THEM ETERNITY! ETERNITY HAS NO PRICE!
WE GONNA SEE A FIGHT OR WHAT?
RUMPUS! RUMPUS!
YOU KNOW PERFECTLY WELL WHAT HAPPENS AFTER. YOU'RE IN ON THIS WHOLE SCHEME!
WHY, IT WAS MY IDEA! I OWN BOGUS INDUSTRIES.
PROTEST ALL YOU WANT, BUT IF AUDIENCES DON'T GET A HERO THIS YEAR, THEY'LL LYNCH YOU BOTH!
DEAR FANS, I HAVE A SPECIAL ANNOUNCEMENT TO MAKE!
THIS YEAR, WE'RE GOING TO HONOR THE MOST POPULAR HERO IN ALL FAMOUZ. I'M TALKING, OF COURSE, ABOUT...
...YOUR HOST! HE'S THE MAN OF THE YEAR! AFTER ALL, HE'S EARNED HIS OWN STATUE, HASN'T HE?

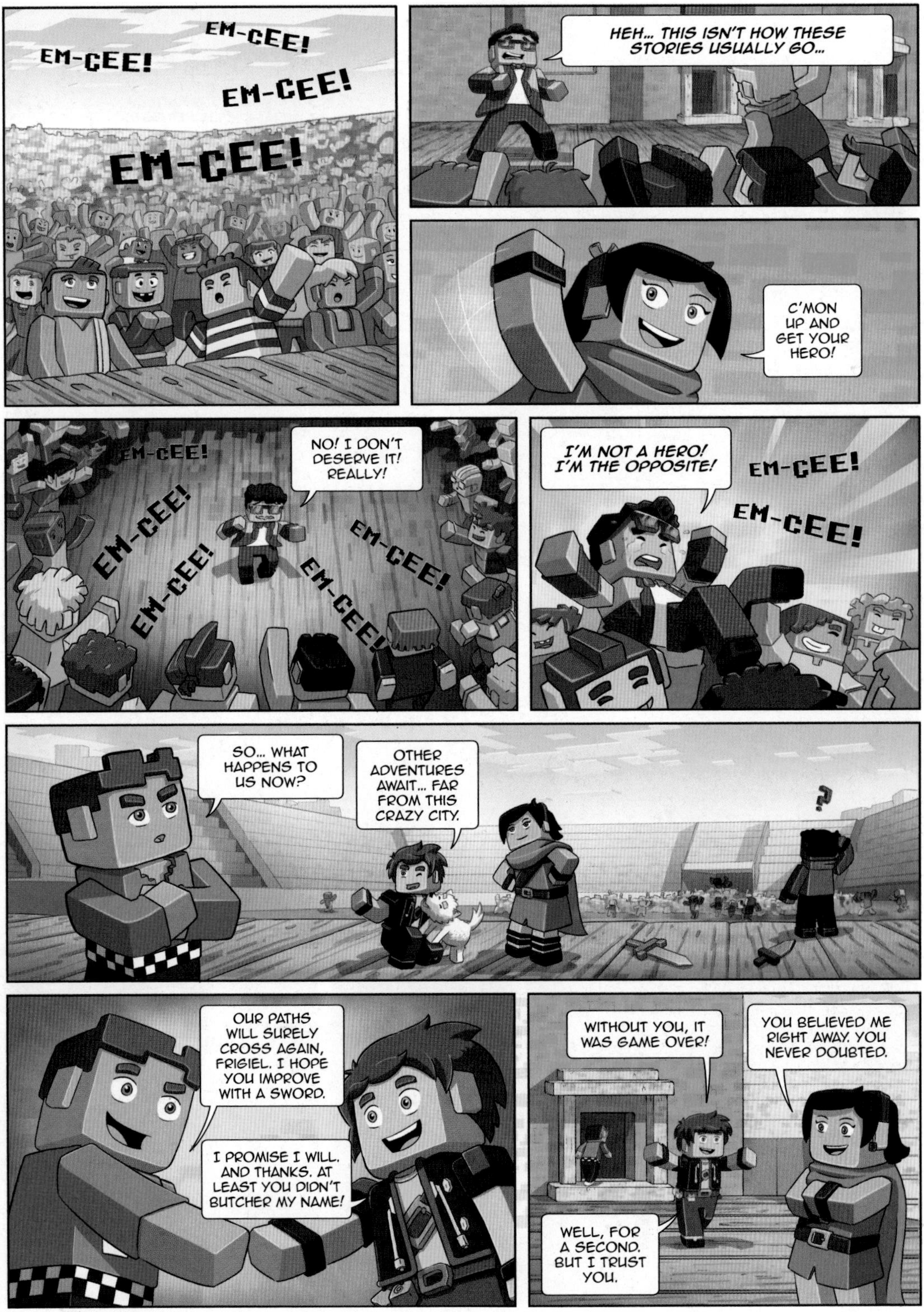
EM-CEE!
EM-CEE!
EM-CEE!
EM-CEE!
HEH... THIS ISN'T HOW THESE STORIES USUALLY GO...
C'MON UP AND GET YOUR HERO!
EM-CEE!
NO! I DON'T DESERVE IT! REALLY!
EM-CEE!
EM-CEE!
EM-CEE!
EM-CEE!
I'M NOT A HERO! I'M THE OPPOSITE!
EM-CEE!
EM-CEE!
SO... WHAT HAPPENS TO US NOW?
OTHER ADVENTURES AWAIT... FAR FROM THIS CRAZY CITY.
?
OUR PATHS WILL SURELY CROSS AGAIN, FRIGIEL. I HOPE YOU IMPROVE WITH A SWORD.
I PROMISE I WILL. AND THANKS. AT LEAST YOU DIDN'T BUTCHER MY NAME!
WITHOUT YOU, IT WAS GAME OVER!
YOU BELIEVED ME RIGHT AWAY. YOU NEVER DOUBTED.
WELL, FOR A SECOND. BUT I TRUST YOU.

NOW THIS IS DEFINITELY HAPPINESS, THIS TIME.

GOOD FRIENDS, A SUNNY DAY, WATERMELON JUICE...

...AND THE FOUR OF US STILL ALIVE.

THAT'S HOW I LIKE IT.

STILL... WHAT A WEIRD IDEA, THAT TOURNAMENT.

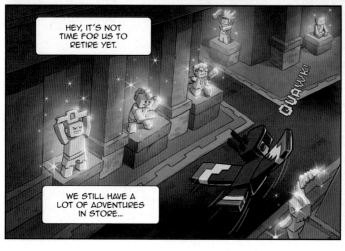

HEY, IT'S NOT TIME FOR US TO RETIRE YET.

WE STILL HAVE A LOT OF ADVENTURES IN STORE...

QUAWK!

SQUAWK!

FRIGIEL AND FLUFFY WILL BE BACK SOON!

BONUS MATERIAL

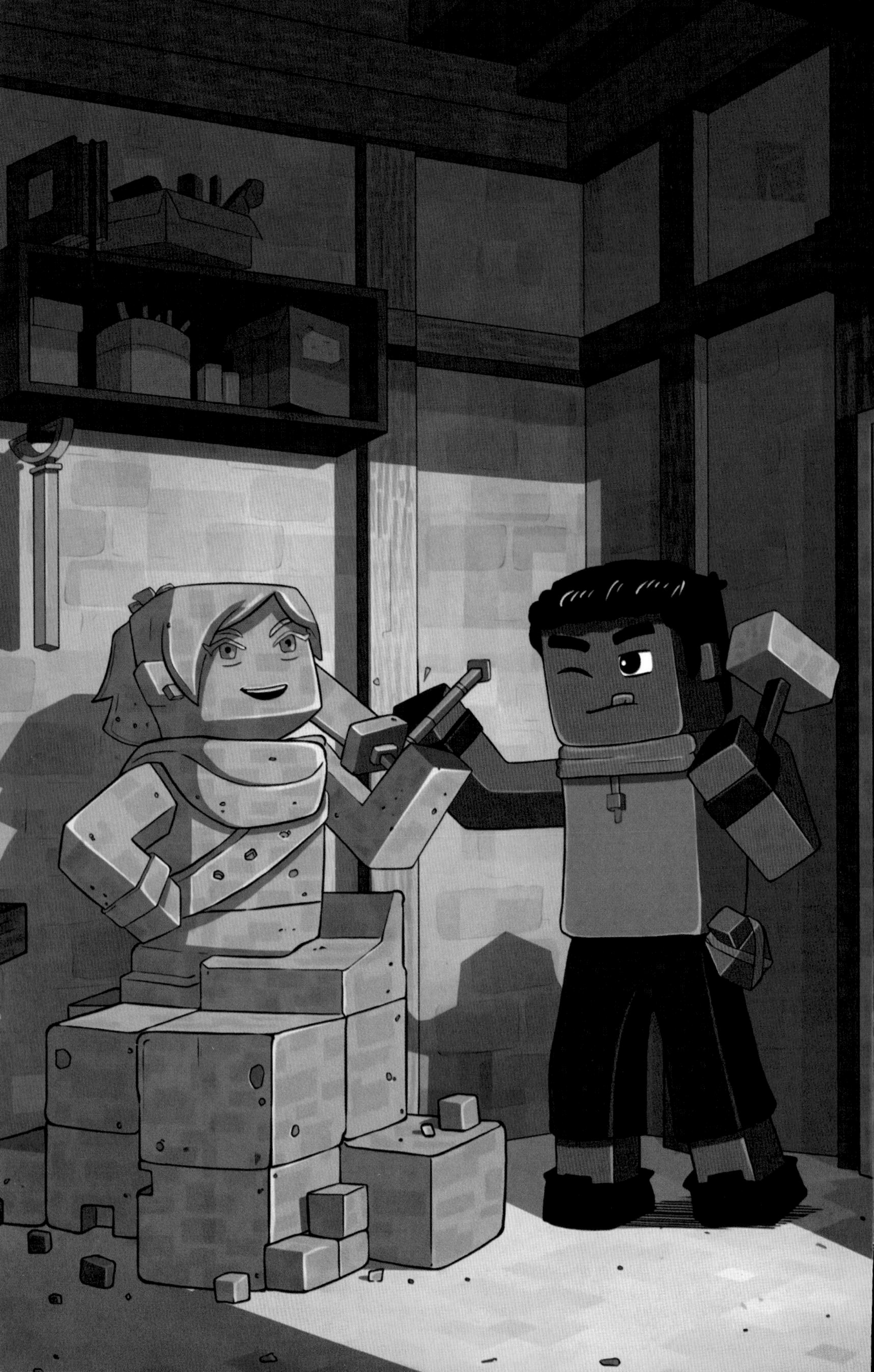

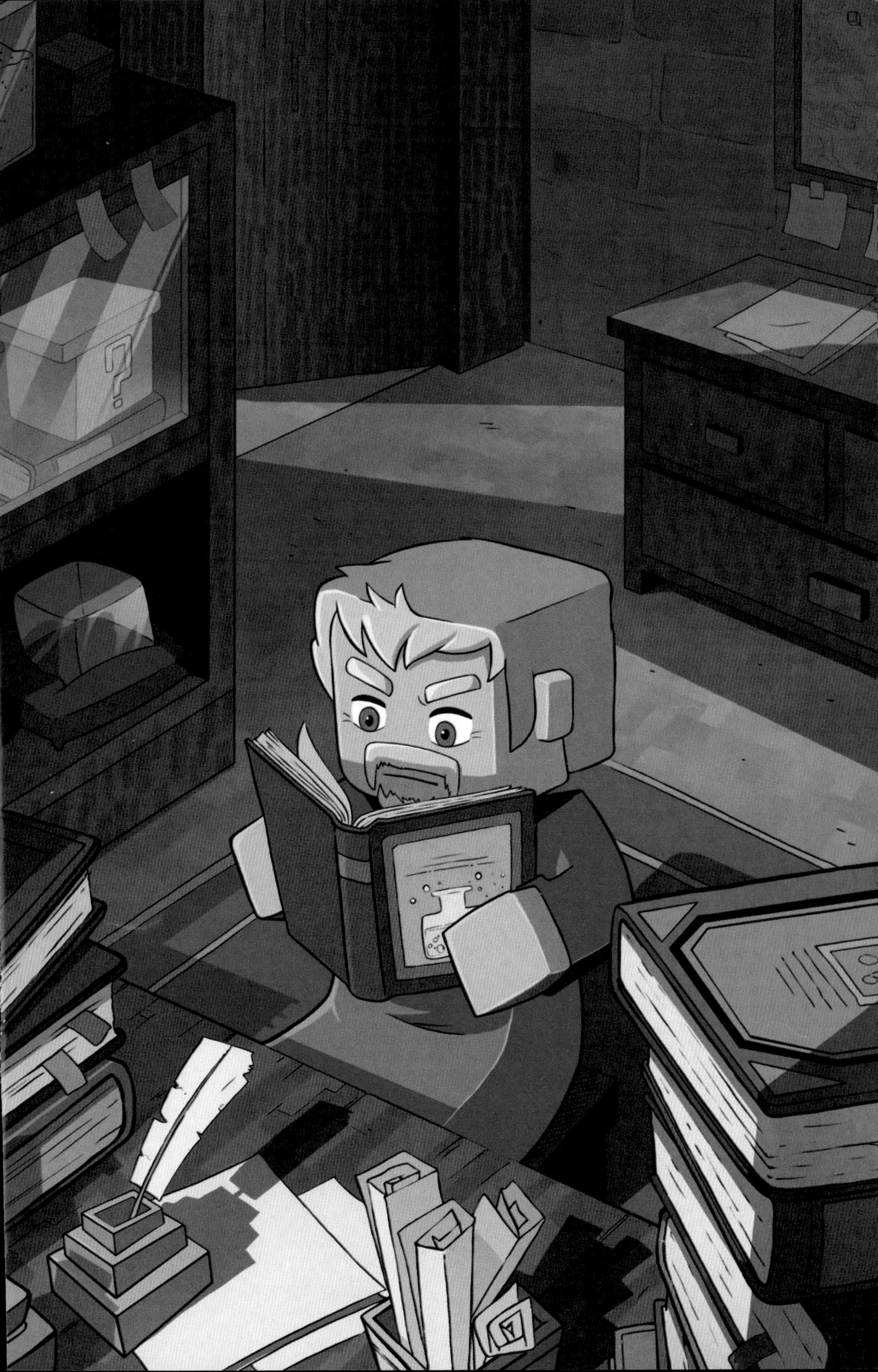

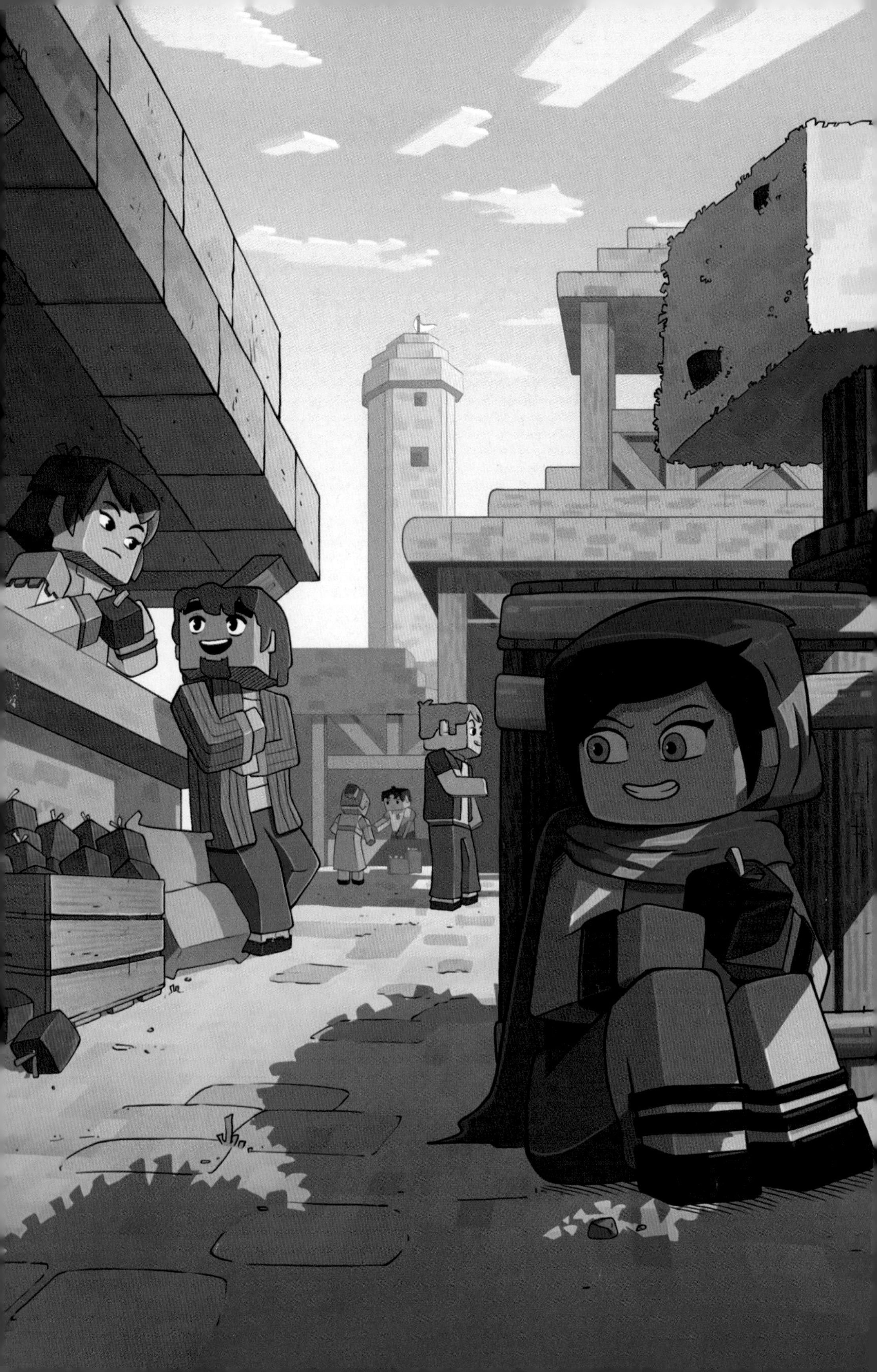

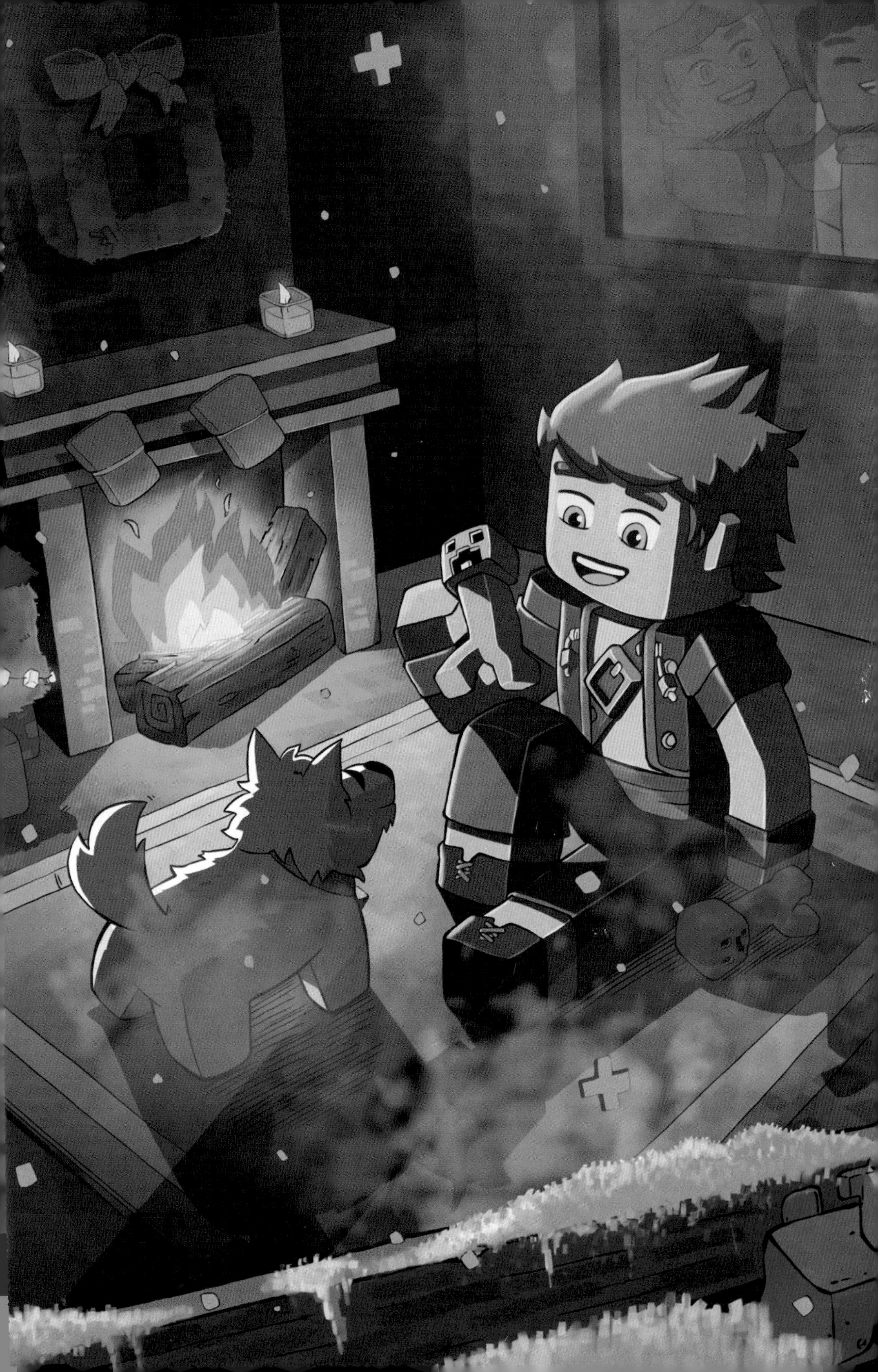

NEXT ON

THE MINECRAFT-INSPIRED MISADVENTURES OF

FRIGIEL AND FLUFFY

**NEW ADVENTURES FULL OF HUMOR AND TWISTS AND
TURNS AWAIT OUR HEROES IN VOLUME 2!**

Featuring two new stories:

THE ORIGINAL BLOCK

**Having recently acquired an old mine, merchant Davidi lets Frigiel
and his friends watch after it for a weekend. But looters, creepers and
other creatures invade, and our heroes, despite themselves, will have
to explore the mine's depths and discover well-hidden secrets.
Will they get the legendary original block? And what if they break it?**

THE FROZEN KINGDOM

**It is snowing on Lanniel and everywhere else for that matter...but how?
wvlt's impossible! With his grandfather away, Frigiel receives a letter from the
Ice King who promises them eternal winter if the village does not pay him a big
ransom. Our heroes venture out to learn more about this mysterious blackmailer.
But they will have to face many dangers along way, and in the freezing cold!**

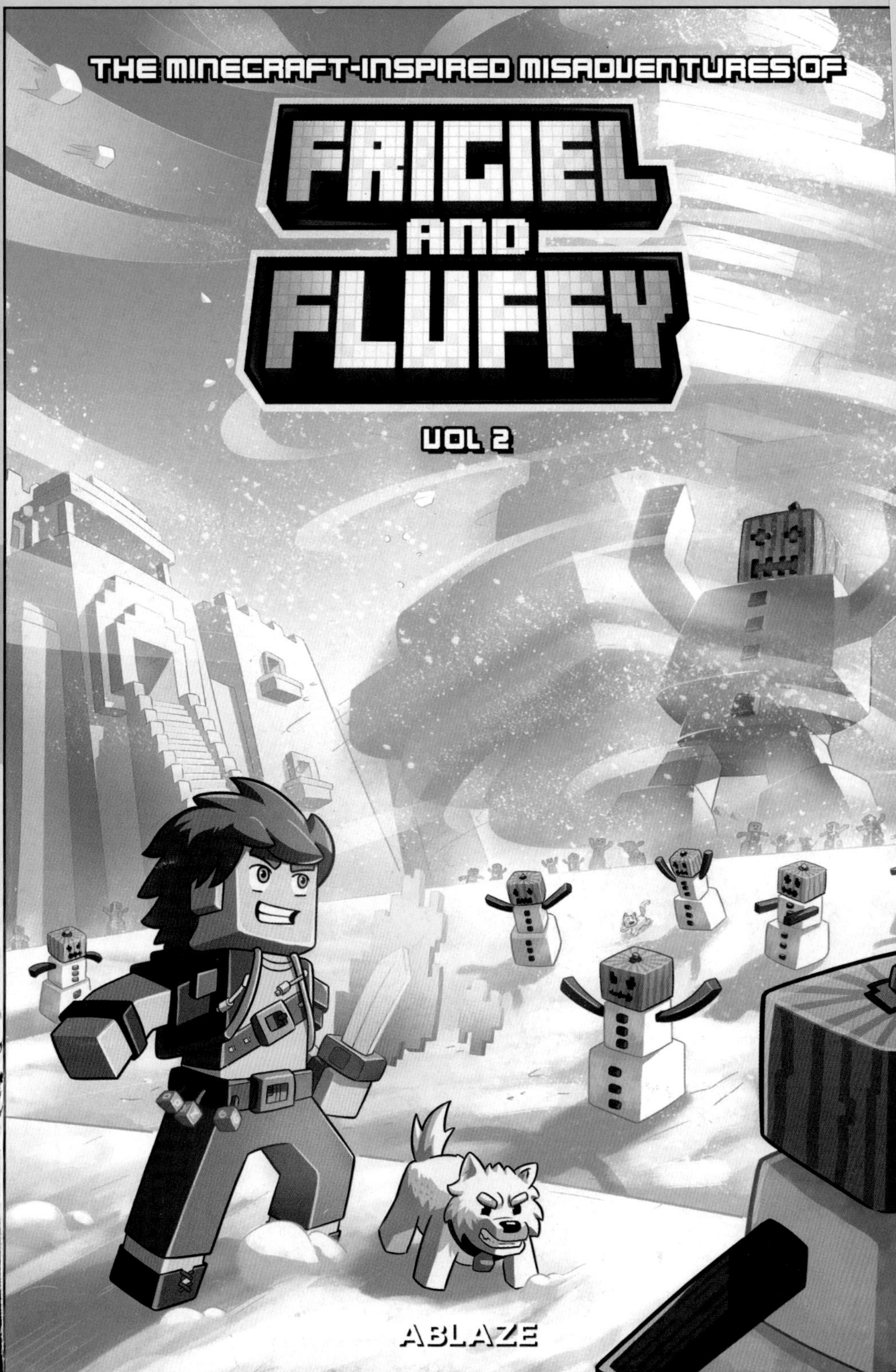
THE MINECRAFT-INSPIRED MISADVENTURES OF
FRIGIEL
AND
FLUFFY
VOL 2
ABLAZE

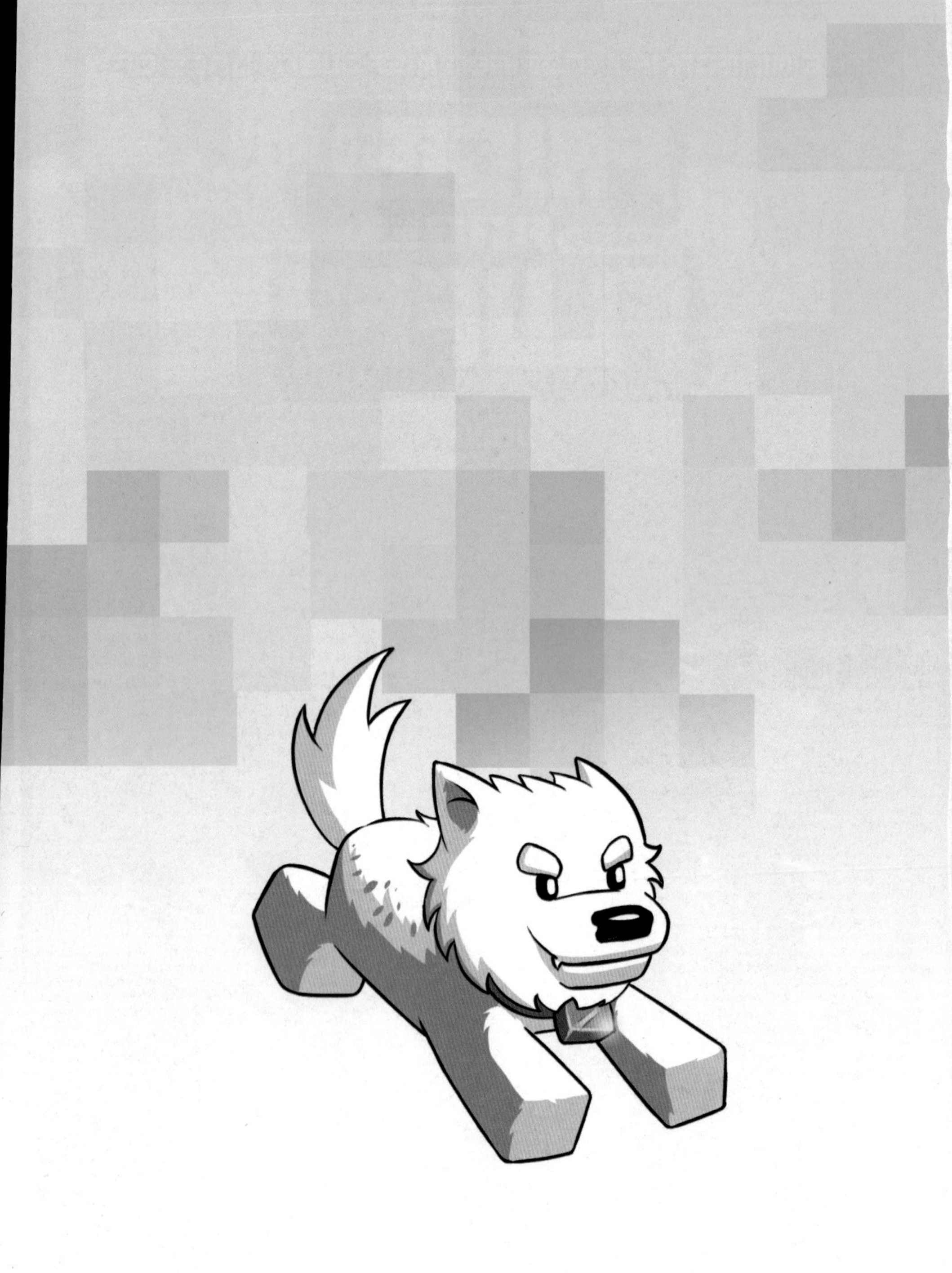